THE
TRAVELER'S
CUP

AC BALDWIN

This is a work of fiction. Names, characters, organizations, places, events, and incidents are either products of the author's imagination or are used fictitiously.

Published by Inkshares, Inc., Oakland, California
www.inkshares.com

Edited by Carlisa Cramer and Chersti Nieveen at Writer Therapy
Interior design by Kevin G. Summers

eISBN:2017962527
ISBN:9781947848238
LCCN:2017962527

First edition

Printed in the United States of America

ACT ONE

CHAPTER 1

I WASN'T VERY BRIGHT. I think a lot of people would agree with that after my complete lack of judgment at the Cup Festival. It wasn't exactly a secret that I was ignorant and shortsighted, and that I'd never had an original thought cross my mind, but I honestly didn't think it would matter. I didn't think much mattered those days.

The majority of my time, before all of this, was spent being served sweet wine around the garden baths behind our family palace. My friends joked that our family's Grey were my closest acquaintances. You could say I wasn't exactly known for community involvement, but not many of us Lumen were—we just took life one day at a time.

The day this all began didn't start any differently. Goblet in hand, I hung my feet over the ledge of the bath, careful not to let the oil come in contact with my body paint. I set my robe aside and relaxed under the rising sun, feeling its warmth on my back. This was the last full day of the festival, and that was about all I could stand. When most of your days were spent oscillating between rest and sleep, all the walking and socializing could take its toll.

I toyed with the idea of lounging a couple more hours, but if my friends or my mother found out I'd missed the whole morning, I'd never hear the end of it. *The Cup Festival is the most important celebration we have, Damaus*, she had lectured several times.

With one last swig, I stood and stretched, trying to gather the energy to find a decent robe and put on my gems when I felt something on my shoulder. I turned hard, slipping on the yellowstone below. Next thing I knew, I was plunging into the warm, viscous bath, trading my mouthful of wine for oil.

I reached the surface and spat. Roeni, a lifelong friend, was grinning like a fool. "Looking good, D. I came to get you to hurry up, but I guess you'll have to redo your paint." He quickly averted his eyes and went inside.

Around me, fresh flakes of pale blue were spreading over the surface of the bath oil. "You'll be waiting awhile!" I called after him.

Embarrassed, I reached for my discarded robe. No one saw a Lumen without their paint. Some of us were only a few shades away from grey, and I wasn't about to put myself up for comparison. I made sure my face was covered as I passed a cackling Roeni on my way up the south staircase to my chambers.

The first dozen dress robes I tried on wouldn't do. Most were too big. According to my mother, draping baggy robes over my body was optimal for my fashion and comfort. The first few that did fit were missing gem casings or were sewn with fabrics that hadn't been popular in half a decade. Reluctantly I pulled out a navy one that was more bearable than the rest and set it on the dressing table—a large circular surface in the center of my garment room that spun in place. My gems and paints were still sitting out from earlier that morning.

I picked up my usual base paint—a pale blue—and began to lather it on my naked body. It hadn't all come off in the fall, but that made applying the stuff evenly even more of a pain. Once it was on, I stood in the room's personal-sized sun atrium to expedite the drying, since my plan to dry naturally in the garden clearly wasn't happening.

When my body had dried enough, I took a smaller tube of paint—this one a soft violet—and began to apply our family's facial strokes. Then there was the glue, followed by my new gems. With my face complete, I secured my robe and set the remaining gems in their casings. I spun the table around to find the right footwear below. If I walked as much today as I had the day before, I was going to want something sturdy. I pulled out my worvil-skin boots and yanked them on. Then I slipped a small package into my pocket and headed back downstairs.

"You took almost an hour to get a bit bluer." Roeni was tight-lipped and had clearly lost his patience long before I arrived.

"Yeah, well, you indirectly threw me into a bath," I retorted. "Consider us even."

"I'm not the one who's keeping Westalyn waiting," he noted, nodding out toward the garden.

I followed his gaze to the sundial. Time-telling had never been a skill I considered worth learning. "It's . . . uhh . . ."

"She's been waiting a third of an hour already," he said. "Wow, Damaus. Please tell me you at least have a courtship gift."

I nodded, but my chest tightened. My mother had made it abundantly clear that keeping a potential courtship partner waiting would be wasting their time. It wouldn't be the first time someone else had swooped in on one of my courting prospects, but this was *Westalyn*. She was somehow cool, or something.

"Let's go!" I spun and headed through the hall toward the gate.

The sun heat on Palunia was no joke. The walk to the Chi Soha palace was a frustrating one because it actually took us farther from the town center, which gave me ample time to mess things up with Westalyn on the way back.

"You should have requested a chariot," Roeni said after we'd walked a few minutes, our heads and bodies covered by our cloaks.

"We'd have been waiting another hour," I groaned. "One of of our slugs died this week, and Mother and Jona took the other two this morning."

"A shame," he said. "We'll be begging your courtess for shelter at this rate."

"You mean we'll be happily escorting her to the festival," I said. "She's gonna be furious."

It didn't lighten my mood when the Chi Soha palace came into view behind the upcoming dunes. My family's home was boring—obtrusively geometric and built with brick and yellow-stone. Their palace, on the other hand, was made of shattered glass, reflecting the land around it in mind-bending arrays of color. It was irregularly shaped, with angled slides and stair-cases between its low towers, which all sat at different heights at the base of one piercing, fractured central tower. It was bested in height by only one other family palace—and that one was little more than a needle to the sky.

I tried to regulate my breathing as we entered the palace grounds. We didn't have to go far. Westalyn was waiting in the entryway, watching our approach. Her arms were folded, which, paired with an unreadable expression on her face, made me considering running to the festival alone. I could work in the water pits—it couldn't be as bad as disappointing her and, by extension, my mother. But my feet betrayed all reasoning, and the next thing I knew I was looking her in the eye.

"You're late," she said with hardly any inflection. It was a curious thing about Westalyn—she stated things as fact. There was never any nuance with her.

"I—I'm sorry." I bowed slightly in my shame. "Will you still come with us?"

"He doesn't have a carriage or chariot either," Roeni pointed out. I wanted to turn and glare, when Westalyn stepped toward me. I froze.

"Good," she said. "I prefer to walk." And with that she led the way to town while Roeni and I skulked behind her, fighting with our eyes.

The buzz of the town could be heard long before the tents came into view. Chatter and Grey noise that some called *music* began to fill the deepening silence we'd maintained for half an hour.

"Can you really get us access to the stage?" Westalyn asked me when we passed the city gate.

I coughed on my response. "Well, I think so. Jiyorga's an uncle of mine. We should at least be able to look around while they set up for tonight's Drawing Ceremony."

"I told Quorian and Masus to meet us there," Roeni said. "They probably came from the north though."

Westalyn eyed him, and then me. "Will they be joining us all day today?"

"Uhh . . . no?" It hadn't occurred to me to spend time alone with her. When I thought about it, I could see how that made sense as potential courting mates. It gave me an odd feeling though.

We walked quickly through the tents with a sense of purpose, still led by Westalyn. I was grateful she felt the same way I did around crowds, because despite his supposed hurry,

Roeni had to examine every gem and cloak along the way. The only thing that caught my attention was a fresh spread of delicious-smelling sweets, but I wasn't about to insist we stop when I had a chance to land a courtship—a feat my mother considered to be my purpose in life.

After a final push through the densely packed row of tents, we sputtered out into the middle of the city, which was delightfully and eerily empty. I'd never seen so much of the dusty yellow ground here before. Red-cloaked city guards were actively clearing out anyone who stumbled in, even though the Drawing was still hours away.

"Excuse me." I stopped a guard approaching the three of us. This was my chance to start being impressive. "Damaus Ju Demma—nephew of Jiyorga N'a Otero, son of Damonia Ju Demma. I'm due to help with stage preparations."

The guard looked me up and down, then gripped my chin and pulled me toward him, his wide orange eyes reflecting the turquoise in mine. I could tell he was examining my facial paint, trying to remember what the Ju Demma symbols were. "This," I choked out so Westalyn and Roeni wouldn't hear, "is no way to treat a descendant of the Oteros. Unhand me now and let us walk, and I'll see that Jiyorga doesn't send you to the pits."

The guard hesitated only a moment before letting go of me and starting toward a group of drunken older women. Roeni gave me a congratulatory side-eye, but Westalyn's gaze seemed skeptical at best. Maintaining the illusion of confidence, I led them straight through the middle of the open festival grounds toward the stage.

Pillars were being erected from the dirt by groups of Grey workers, commanded and closely supervised by more red cloaks. The tops of them were set with fire pits and would be ignited after the Drawing, as a sort of prayer for the travelers' safety when they left our planet behind. That clearly hadn't been working, given that no travelers had ever made it back to Palunia, so it was mostly ceremonial at this point.

We passed six rows of two pillars, one for each traveler, before arriving at the base of the stage. It stood more than twice as tall as me, and still a wall of nearly invisible glass separated us from it by several paces. On the far ends were two more guards, standing at the glass wall's openings. Now I just had to convince them to let us through.

I led the group to the right, toward a guard who didn't budge at our approach. I searched my mind for important-sounding words but was spared the opportunity to test them. A short man, painted vibrant magenta, was hobbling from the stage down a staircase toward us. His white-painted lips were pursed, and his cheeks were more on the violet side than I remembered. He huffed a little as he directed his guard aside, his decorative turquoise robes contrasting almost painfully with the red hues of the guards' cloaks.

"Damaus Ju Demma," the man grunted. That was the closest thing to a greeting you could get out of Jiyorga. "Apparently, against my better judgment and near impeccable memory, I asked you to come help with the stage setup. Supposedly I even asked you to send ahead the neighborhood hooligans because you and these two couldn't possibly offer enough . . . *help*." From the top of the staircase, Quorian and Masus waved.

"I thought you could use a hand in your old age, Uncle," I retorted. "Unless you want to do this all yourself."

"What do you think the Grey are for?" he asked, scowling and starting back up the stairs. I exchanged a shrug with Westalyn and Roeni before we followed.

"Come on," I said, patting Jiyorga on one of his gem-clad shoulders. "You'd love a chance to boss me around like you used to. It's a shame we don't reenact those memories more often."

Slowly and without a word, he led us the rest of the way up to the stage. I wasn't sure if that was because he'd had enough of me or that he couldn't breathe and speak at the same time. For as long as I could remember, Jiyorga had always been, well, old.

The stage was outlined with citrus-colored gems. Sheets of rich, beautiful fabrics had been draped along it as curtains. This year they were deep green and vibrant orange. Standing in front of them were Quorian and Masus, who were giddily fidgeting and grinning at us.

"Damaus!" Masus was lanky and tall, with robes that hardly fell to his wrists and ankles. His hood was oversized at least, keeping his head and face out of the scorching sunlight. He was a full head taller than Quorian, who intentionally chose fabrics that were decades out of fashion. This time he'd chosen a patterned robe. If that wasn't bad enough, the pattern in question was a series of diamonds, yellow and orange. It was nauseating to look at.

It wasn't my first time on the stage, but it was the first in six years. The Cup Festival was a triannual event, and last time I'd spent the entirety of it eating and drinking with my friends.

"Come," Jiyorga said, snapping me back to the moment. He slipped between the curtains and out of sight. I motioned to the others to follow as I pulled a soft, orange panel aside and entered.

There, at the very back, in the center of the stage, raised on a pedestal, was the Cup. It gleamed green in the sunlight, and its gems shone brightly in a rainbow of colors. The others gasped, and I sucked in a little air myself. I had to fight off the impulse to walk up and stroke the surfaces of the gems.

"A real beaut, isn't it?" Jiyorga said. "You five want to help me with it?"

"Yes!" they all offered in unison.

"No," I said. All eyes turned to me. "It's not what you guys think. It's been polished and raised, which means there's only one thing left to do."

Jiyorga scoffed. "You should be honored."

You mean I should have seen this coming.

"He wants us to put the names in. The names of—what is it now? Forty thousand Grey? All different slips of parchment, one at a time."

"They started it already," Jiyorga said, nodding to a group of Grey seated at stage right, folding up pieces of parchment. "Should only be about twenty thousand to go now."

"Still seem glamorous?" I asked Quorian and Masus, after Jiyorga had wandered off.

"Yeah, actually," Masus said. "We get to touch the thing! We even get to see real amber!"

"You're part amber," Westalyn reminded him.

"But I've never seen *pure* amber. Given by the great wizards to power our planet. I wonder how much is in the Planetary Reserve. If we only need a drop in the air to live for days . . . and there must be thousands or millions of drops in the Cup . . ."

We left Masus to his revelation and tried to figure out a plan. "Someone needs to take some of that parchment from them," I noted, nodding toward the silent, pale-skinned, over-sized beings in torn, grey robes. No one moved.

Roeni sighed after a moment. "Fine. But you all owe me."

"Is this okay?" I asked Westalyn. "We can see about getting out of here if you want."

"It's fine," she said. A smile came across her face. "We're doing our people a favor this way—helping to get our ancestral treasure back."

"Do you really think anyone's going to survive? Ever?" It was plenty entertaining, watching Grey sign up by the thousands for a death adventure, but *no one* had returned, and this had been going on for a thousand years.

"We've got to get it though," Westalyn maintained. "We'll keep hosting the Cup until we do. Whatever it is, it's rightfully ours. You know how savagely our homeland was taken from our ancestors. Who knows what was left behind. Books on our history? Technology that could renourish this planet? Better ships? Maybe water for the Grey—you know they're dying at a higher rate than ever, and the pits will run dry. And I hate to say it, but Masus may be on to something. Exactly how much amber have we been blessed with? Maybe the Grey have longer than we do. Lor is made of amber, through and through. I doubt the treasure is gems and gold, Damaus. I think, if we've kept this up for so long, it must be something we really need."

I studied her. She was serious. It was ridiculous. "Westalyn, if we ran out of amber, we'd die. I doubt the contessa would place the fate of all Lumen in the hands of some clearly useless Grey."

The look that came over her face then made it obvious I'd said something wrong. Thankfully Roeni had come back with a chest filled with parchment. "They folded these ones," he said. "We can drop them into the Cup."

Masus and Quorian danced in place as we approached the pedestal. There were stairs on its side. Roeni hesitated.

"Only one name at a time," I told him. "Make sure the slip is covered in the amber before you place another."

He nodded and climbed slowly, each step a deliberate, conscious effort. He kept his eye on the Cup, staring at it with a reverence I felt, too. It was huge—it had to be to be visible to a hundred thousand festivalgoers. The pedestal was taller than I was, and the Cup was about my height. We all stared as Roeni took the first slip of parchment and let it fall from his fingers. He exhaled and waited, then dropped another.

We all took turns, rotating every few minutes at first. Then, after the reverence wore off and monotony set in, our shifts extended to half an hour.

"What do you think would happen if we put our own names in?" Quorian asked after a while.

"They'd sink," Masus said. "Amber's a life force, but it isn't magic."

Quorian rolled his eyes. "I meant, do you think they'd be drawn?"

Westalyn laughed. It was the first time she'd smiled or made a noise in hours. A good sign she might forgive me soon.

"We'd never be drawn," Masus replied. "But if by some chance we were, I think Jiyorga would draw another and make us tear down his stage with no help from the Grey."

"Or send us to the pits," I groaned. "Jiyorga can be a vengeful brute, so I'd say either scenario is likely."

"Just imagine his reaction though," Roeni said, coming down from the pedestal. "He's taking the ceremony way too seriously, as always, and then he draws Masus's name."

"I'm not putting my name in that thing," Masus protested.

"I could put us all in," Roeni offered. "Damaus, do you think your own uncle would make that big a fuss? He'd probably just throw all the blame on you."

"Don't put us in!" Masus was standing now. "If you guys want to fool around, go ahead. But I won't have my name called out in the Drawing."

"I thought you said we'd never be drawn," Westalyn noted. We all stared. None of us were brave enough to keep egging Masus on once his mood turned serious. She was enjoying this.

"Nearly never," he said through clenched teeth. "Five of us and over forty thousand of them? We'd have a better chance of seeing rain. I just don't want to risk the embarrassment or Jiyorga's wrath."

"It hasn't rained in four years," Quorian pointed out. He was always keeping tabs on obscure events.

"I know," Massus said. "This is about . . ." He closed his eyes for a few seconds. "About six times less likely. But the answer is still no," he added as we stared eagerly. "I'm not doing it. Let's just finish up and go. I'm way too hungry considering it's Drawing Day."

I caught the look of disappointment in Westalyn's eye as the group went back to folding parchment. Next thing I knew, I was on my feet. I took an empty piece of parchment in one hand and ink in the other, and scrawled my name. I ran up the staircase to the Cup and glanced down at my friends with a wink to Westalyn. Masus swayed a little, but the others cheered.

Roeni laughed. "He won't do it!"

Westalyn laughed, too. I gritted my teeth and loosened my grip. The slip of parchment tumbled downward. The laughing stopped. I watched with bated breath as the liquid amber took my piece and sucked it under, burying it among the rest.

Everyone was silent for a moment, and then the laughter erupted again. I even caught Masus choking his enjoyment down as I took a bow.

"I can't believe it," Roeni said after catching his breath.

"You're so careless," Masus added. "You'd better hope Jiyorga doesn't draw your name. We won't be visiting you in the Southern Pits, you know."

"You liked it," I teased.

"It is the most interesting thing that's happened today," Westalyn acknowledged. I stood up straight and felt my face go flush. She was actually smiling at me.

"*Damaus!*" I nearly toppled off the pedestal stairs. In my romantic fugue I'd failed to notice Jiyorga approaching. I froze, wondering how much he saw. "Are you finished yet? Even the Grey would have managed by now."

"Ah, well . . ." I stammered. "There's only a bit left. Why not let them take over?" I hopped down the stairs two at a time and placed a hand on Westalyn's shoulder. She gasped at my touch but didn't pull away. My mother wouldn't believe me if I told her I'd already managed to lock in our courtship.

CHAPTER 2

I TRIED TO contain my excitement as we left the stage area and headed toward the far tents. I just had to keep Westalyn happy until after the Drawing. Then I could make my official request at the family feast.

We enjoyed Drawing Day the way I usually did—overeating and discovering new forms of entertainment at the rainbow tents, where the Grey put on shows and created the latest fashion items for us Lumen. The only difference this year was that my usual wandering eye had settled on one person.

The whole week had been high-energy, but everyone knew you had to conserve some stamina for the finale, which was just getting started. In every direction Lumen were grabbing fabrics and jewels from Grey creators. There was laughter and what they called music burying the usual silence of the city. When the biggest, loudest festival only happened once every three years, it found a way to surprise you every time.

Supposedly our early ancestors, after arriving on Palunia, quickly put the Grey to work, citing that they weren't very useful otherwise and that they actually seemed to enjoy it. But a few decades ago, a scientist by the name of Garona Ju Demma, my high-uncle as a matter of fact, discovered that the Grey had a myriad of hidden talents. Apparently the pastimes they referred to as "singing" and "painting" made them intelligent in a way we weren't. I never really believed that, but it did make them a great source of entertainment.

During the last Cup I was only fifteen turns old. Since I spent most of it playing games with friends, I'm not sure I even heard the names. Not that it would have made a difference. I don't think a single Lumen could pronounce a Grey name, let alone associate their names with a face. The only way you could even check someone's name was by their birth marking, and it was rarely called into question. But year by year, with each ballot read, another Grey would eagerly run to the stage, and the crowd would cheer for him, or her, or whatever gender they happened to be. That was how it was with the Grey. No rules to uphold them as a society, and so easily satisfied.

"You're lost in thought," Westalyn noted. I turned to her, blinked, and flushed. She was intimidating: articulate, intelligent, physically strong, and a whole head taller than me. "How about a stick of ginger glass?" She touched a painted hand to my shoulder. I stammered and began digging into the purse inside my robe. My fingers clasped a roll of stones, which I handed over to her. She took two dark pieces from inside and placed the remainder in her own purse. I was vaguely aware of what she was doing, but mostly I was aware of *her*.

Her base skin tone was a delicate periwinkle, which she accented with lilac stripes painted vertically down the sides of her face along her magenta eyes. As was Lumen custom, she must have shaved her head daily. But what I found curious about her was that she left a short, pointed patch of hair hanging over her left ear—a tiny streak of rebellion. It was white in color, and I couldn't be sure if she painted it that way or not. I didn't get many glimpses at it since, like any sensible person, she kept a hood—khaki-colored in her case—draped over her head to block the ruthless force of the sun. That was the other thing: most Lumen declared their status by how fashionably colored their robes were. But that didn't seem important to Westalyn. And why should it be? She glimmered all on her own.

My eyes followed her movement as she reached down to take a stick of crystalized ginger from the Grey woman at the booth. The contrast couldn't have been more extreme. The woman was large with frizzy black hair and a mole on the very tip of her pale grey nose. She was sitting on the ground behind her booth, hunched over it, like her back was stuck that way. She only had about four teeth left, which I only noticed when her face broke into a crooked smile. "Nice day!" she squawked mindlessly after us as we continued through the network of tents. Occasionally a Grey would speak words, but they were imitations, usually parroting phrases spoken by us Lumen.

The next section was exposed, and still there were Greyfolk sitting on the ground and singing on the open sandrock. Most of the Lumen I knew lapped that nonsense up, but I couldn't understand what the big deal was. Why waste something as useful as a voice just for the sake of making noise?

"It doesn't make sense, does it?" Westalyn said, her face flat as usual.

I smiled and shook my head. "Not a bit."

We walked past some Grey who'd draped themselves uncharacteristically in colored fabrics—dated pieces that Lumen must have exchanged for new cloaks and scarves. They were scattered on the ground, making awful noise with their voices and literally pounding sand. Some were doing it alone, while others sat in variously sized circles. In the largest circle there were a few drunken Lumen dancing. Others were trying to learn to make the squawking noises or hit the ground in unison with those leading the songs. Westalyn and I darted past into the next section of tents.

When we got there, we both let out a sigh of relief, catching each other's eye. I smiled as she turned away, but I thought I saw a grin on her face, too. I let her lead us through the tents. We looked at scarves, boots, decor, and gems, and we bought a little of everything. The displays went on for so long that we kept regretting our purchases because every booth's products seemed to get bigger and better. Soon our arms were full of things and we were getting tired.

"I guess we could go to one of the shows," I said, taking a multithreaded scarf from her and adding it to my pile. "Get a break and try to enjoy the irony of it?"

She laughed, then slowed to look at something. "Yeah, that works." I followed her gaze to a gem set nearly identical to one in my pocket—her courting gift. "This is beautiful."

"Six hundred!" the Grey man at the booth wheezed.

"So expensive," she muttered, staring at him.

"Shall we?" I offered to take her arm with my left while carefully balancing the items in my right. I thought she looked vaguely disappointed, but she snapped out of it and joined me, heading away from the shopping booths, toward the big show tent ahead. We passed a few Grey sitting in the bare sun, begging for the remaining food of passersby. I'd almost forgotten about the festival food. Tonight was going to be perfect.

The tent curtains all drew closed, leaving the inside black. The crowd around us quieted. I turned to make a joke to Westalyn when a faint light appeared from above, and a shadow rolled back off the top of the tent. It had been double-layered. The remaining layer had small holes cut into it, allowing tiny rays of sunlight in directly onto the floor at the bottom.

The crowd, except for us, cheered. Westalyn clapped politely, and I followed suit.

The show began with a single Grey taking center pit. He looked like a young man, around my age. But instead of being trim and fit, he was skin and bones. His knees shook visibly as he stood there with a thousand Lumen eyes on him. Then two more Grey, both tall and wide, came up behind him with a roll of parchment. They unrolled it and faced the audience. Two Grey women brought out cans of paint, and the shaky man got to work.

He splashed reds and browns up on the left, blues and golds on the bottom right. This continued for some time as the crowd sat in awe, all eyes on the vibrance before them. When the parchment was well-soaked, he began to spread thick layers of paint into new shapes. I thought the colors were nice, but the woman on the other side of me was in tears. Westalyn sat transfixed, her mouth hanging slightly open.

"What do you see?" I asked, hoping the piece was subjective. I was wrong.

"It's an ancient garden, Damaus," she said, not taking her eyes off it. "Don't you see it?"

"I suppose, now that you say it, yeah," I mumbled.

The Grey man had turned the blue and gold into green grass and sun, and the orange gradient was turning into some kind of flower. Or maybe a group of them. Some of the brown might have been dirt. It's not like I'd ever seen a real garden. We had a couple artificial pods here on Palunia, but supposedly our home planet, like many worlds, used to have entirely green surfaces.

When he finished and held up the completed canvas, the tent burst into applause. Westalyn's expression had deepened, but I didn't feel much. It was nice to look at, I supposed. I clapped along with everyone else, determined to *get it*.

We stayed for five acts in total. After the canvas painting, several Grey lathered themselves in paint, robes and all, and began rolling their bodies around a large tapestry that had been draped over the stage. The finished product was supposedly an ancient forest, but I failed to see that, too. Then there were the singers, letting out nonsense melodies without any real words. Some sang alone, some as an ensemble, and the last act had to be a hundred of them, singing in various pitches and using a variety of instruments. Despite my reservations, I found myself tapping along. I was almost disappointed when it was over.

We had to leave the tent carefully with so many goods in our arms. Westalyn walked gracefully, and I tried to follow her lead. I only dropped one scarf on an unsuspecting Lumen woman, who pouted slightly when I took it back. I was tempted to let her have it and find out which family she came from, but I'd gotten this far with Westalyn already. This was all a first for me, and I was trying my damned hardest not to throw it away.

"What now?" she asked when we got outside.

"We should eat," I said. I was famished and not about to miss out on the variety of delicacies at the food tents. "But first, why don't we put all this in a storage cart so we can get around more easily?" *And fit the many dishes into our hands.* One meal at a time wasn't going to do.

Westalyn didn't say much but kept me company as we stepped into one of the narrow paths between a row of vending tents. I recalled spotting the storage carts on one of our passes through, but I couldn't recall exactly which direction we were facing at the time. It was nice to get out of the main crowd for a while, but it meant walking alongside booths of Grey workers, who kept eyeing us. It was something they always did, I supposed, but I'd never noticed so many do it in succession. Was it hatred? Fear? Or just a lack of understanding?

"There!" she said, nudging me to the right. I had to turn my whole body to see past the heap of goods in my hands. We were only one row over.

We squeezed through a group of Lumen shoppers and carefully dropped all of the new fabrics and jewels into an empty cart. Westalyn went to pay the Grey woman working the stand with what remained of my coins. While she looked the other way I slipped the package containing the courtship gift from my pocket into the cart, beneath the first scarf on the pile. I was still fidgeting when I saw the canvas color of her cloak in my periferal. I tossed the hanging sides of the scarf inside quickly and closed the lid.

"What were you doing?" she asked with one eye narrowed.

"Just reorganizing," I said, putting an arm around her shoulder. "Shall we eat now? I want to make sure we find a good spot for the Drawing."

She let me lead. It still felt weird to touch another person at all, let alone so familiarly, but this was about to be a new part of my life. Westalyn and I, openly courting, conceiving young, and then separating for whatever our life tasks may be. I'd raise the children in their youth, and then when my time came to work, motherhood would begin for her. I expected she'd travel and learn. Maybe she'd take to space; that seemed a very Westalyn sort of life task. She always seemed to do best on her own.

We headed for the first row of food tents. They were organized by color. "Do you want something blue?" I asked, heading for the most expensive.

"I was thinking orange," she replied, looking past the most beautiful, ornate sweets I'd seen in my life. Her eyes settled on a set that looked a lot like my morning meal.

"Orange?" My family's palace was *filled* with orange and red foods. Most Lumen palaces in Centrisle were. "Do you have orange at home?"

"Yes," she said as we passed the line of wine fountains, in every shade of every color, all offering a slightly different mind state. I grabbed a cup full of violet wine while keeping my best eye on her as she continued through the crowd.

"Damaus!" A hand clasped on my shoulder, forcing a flinch out of me. I jumped before recognizing the touch as my younger brother's. Quorian and Masus were coming up behind him with a few other friends of theirs.

"Jona," I greeted him, looking back for Westalyn. She was lost in the sea of Lumen. "I need to go."

"Mother wants to see you before the Drawing," he said. "She seemed to think it was worth tracking you down for. Which, you know, is exactly how I like to spend my afternoons."

"Are you seriously spending your fair day looking for me?" That would be an awful waste of food and wine.

"She wishes." He grinned. "I got lucky, but if she asks, it was agony."

"Yeah, okay." I waved him and the others off and squeezed toward the orange food tents. My chest tightened. I hoped Jiyorga hadn't discovered I'd placed my own name in the Cup. I wondered if my mother would separate me and Westalyn for eternity or just kick me out of the palace. I sighed and soon distracted myself with more food and wine.

Since Lumen rarely touched each other, our crowds were at least a lot more organized than the Grey. There was no shoving, elbowing, or nudging each other around. There was, however, a lot more scowling. We Centrisle Lumen didn't always handle the tourists as well as we promoted. This was all a spectacle to them, coming into our city and stomping all over it. Eating our food, drinking our wine. Granted, a lot of it would go to waste otherwise, but dammit, it was our waste.

I narrowly dodged elbowing an attractive Lumen man the locals all knew as Barena when I spotted her. Westalyn was taking a simple plate from a stand near the end of the line. I hurried over as quickly as I could, wine somehow still in hand. If men like him were standing around these tents, I couldn't let her out of my sight for long. Rumor had it his latest courtship had fallen through.

"Westalyn!" I called to her. I saw her eye me, then go back to exchanging some words with the Grey behind the stand. I froze. I had never been glossed over for one of *them*. "Westalyn!"

When I got to her, I was panting too much to speak or drink. She looked at me with what could only be pity. "Yes, Damaus?"

"I . . . I lost you. Sorry, my brother . . . What are you talking to them about?" The Grey behind the booth shuffled around cleaning things.

"I told them the food was good," she replied, and I thought I caught a slight sigh of exasperation.

She was holding a small plate with a single orange square, which she had taken a single bite from.

"Tell me you're having more than that," I said.

"I might," she replied stiffly. "Do you want to try?"

"You want me to share your food?" That was the most bizarre request I'd ever heard. I was almost repulsed enough not to take the next sip of wine. Almost.

"Why not? You want to court me, don't you?"

I felt myself burning up. I hadn't formally asked yet. And I certainly hadn't heard of anyone—including courting partners—sharing their food. "I—It's okay. I don't care much for orange."

I did, however, stop at nearly every other colored row. Blue fruit, violet jellies, yellow pastes, and pink breads took over my many plates. Each time we headed for the next row we stopped for wine. Westalyn reluctantly tried about a sip of each one, while I took generous helpings in my own cup.

We must have spent two hours eating and drinking. Or at least I did. I think she was satisfied with about two squares and a cup in total. Still, she didn't complain, which helped solidify my confidence in our pairing.

"Damaus," she said as I spread green paste onto a red roll, "we've only got a few minutes before the Drawing."

I paused with the roll in front of my mouth. "What?" I was supposed to meet with my mother. She'd be in the front row, and it would be way too crowded if it was minutes away. "How do you know? I didn't hear anything."

"The sundial, Damaus," she groaned, nodding to one just outside the tents nearby.

"Well, let's go then!" I grabbed her wrist, dropped my plate and cup, and started for the gates.

"Damaus!" she cried. "Let go of me!"

Startled, I took my hand away immediately. A few eyes of passing Lumen were on us. Of course they were. "What? I'm sorry . . . ?"

"You hurt me," she explained. "I can walk by myself just fine."

Confidence a little shot, I walked alongside her, letting her take the lead. Tens of thousands were already far ahead of us, crowding beneath the stage. There were still red guards around—definitely more than earlier—but they were lost in a sea of colorful pastel robes. We settled in near the edge of the crowd as more and more Lumen came in from behind.

Our section was huge. Even with so many gathered, there was plenty of room behind us. The Grey section, on the other hand, was smaller, though it housed many more bodies.

The best part of the Drawing was witnessing and being part of the crowd. We Lumen had our standards of dress, but to see the full range of ways modern style could be interpreted was incredible. It also made me realize how underdressed I was—my mother would have encouraged me to wear the whole gem collection and add a couple of colored scarves—but there was something to be said about blending in and just *observing*. This year the popular cloaks were citrus orange, faded leaf green, deep violet, and metallic cyan. I wasn't setting any trends with my outdated navy, but Westalyn, despite her colorless cloak, stood out far from the rest. She was most radiant in clothing that didn't detract your attention from *her*.

I studied her face, but she wasn't looking at me. Her eyes were fixed ahead and glazed over, and she seemed to be struggling for balance. "Westalyn?"

"I'm fine," she said, short on breath, blinking up at me and then away again. "I don't do well in crowds."

I placed a shaking hand on her arm, and we watched the stage together, just as the front layer of curtains pulled back. The solid dark wall turned to one with many shades of green, yellow, and orange, hanging in panels, forming a marvelous gradient on either side of the stage. The back of the whole display was encased fire, blown from Grey fire-dancers under the stage. The crowd cheered loudly, and Westalyn did, too. Following her lead, I called out with the rest.

Two red guards entered the stage, wearing rich scarves and tall hats in place of their hoods. They approached the center, walking on either side of Jiyorga N'a Otero, who they helped onto a raised podium. Behind him four more matching guards rolled out a golden chariot, covered in gems. We all knew what was beneath the sheet on top of it, and the cheering grew louder. The guards tore the sheet away, revealing the gleaming Cup. Using chains and the stairs behind, they lifted it back onto the platform we had found it on this morning, which was now covered with dark cloth. The ancient artifact radiated against the fabric, shining out with greens and the rainbow of gems it occupied.

The crowd cheered for several more minutes, while Jiyorga soaked it in from his place next to the Cup. When he decided he'd had enough, he raised gentle hands to us and the cheering fell to silence. It was finally time to select the twelve.

"Citizens of Palunia, welcome to what I can only hope will be the end of an ancient and perilous journey. A journey we keep fighting toward, time after time, triannually, hoping against the odds that our travelers will seize our ancestral treasure from those who banished us, and in turn also seize the Traveler's Cup."

"He must have some kind of blessed artifact to project his voice this far," Westalyn murmured.

"Yeah," I said, though I realized I'd never seen what that was.

"The Cup looks different from back here," she noted.

"It's because of the sun," I said. "We always have the Drawing at this time because it collects, and reflects, the most rays. It's beautiful, huh?"

"So who wins in the end?" she asked as Jiyorga drew the first name.

"What do you mean?" I whispered, not taking my eyes from my uncle. He read out something Grey that sounded like *Marlithan Izeyrin*.

"A single traveler gets the Cup, isn't it? Why send twelve? How do they determine who the winner is if they all make it back? Shouldn't a full crew return if they manage the mission?"

Another Grey, *Helragizan Thuli*. Then *Rodiger Hozayathin* and *Welsia Modolin*, followed by *Militaw Throzen*.

Westalyn's eyes were on the Cup. It really did shine brighter than it had that morning, reflecting the rays of the lowering sun back into the sky. It was barely a speck to our eyes with how far back we were, but it was a speck that stood bigger and brighter than any gem beside me. Once you got a look at its perfection, it was hard to look away.

"Maybe it's the person bearing the treasure," I whispered, offering a slight shrug. Three more Grey names had been spoken. Then two others. They all sounded the same to me. I was wondering, in that brief moment, what it might be like to claim the Cup. The truth was, I didn't know the answer to Westalyn's question. I made a mental note to ask my mother after the festival.

"One name to go," she said, breaking me out of the imaginings in my head. When the name was drawn, I realized I was squeezing her arm. The audience had become tense. Following the last name would be the final feast, which would last the night, leading to the Grand Procession. I exchanged a smile with Westalyn, eager to burn this moment into both our minds. This was an important day. When the feast was underway and they lit the sky fire, I'd ask her to officiate our partnership and bear my child.

I snapped out of my daydream as someone called my name. I spun around, searching the crowd for the speaker. Those behind me looked at me and then upward. I turned back again and saw only Jiyorga peering out into the crowd. Was it him? Did he need my help?

"Lord Damaus Ju Demma," he repeated. His white-painted lips were almost certainly pursed together on his round, plum-colored face. He waited. The Lumen who had noticed me were signaling to their friends. I even saw a few Grey eyes motion over toward me.

Realization set in. Horror began to rise up from the pit of my stomach as I remembered the dare. Remembered how impossible it seemed, how much of a joke I'd made out of the whole thing. My mother was the first person I thought of. She'd be nearby and worried. I placed a hand on Westalyn's shoulder before pushing through the scoffing Lumen beside us and rushing to the front of the crowd.

There were six red guard, at the staircase now. "It's me!" I snapped at them. "I'm Damaus Ju Demma."

One looked over to the front row, and I followed his gaze. It was my mother and my brother Jona. Jona was flabbergasted as usual, but my mother looked more angry than I'd seen her in my life, and I'd given her a plenty of opportunities before. She nodded viscerally at the guard, who opened the gate and accompanied me up the staircase, each step a moment to revel publicly in my shame.

Jiyorga didn't immediately come to meet me. I stood firm at the side of the stage, behind the curtains. He was in my line of sight, and I glared at him until he left his position at the podium, making a joke about going to get me. The crowd's laughter was nervous, laced with the suspense one got at a Grey acrobatics show.

"It was a joke," I said, when he came into earshot. "Hurry. Laugh it off and call the next name."

He gave me one stiff nod before grabbing the neck of my robe and tugging hard. I lurched forward into sight, then regained my balance and joined him bitterly for the walk to center stage.

The crowd below was silent. I was angry and embarrassed, but not worried. They couldn't make a Lumen go. This would be the last time I helped Jiyorga.

"That concludes the Drawing of the Traveler's Cup!" he exclaimed, raising his pudgy plum hands to the sky. A few of the Grey cheered with as much enthusiasm as they would for their own. It was a nice touch. The Lumen were staring at me, horrified. I looked for Westalyn, but I couldn't find her among the crowd.

I was frozen in place. I kept waiting for Jiyorga to laugh and say he was kidding, or to tell me, "Never mind," but he just stood there. The first thing that went through my head was that the punishment for fleeing the Cup was death. The prize for going was, well, likely also death, but my chances would be marginally better. Not that I was going.

On shaking legs I tried to stand with confidence. I probably looked like a sweating, pleading child the way my mouth was forced into a smile, but I fought to maintain my composure. Jiyorga's eyes didn't leave me until two men wearing crimson cloth came to him and began whispering. I stared at the stage floor, not wanting to make eye contact with anyone, especially not my mother.

Then Jiyorga turned to face me, adjusting his pastel cyan robes, as though he'd snapped out of the charade of the ceremony and just realized there were thousands of eyes on us. "Lord Damaus Ju Demma." He addressed me, his throat struggling through the words. His white lips contrasted sharply with the blackness inside his mouth as he spoke. "You are hereby stripped of all rights, of all titles, of all claims, of all friends and family, and granted the honor of participating in the Traveler's Cup. Do you have any words for your community?"

My confidence faltered. I forgot about the speeches. For most of the Grey, the speech consisted of little more than a grunt. I wanted to scream and yell, but I couldn't spit curses at my own community, in the face of my family. "I—" I stammered, not sure anyone even noticed I was speaking. Then, as he opened his mouth to dismiss me with the patronizing banter that always followed these ceremonies, I coughed. And I remembered words from my childhood. Words a Grey prisoner had given when I was about five years old. What he said had stuck with me, because he was the only one who had spoken with dignity and in full phrase. The only one who had gone with confidence, who had used true Lumen words on this stage. I didn't understand it, but he couldn't have been all Grey. And right now I supposed I wasn't all Lumen. I opened my mouth, and his words came pouring out. "Let the fire of your sleeping god rain on me."

There was a gasp from the crowd, which startled me into looking up. There in the front row, clad in a brilliant silver robe, was my mother, and she was spilling tears of anger. Jona was, as usual, dumbstruck, but for once he looked part of the crowd. Every jaw was hanging, and every body stiff. Some of the Grey had grim looks of satisfaction on their faces, and they began to cheer. To repeat my words, or at least the cadence of them. It seemed so foolish now. What had I even said?

I didn't have time to think it over because the next thing I knew, I was being dragged away by the red guards. When we reached the other side of the stage, behind the curtain, I lost my balance. One of the guards had slipped. I turned to see Westalyn gripping his arm and spitting words into his ear. The men loosened their grip and allowed me to walk but at their unnecessarily quick pace. I craned my neck back toward Westalyn, whose eyes followed me to the staircase. She had her arms crossed and was staring expressionlessly.

CHAPTER 3

THE GUARDS HELPED me onto a chariot for one. It was chained on three sides, connecting it with eleven others. We were arranged in three columns, four rows, and headed at the front by an oversized sand slug. This slug was thick and tall—at least thirty years old—and hard around the edges where its natural armor had formed. Like all aged slugs, that meant it could move fast. I'd never seen a slug take more than three chariots at a time, and those ones were aged specifically for events like the festival.

The chariots were gold and decorated with gems. Mine was encrusted with emeralds, gleaming deep green in the remnants of the sun that was fading behind us. I secured my footing, slipping my worvil-skin boots into the riding slots. I heard a *clink* as one of the guards locked a wall of chains closed behind me.

"Don't think my title won't be restored in an hour," I warned, meeting his gaze.

He continued to the chariot beside me—this one gold and garnet—where a Grey woman was standing completely still.

She had hair on her head, long, stringy, and black, and her clay-colored robes bore no hood. She was hunched over the front of the chariot, clearly lacking riding experience, and her broad shoulders made her look a bit like a rolling desert beast. She was sorely out of place in a Lumen chariot. They all were. All but me. *Clink, clink.*

"When this is sorted out, you'll be sent to the water camps!" I shouted toward the guard, now three chariots away. *This is ridiculous, Jiyorga,* I seethed.

Once we were all in place, the two guards boarded their own chariots, led by smaller but well-armored slugs. The guards raised static charged whips in unison and struck downward at the same time, sending a flash of light from the point of their whip to the creatures in front of them. The slugs began to move. Again both men raised their whips, waited for a change in the electric winds, and pointed them at the oversized slug in front of the twelve. The static left the straps, as it had with the last strike, and flung toward the invertebrate puller, this time narrowly avoiding the front row of Grey. And the slug began to pull.

I'd traveled plenty in my mother's chariots with our family's slugs, but they weren't this well-grown by a long shot. It was too much of a gamble to keep a slug to the end of its life. Some highborn Lumen would pay a wealth of gems for anything over twenty years. The older they got, the tougher and better at pulling they were. But it was a risky purchase because they could die at any time. So most sold them before the twenty-year mark, as soon as they could verify the armor was coming in solid. Watching this one pull twelve chariots at the same time was sort of breathtaking.

I'd never really bothered thinking about what happened to the twelve after the Drawing. As a Lumen it had always meant stuffing myself full of food and celebrating under the sky fire with my brother. It meant staying up all night with friends and family and topping the whole festival off on the last day with the Grand Procession.

This was far from a celebration. The setting sun was still hot on my back in the open desert, and I kept thinking of Westalyn's gift, locked away in that storage crate. I had to get back in time for the feast, or my mother would banish me from the next one.

Waves of sand *whooshed* over us at a steady rate as the slugs burrowed and dug forward. A great, golden wall enclosed all twelve chariots, completely blocking our sight. The Grey all stood awkwardly and winced as specks of sand flung toward them.

"Stand up straight!" I shouted to the one next to me. Her shoulders twitched at the sound of my voice, but she kept her head down. I sighed. "You're only getting sand in your face because you're sticking your head *into* it. Make sure your feet are locked in the sleeves and straighten your body. Trust me!"

I watched her fumble the position of her legs—they were much heavier than mine. She slowly unbent her knees and pushed herself up, revealing her face. It was round, plain, and, well, grey, without a drop of paint to cover it. Her wide eyes and lips were still tightly closed.

"It's okay now!" I called out. My voice wasn't carrying very far against the *whirring* of chariots on the sand or the occasional shocks of static on the other side of the wall.

She opened her mouth first and promptly coughed out a mouthful of sand. Then she took a short breath, followed by many more gulps of air. Her eyes blinked open. They were deep black pools. Grey lacked colored pigment of any sort, of course—unblessed by the Wizard of Light and all that. But I found myself drawn into them. They didn't glow with their own light, but they didn't suck it in either, like my family always said. They actually seemed to reflect whatever was in front of them. I was looking at my own mirrored image. The thick black brows above her eyes furrowed then, and I realized I'd just been staring at a Grey woman's face.

"Sorry," I muttered. Then I had to struggle not to burst out laughing. I wondered if, in the history of our people, a Lumen had ever apologized to a Grey.

Wave after wave of sand continued to blast over us. Palunia was a sand planet, with desert covering all of its surface, save for a few islands of stone. My family lived on Centrisle, of course, but there were islands at the corners, too. Centrisle was the largest, and the home of all planetary celebrations. It was also the only one with sub-islands. The shipyard was a rough ride to the east, propped up on a platform built of metals that were now extremely rare. To the north, where we seemed to be heading, were three noteworthy landmarks: the outer dungeons, where the vilest offenders went to drown in sand; the Planetary Palace, where the contessa lived as the last royal descendant of the original Lumen people; and the Amber Tower that stretched to the stars, once filled with the holy fragrance that kept us alive, still slowly draining after thousands of years.

The sky was turning its usual evening green, which meant the sun would be just a sliver of light on the horizon behind us. Two bright stars shone emerald and yellow through the blackness of coming night. This time last festival, Jona and I were setting the plates and goblets for the feast. I scowled as my insides seemed to twist. It was bad enough that I was missing the celebration, but that stupid phrase had really upset my mother, and a lot of other people, too. I could only pray to the Wizard of Life that we weren't heading to the outer dungeons. I imagined the crew dropping me off to drown in sand, then going to celebrate. Maybe Jiyorga would like that.

The feast at our palace would start when Jiyorga arrived. Naturally he'd built his own palace a century ago, but no one spent the feast alone. He'd arrive, and my family would cheer, and our allied families would cheer. We'd invited the Chi Sohas to join us this year, so Westalyn would be there, too, waiting for me. Something in my chest twinged.

After the feast there'd be the repeating of the Traveling Chant, wishing luck and prosperity to the Twelve, asking the great wizards to allow them safe passage and all that. To be honest, I had never memorized it properly. Jona and I would make mouth movements and compete for whose could be the most convincing. The loser was inevitably the first to laugh.

Then there'd be the revealing of the new Lumen fashion standards, and it would be encouraged to burn any old robes left in the palace. Mother would, of course, have hidden those of mine she felt I *should* be wearing. It occurred to me then that this might be my last feast living in the main palace. Once I got Westalyn's word, construction would start on a new expansion for us and our children.

I was still imagining what I'd be missing out on when my chariot jerked in place and stopped. We'd come to the edge of a sand crest. The wall fell to dust in front of us, revealing a crater beyond. I was just realizing where we were when static cracked and the slug lurched ahead again, dragging us forward and swiftly down the slope.

A few of the Grey let out odd cries, and I nearly joined them. But I sucked in a deep breath, ready to let the fall happen. The woman next to me kept her footing, surprisingly. Our row was last to pass over the crest, and when we did, the twisted, pointed turrets of the palace towers came into sight. We plunged downward.

Focus on the palace. It was thin and tall, dug deeply into a crater in the sand. *Do not scream.* Its blackstone outer walls captured projections of distant galaxies, which tonight were midnight blue and fuschia. Unlike the other structures on our planet, this one was made of a smooth stone that seemed to have no beginning and no end. I always thought that if I could touch it, it would feel like the surface of a gem.

We hit solid ground, but all eyes were now on the breathtaking structure in front of us. A bit like the Chi Soha palace, the iconic towers were separated. These ones were not attached to a central body but were interconnected together, all spiraling up to the height of the crest. Looking up at it was like looking at the stars and neighboring planets. The palace seemed immeasurably tall from the bottom, where the land was filled with plants and flowers, making it the closest thing we had to ancient gardens on Palunia.

As the slug came to a stop near the palace gate, my attention was drawn to the two frontmost towers. Balls of emerald green light were dancing behind their solid surfaces. They wobbled a few minutes before erupting into perfectly parallel lines and zooming up the towers. They followed the spirals round and round before exploding out the tops and igniting the sky with viridian light.

Of course, I realized. This was where the sky fire came from. That meant the festivities were starting. I wasn't getting back for the feast at this rate. The sky was now completely green overhead, fading slowly into the night sky. Watching the lights from a distance was a must-have experience for anyone during the Cup Festival. Watching from here was breathtaking. From the feast we would have seen the lights exploding upward on the horizon. Here, though, it overtook the entire sky. The dancing orbs inside the towers were mesmerizing, too, drawing my eyes back down at the slightest movement. They must have been coming from some mystical artifact inside the palace.

We'd all heard, of course, that some of our ancient treasures and artifacts were stored here under the contessa's lock and key. I was starting to wonder how true that was and what else she was hiding.

Along with the Grey, I watched, transfixed, as more balls of light appeared in the towers. Again they danced—slowly at first, then gradually faster, until they shook wildly and shot upward as beams of light and twisted out the tops with a *bang*. This happened over and over again. Green, yellow, cyan, violet, orange.

I hadn't prepared a sky fire wish this year. I was a bit caught up in my courting, and all of this traveler nonsense wasn't helping. I wondered what Westalyn would be wishing for. I tried to come up with something, but I found myself staring at the Grey, none of whom had moved an inch since the fire started. I felt my chest tighten, and I had to stop myself from letting my anger slip out at the wrong target.

It was just occurring to me that these Grey may not even realize what they'd signed up for. They weren't really intelligent beings. Were we taking advantage of their stupidity? Did they think they'd just won a moment to prance across a stage and could walk away unscathed? Did they even know that none of their friends had returned after being called in previous Drawings? If they didn't have that awareness, did that somehow make it better? I sighed and found myself glancing over my shoulder to the Grey woman beside me. She was still upright like I'd shown her, and her face—her eyes were looking at mine. Startled, I jerked my head back toward the sky.

Yellow and violet orbs had just lit the sky when I heard a *clink* behind me. One of the guards was unlocking the chains from my chariot. As I turned to face him, he reached out for my wrists. I pulled back, but he was stronger. He wrapped cold, oversized links around my forearms, pressing them roughly into my skin. He moved to the Grey woman next.

"I'm not your prisoner!" I called to him. The woman didn't bother to resist. "You can't treat a Lumen this way, let alone a Ju Demma. I hope you like digging for water."

Grey could become violent and dangerous, of course. It made some sense to chain and bind them, just in case. But we Lumen didn't even *touch* one another. Being sentenced to the water pits would be less embarrassing than this; at least then you wouldn't be treated so inhumanely.

I was shaking.

The chariots were unchained two at a time by the guards, and links were slapped easily over more Grey arms. As the last two were being bound, a creaking sound echoed from one of the distant inner towers. Then another noise emerged, a bit like the *singing* thing the Grey did, but louder and louder. The vibrations in my ear felt unnatural. I staggered a bit as the guards pushed us into a line.

"I can walk!" I snapped, skipping into the lovely procession of Grey. I held a few more words under my breath but tried to embrace the situation with an enthusiasm strong enough to wear the guards down.

In front of me was an almost childlike Grey, surprisingly shorter and narrower than I was, and I couldn't tell which gender they belonged to. According to my lessons, Grey had all sorts of genders, just like they had all sorts of art, or whatever they called it. Behind me was the tallest one of them I'd ever seen. I wouldn't have noticed, except that as he staggered along he bent his neck downward, over my head. Grey stench could be a powerful thing.

"Do you mind?" I growled, shooting him a look. He didn't so much as blink.

"You know what I'd like to know?" I asked him. He stared back. The lack of pigment and paint in his skin made it hard to guess what he was feeling, assuming Grey *had* feelings. "I'd like to know how you would captain a ship. A military-grade intergalactic travelers' ship. Would you know which levers to raise or buttons to press? Do they train you for this? Honestly, I could use some enlightenment, because the more I think about this, the less sense it makes."

His face remained blank at first, and then his mouth opened. More Grey stench, but I watched him, wondering if he understood, and if he could possibly form a direct answer. I didn't find out, though, because the singing sounds began to blare in front of us, commanding all of our attention. Tens of other Grey, of all shapes and sizes, came out in two lines. In their hands were shining gold-colored tubes. They blew into them and manipulated them by pressing their fingers to sets of valves, which seemed to change the sound. The instruments came in about as many shapes as the people did, with the smallest, and *loudest*, ones in front. They stopped walking a short distance from us, and the noise faded to silence.

We all waited, shifting uncomfortably in the sudden quietude. Then the Grey players parted, revealing the entrance to the main tower. In front of it a figure emerged, mostly obscured by the darkness now that the sky fire had finished. But I knew exactly who we were looking at.

The contessa wore a headpiece of solid gold that shone all on its own. It was half a circle—rounded on top and flat on the bottom, with five long, pointed arrows extending from the band on her head outward. Between the arrows, small orbs of light hovered in place, bouncing cautiously between their dividers but never crossing over. Orange on her right, violet on her left, and the central one, which sat a little higher than the others, was glowing bright electric blue, matching the orbs currently resting in the towers.

Lumen usually painted themselves to accent their natural tones: blue, violet, and even pink. The contessa chose gold. Bright, shimmering gold. If not for the smooth texture of her face, it would have been difficult to see where her skin ended and the headpiece began. Her eyes were covered in gold as well—she must have been using some ancient magic to see. And painted down her cheeks were white holy markings that only the founding family could bear.

Her robes were stark white, which only made her more radiant. On her shoulders sat an enormous, cloth-covered pauldron, draped fabrics of red and vibrant orange down her front and over her back like a long cape. Two Grey held the cape above the ground behind her. In contrast with the white and gold, the contessa's top lip was painted black, and the bottom one red. Sharp white teeth reflected the light around her as her face broke into a smile.

"Welcome to the Planetary Palace," she began, surveying the Twelve. Her voice was soft but commanding. She gazed at the group before her, taking time to study each individual one by one. Her eyes found me.

It was like the very sight of me had interrupted her. Her brow narrowed and her lips pursed—a distinct Lumen expression signaling that she was *highly offended*. She managed to raise her left hand, enforcing the silence among us, while she appeared to be gathering her thoughts.

One of the guards shifted in place. It was probably on the tip of his tongue to spill the entire story of my drawing.

"Guards," she let out at last, remaining completely still. "The usual with the Grey. The Lumen follows us to the Celebration Chamber."

Finally this'll get sorted. The two men in red took a moment to exchange hand signals. They were most likely worried about what their punishment would be for treating me so poorly. I hoped Jiyorga would get an earful, too.

The contessa led the procession toward the entrance gate. The Grey were slow-moving creatures, who mostly wobbled their way there. I noticed near the front of the line the round-faced Grey woman still standing with her back straight, while the rest hunched over. Maybe she'd taken my chariot tips as an order. I supposed now that made sense.

The guards had taken the front and back position of our happy little lineup, undoubtedly making sure we didn't run out of the giant crater. I sighed. If I had my say in their punishment, it was going to be relentless.

We passed the two front towers as the orbs faded from blue to violet, calmly dancing in place behind the translucent dark stone. The contessa set foot in front of the tower with the door. She brought her hand up to it, and it opened inward before she could make contact. She led us inside.

"No guards here, Your Fairness?" one of the red asked, clearly not knowing how a Lumen could get by without someone like him.

"This palace obeys me," she replied. Her voice had a quality to it that made me want to hang on every word. She was young of face despite being centuries old. It wouldn't surprise me if she were part wizard or something.

As she walked through the entrance, orbs of light illuminated around her, matching the color of those in her headpiece. We were crossing a narrow corridor over an enormous dark pit that stretched the entire base of the tower. Other corridors ran parallel or crossed one another at various points throughout the room of black emptiness. The more orbs we lit, the more shaky my legs became.

At the end, we reached a long, downward staircase. A crater halfway through the planet's surface wasn't deep enough for royalty, apparently. I had heard rumors that the sand dungeons weren't limited to the prison. Maybe the Grey would be spending a night half-drowned in the cold desert while I was given a glass of mead to set this thing straight. My insides twitched again at the thought.

When the front of the group reached the bottom of the stairs, a yellow orb began to glow in the corridor ahead. At least I thought it was a corridor. It wasn't until my own feet hit the stone floor that I saw we were in a room. A single room taking up the length and width of what had to be an entire tower.

The walls, like the floor, were made of rough, dark stone wedges—individual pieces that just happened to stay together, by the look of it. Along the walls were many strange instruments. The contessa motioned to her crew of Grey to put theirs back, but there were hundreds of others. Some gold-colored with valves, and others completely different with strings, skins, keys, and other components I'd never seen. It was hard to tell from where we stood, but it looked like the far wall was empty. In the center of the oversized room was a floating tray, filled with paints and brushes. Toward the back of the room the floor was covered in rich fabrics and pillows, surrounding tables filled with books and writing pads.

The guards began removing the bindings on each of the Grey, but not me.

"You're putting them to work? On their last night here?" It was out of my mouth before I knew who I was speaking to.

The contessa held my gaze long enough to watch me crumble with embarrassment, then spoke. "Friends, please make yourselves at home here. Meals and mead will arrive in due time. Let the guard know if you have a favorite and we'll make it happen. You are the reason we are going to get our treasure back this time, and we offer what little hospitality we can in exchange for your sacrifice."

I had to stifle a laugh. The Grey tell someone what they want? Even if they could speak fluently, I had no idea what a Grey would want. An order of rocks? Some slop from their home palace pale? I'd never seen a Grey take a bite of any of my family's food.

I followed behind the contessa and the two guards. As we exited I remembered there was no door—nothing to lock. What if the Grey roamed free? Could the contessa just will them to stay? Confine them mentally in the bottom of this tower?

We made our way back up the staircase. When we got back to the open corridor, a new set of stairs appeared in front of us. It formed out of nowhere, jutting off the side, extending to a nearby floating bridge. It was steep, too. Funny how I hadn't really made note of the distance going down, but each step on this was excruciating. It was downright embarrassing, watching the contessa and guards ascend it effortlessly while I trailed behind, coughing and wheezing. I wasn't trained in resistive combat like the red cloaks, and I didn't have the advantage of living here. We regular Lumen weren't cut out for this sort of exercise.

When we finally reached the bridge, myself in a heap, we took a right, heading back toward the palace entrance. I was exhausted, but it was almost a relief to walk in a straight line. I just had to keep my nausea under control so I wouldn't fall off the edge. Doors started to appear as we walked along the sides of the free corridor. Not exactly doors—more like the outlines of doors, drawn in thin white lines of light. They all had different shapes at their centers: suns, stars, moons, planets, and various space creatures. I found myself studying each one we passed, mesmerized by them. I nearly bumped into one of the guards as we came to a stop in front of a door with a star and a key on it.

The contessa took something from within her robe around her neck and raised it to the door. The thin lines began to radiate, filling in the door-shape solid white and then materializing into an actual slab of stone. It opened without her touch and she entered.

With how well the Grey had been treated, I prepared myself for luxury as I trailed behind her and the guards.

No light appeared at first. I had to follow by the light of her headpiece, but it didn't activate any other orbs this time. I saw her take something in her hand again. A moment passed in silence, and then at once the room became white. I shielded my eyes in shock.

When I managed to lower my chained hands away from my face, I saw that she was holding a staff. A long, majestic staff that couldn't have come from Palunia. Another ancient treasure, no doubt. It was silver in color, with red runes encased upon it from bottom to top. The top of the staff was a flat circle, which acted as a bed for the light source. It was some kind of white gem—not too large on its own, but powerful in its light. I'd never seen a white gem before, but it was too bright to get a closer look.

After a few minutes of gawking at the staff I finally noticed the room. It was a fraction of the size of the lower one. The walls here were plain sandstone. The contessa was now sitting in an old burgundy fabric chair, and she motioned for me to take one across from her. There was no goblet in her hand. Behind her a wall of bars enclosed a row of prison cells. Stunned, I gulped and took my seat without a word.

"Guards, will you leave us?" she requested. Her eyes were still covered, but I could *sense* her looking behind me toward them. When they stepped out, she set the staff casually across her lap. I was still drawn to its light, but the brightness kept stinging my eyes and forcing me to look away. As the door swung back into place, it resealed itself and disappeared into the sandstone wall.

CHAPTER 4

I STIFFENED. I had met the contessa once as a child, but it had been with my mother, and I was too young to remember most of it. We were a fairly important Lumen family—one of the most important, thanks to Jiyorga—but that didn't mean we were cozy with ancient royalty. I'd never been so humiliated and nervous in my life. I could feel her eyes on me, but I couldn't bring myself to return her gaze.

"What do you wish for, Damaus Ju Demma?" she asked. Again, her voice was soft, but it echoed powerfully off the chamber walls. I couldn't remember if she had ever bothered with honorifics or not, but it was odd not to hear "Lord" in front of my name.

"If I could, I'd like to turn back time about a day," I said, studying the floor. This floor was dark and smooth, like the palace's outer walls. Though it was translucent, in the darkest shade of violet-blue, I couldn't see the next floor below; instead, I saw what looked like a great pit of fire throwing red and orange embers toward its surface. I instinctively jerked away as one came toward my foot, but I didn't even feel its warmth before it fell back down. If the contessa noticed, she didn't acknowledge it.

"I suppose you would," she noted. Now I forced myself to look at her, wincing an embarrassing amount at the light of her staff. Her dark painted lips pressed together. "Do you remember your first visit here, child?"

"A little," I said, attempting to lean back and act comfortable. It was difficult wrapped in chains. "I think you summoned my mother for something. I don't remember the . . . exact circumstances. Which I think is fair, given that I was only about three turns of the sun old."

If she was amused, she didn't show it. We weren't sweet-talking yet. It kept hitting me that this was the most powerful being on the planet, blessed by all ancient wizards, and yet the only way I knew how to respond to such an absurd situation was to keep cracking nonsense at her. If Westalyn or my mother could hear what a fool I was making of myself, they'd drag me out by the ears.

"Three and a quarter trips around the Great Sun, yes," the contessa continued. "At your mother's request."

"I wasn't aware one could request a meeting with the contessa," I confessed.

"It is unordinary," she said, getting to her feet. I didn't know whether to stand with her out of respect or shrink back into my seat. I stayed put.

The fabric from her pauldron trailed behind her on the floor as she crossed to the center of the room. Facing away from me, she began to turn the staff in her hands. She spun it slowly at first, then doubled the speed. Faster and faster it twirled like a whirling baton of light. She kept her arm relaxed; it was more like she was conducting it than forcing it to spin.

It started to spin more quickly than she could keep up with, and she took a single step backward. Arm still extended, she positioned her hand adjacent to it with her palm toward its center and motioned her wrist toward it. The staff followed, lowering itself flat onto its side, and continued to spin horizontally.

I watched with my mouth wide open as the fires below the floor all pulled in the direction of the rotating staff. Orange-hot runes began to form on the floor a short distance below where it hung in midair. Two thin circles formed around the runes, much like the first light of the doorway, enclosing the markings in a white ring. Then to my horror, the inner circle opened up and liquid fire exploded up into the chamber. The contessa didn't move, but I thought I heard her whisper something. A white, cylindrical column of light fell from the staff to the floor, causing the flames to vanish and the floor to close again. I blinked and saw that the runes were gone, but where they had manifested on the dark surface sat a small box.

The contessa didn't speak. I had a million questions and yet zero words. My eyes hung on the box. There wasn't even a trace of smoke. I wasn't sure if that spoke to the power of the staff, or if the fire had been some kind of illusion.

"Come, Damaus Ju Demma," she beckoned. Her arms were relaxed at her sides. I realized then that the staff was gone. The room was only lit by the fires below.

Stunned, I made an attempt to stand. It was surprisingly difficult. I could hardly move my legs, and the casings on my arms felt extremely heavy. Something was wrong. I could feel my face burning up with embarrassment and wondered for the first time since the festivities began how my paint was holding up.

I managed to stand on the third try. Then it was like learning to walk for the first time. One foot in front of the other, careful not to lean too far forward or back. Thirteen awkward steps in total before I was face-to-face with her. I grimaced as I dared to look her in the eye—or where her eyes should be—wondering what thoughts were hidden behind all that gold and glimmer.

"Do you know what this is?" she asked, motioning down at the box. It was a bluestone chest with a rune on its top above a star-shaped steel lock.

"No," I said. I held back all of the questions and exclamations I wanted to shout at her. I wasn't even sure I could shout; she was probably controlling my speech, too.

She turned toward me, and I could feel her staring into my eyes. I found myself wondering if I'd seen her take a breath. Almost as if hearing my thoughts, she turned away again and began pacing toward the back of the room, toward the bars that separated this part of the chamber from the cells.

"Lumen are interesting creatures," she said, clearly not including herself in that assessment. "Tell me, Damaus Ju Demma—have you ever kept a *secret*?"

"A what?" She was mixing languages. Ancient words only she would know, most likely. It sounded like something out of one of my childhood lessons.

"A *secret*," she repeated. "A truth only you know to be true. Maybe your truth, or one of someone dear to you. A truth kept from the pervasive eyes and ears of our society."

She was speaking in riddles. "I don't think so," I said.

"It is my duty, as contessa of Palunia, to bear this burden. Lumen are interesting for many reasons. One of which is their distinct inability to keep these secrets when asked. Tell me—what were you planning to do this evening before your name was called?"

She was baiting me. It was difficult to keep from snarling my response. "Before all of this," I said, "I was going to watch the sky fire and ask Westalyn Chi Soha for her partnership. Then we were going to feast with my family and watch the Procession in the morning."

"Why do you tell me this?" She fixed her gaze to mine and waited. I was getting frustrated.

"Because you asked."

"Yes." She sauntered to the chest and turned to face it before kneeling on the floor. "What do you suppose would happen if you came to know information that would destroy us?"

"Destroy us?" That was a little dramatic. "I wouldn't know." She more than outranked me, but I had never been spoken down to like this. My patience wasn't going to last much longer.

"You wouldn't know, but there was a time when you did know, Damaus Ju Demma. Because on your first visit here, when you were only a young lord of three and a quarter turns of age, you came to me in this chamber, and you sealed away a secret. You handed to me the burden of that secret, and together we placed it here, inside this box."

The contessa slung her right arm outward and extended her fingers gracefully. White light materialized just outside her palm, forming a key. It solidified, long and gold, with red and violet gems down its shaft. Inside the bow at the top where most had empty holes remained an embodiment of light. She grasped the key in hand and bent forward, sliding it into the star-shaped lock.

I waited.

The key clicked sideways inside the lock. I watched as the contessa placed her hands on the sides of the chest and lifted the top open. I admit I was scared to step forward for a lot of reasons, but I couldn't help myself. I approached, knowing I was too close, knowing no one was supposed to stand next to the contessa of their own accord. But she allowed it.

"Listen," she said.

Doubtful, I tuned out my own thoughts and took in the sounds around me. There was a faint noise coming from inside the box. It sounded a bit like those awful instruments of the Grey, but lower in volume and somehow gentle. As she opened the box further, it grew louder. I watched, determined to see what was inside. But there was only blackness, even once the lid had slid into its resting position.

It was black, but it wasn't nothing. The chest was stone-colored, while what came from it was dark, like a shadow with no true form. I just stood there, dumbstruck, desperate to move but forgetting how.

"This is one of those . . . truths? A shadow?"

"One of the secrets, you mean," she replied. She was way too calm for this. "Here I have the power to contain it and to control it for a time. But to let these run loose would be the downfall of our world."

"And here I thought running out of amber was our biggest concern." Too much thinking aloud. I had to get ahold of myself. Running out of amber was only a rumor. Saying that to the contessa was practically an accusation.

"It's . . . related," she said, placing her left hand back on the lid of the box. As she did, the light from the key in her right seemed to repel the shadow back inside. There was a thud, and the chest was closed again. "I will not show you any more. We can't know what would happen if a Lumen were to relearn a powerful secret. I will only tell you this. What you came to me with so many turns ago was a detrimental truth involving one of the creatures you call Grey. One such being was not as he seemed. He sought to overtake us. He would have succeeded, too, if his name had not been drawn. I suppose the Eternal Wizard of Chance sought pity on us that day. That is who I offer these secrets to, in the blessed flame of Draconia."

"And how exactly did you manage to transport enchanted fire to Palunia from Draconia?" I blurted, instantly wishing I could cram every word back into my mouth. I took a deep breath. "Sorry. But why tell me all of this?"

At first, she didn't answer. She turned toward me, and I could feel the warmth of her breath on my face. I held my place, but every social instinct made me want to jump back or run. "The words you said today."

I didn't know what she meant at first. Then it hit me and twisted my insides in a knot. My mother's shocked expression flashed inside my head, and I wanted to take it all back. "I'm sorry. I was only repeating—"

"That same Grey," she finished for me. "While I will not give you the details of the plan, you will know that he sought to kill all Lumen and make a paradise for himself. He was, undisclosed to us, attempting to build an army of Grey. Most of them are simple creatures, but we can't mistake that for indifference. Give them a cause and they'll parade around it in the hot sun.

"We didn't know, of course, until we drew his name. But before that, he had a conversation none of us were privy to with a young boy of three and a half turns. Our scholars still want to know how he came to command so much of our language when most Grey struggle to care for themselves. When he was selected to partake in the Cup, he spoke his final words."

"Let the fire of your sleeping god rain on me," I muttered, slowly feeling out each word this time. "I find it a bit strange that I remember that line and nothing else from your story."

"The other memories are here," she said, lowering her palm toward the box. "Have you ever, Damaus Ju Demma, spoken of something you thought to be common knowledge, only to find that a relative or acquaintance had never heard of it? Often that's just a gap in learning, but sometimes . . . sometimes the memories have had to be sealed away, for the individual's sake as well as the planet's."

"A gap?"

"I cannot remove the secret without removing the context in which it belongs." She placed her hand delicately on the box lid.

"What does that mean?" *And what exactly did you have to do to get the information out of me?*

"This is a truth I need not relay to a prisoner," she replied, getting to her feet. She extended her arm, allowing the key to hover in front of her palm. It turned to light and formed the shape of the great staff.

My mind was overloaded. "A what?" I wasn't sure I'd heard right, and my eyes were transfixed on whatever arcane object could be both a key and a staff. The thin circles and runes reappeared, tracing a ring around the box on the floor again. Light descended from the hovering staff and the chest began to fall. On its descent, a column of liquid flames shot up next to me. I jumped and toppled backward, letting out an embarrassing yelp, and checked my robes to make sure they hadn't been ignited.

When the column dropped back into the floor, I forced myself into a sitting position. There was no sign of the chest. I studied the staff again, despite its brightness. The light bore into me, but I just kept on staring at it. It was coming closer to me. I closed my eyes and everything went white.

My head felt heavy. My body was stuck in place, like I'd been hit by an armored slug. Wisps of white light floated across my closed eyes, which stung less every time I forced them open.

I was still there, in the same room, but now I was behind a row of dark, metal bars. She had called me prisoner. This either had something to do with those *secrets* or it was because of the Cup. *Why did I have to put my name in the Cup?* I wondered now how much they could charge me with. It was laughable to think that I'd believed I was having an amicable chat with the contessa of Palunia.

I tried to remember a case of a highborn Lumen being incarcerated, but there hadn't been any in a long time. A couple cases from the history texts—like Roala Nu Horga, who'd made an attempt on the old duke's life. Or Terisi Gi Almo, who had been arranging to have Lumen he didn't like killed by Grey assassins. He was presumably caught because Grey would make terrible assassins. Most uncooperative Lumen just got sent to the water pits for a few weeks.

But I think I was the first in recent history to be locked away. At least I could go down famous for something if they had me killed.

I sighed and shook my stiff head. I probably wouldn't be executed. It would set a bad precedent. My thoughts were swimming around, contradicting each other, and I was forgetting them as quickly as they were coming to me. I just needed a bit more rest.

It was hard to judge how much time had passed in the room. There were no windows or sundials (not that I could read them). Just dim orange light flickering from the fires below. I kept waking up every so often, wondering if the contessa was coming back, wondering if anyone would bring me food, needing to know what was happening outside with my family and Westalyn. Had it been an hour? A day?

After waking up the fourth or fifth time, I checked if I could still move all my limbs. They seemed to be in place. Still chained, of course, because bars weren't enough. I sighed and leaned back against the wall, observing the room around me. Then I heard the noise.

It was like a soft pattering. A bit like the way I remembered rain, but slow and heavy. *Pat, pat, pat.*

Exactly what kinds of creatures live below this floor? I wondered. *Did something get through? Or is it coming from the other side?* Through my exhaustion I managed to find fear.

The thing gradually came into view. It was a shadow, not far off now, and it seemed to be approaching me. Was it the *secret?* Was it coming to reveal itself to me? Maybe the contessa's box wasn't enough to contain a Lumen's rightful knowledge. I tried to get up, but my chains jerked me back. I was locked to the damn floor.

"Hello," I offered, my voice quivering. "Are you the . . . the secret?"

The being took a step closer—*pat, pat*—and then another. Soon it was on the other side of the bars. An ember rose up beneath us then, illuminating its features.

"You!" I gasped, my voice hoarse and useless.

Then I was unconscious again. Or at least I don't remember what happened next. When I came to, I forced my eyes back open, but there was no sign of her. The Grey woman who had ridden in the chariot beside me.

I didn't wake up again until I was being forcibly removed from my cell by a couple of red guards. They unclasped the lock from my chains, pulling them out of the steel ring on the floor. They retightened the chains with so much force they were denting into my skin.

"Hey!" I barked. The contessa was one thing, but I wouldn't take outright abuse from red cloaks. They ignored me, of course, and set the lock back in place.

Then I was yanked to my feet. My head was throbbing and spinning, and I thought I was going to be sick. "Slow down," I muttered. I was losing consciousness again. *Dammit.* Whatever the contessa had done to me, I hoped it wasn't permanent. Each time they pulled, I came to again, but it was painful. I couldn't really walk. They practically dragged me along to the other side of the chamber through the doorway.

However much time had passed in the cell, it had given me so many strange dreams. Flashes of the ancient wizards, of faraway planets, of my mother, and . . . of that Grey woman. That one had felt closer to real. I highly doubted the contessa would give the Grey free reign of the palace. But then again, they had a feast while I sat in a cell, so anything was possible.

"Wh—where . . ." We'd gone the length of one of the floating corridors. My voice was strained. My feet kept hitting the stairs as they forced me down to a lower level. Maybe the same one we'd left the Grey in. I couldn't focus on my surroundings long enough to figure them out. I blacked out again.

CHAPTER 5

I CAME TO in a stone chamber, with the eleven others who'd been drawn. The Grey stood in their usual tattered, colorless robes, their heads covered in black, grey, and chestnut hair.

"What is this?" I choked. I was expecting to be thrown in a desert cell or taken to the high court for a water pit assignment. This . . . this was worse.

Behind me I heard a familiar voice. "Guards?" I blinked, my thoughts still foggy. I managed to turn my aching body and spot him: Jiyorga N'a Otero, looking as decadent as always, today in a vibrant orange robe that turned to deep red at the bottom. It trailed far behind him, and on his shoulders our family gems were carved into large spikes. I watched his white-painted lips as he spoke. "Are they all chained?"

"All but the *lord*," one of the red replied.

"Hey!" I tried to shout, but it came out slurred. Jiyorga's eyes locked with mine and I hoped he saw my anger. He gazed at me for a brief moment before turning away.

"Get them all bound," he said. "The Grand Chariot is ready."

"Gebackere!" I tried to yell after him, but nothing was coming out right. *Damn the contessa,* I willed, and waited for the Great Wizard of Thought to strike me down. *Damn all these Lumen who'd turn their back on one of their own over something so trivial.*

My forearms were throbbing in the tight chains, darkening under their pressure. There were hardly any patches of paint remaining on my hands and arms, and my navy robe was starting to fray at the sleeves.

I winced as one of the guards jerked me toward the Grey by my chains and hooked another chain between the closest one and me. The twelve of us were divided into two chained rows, and I was at the back of my line.

But I kept blacking out. One moment we were stationary, and the next we were outside. I was walking barefoot in the sand. I couldn't remember when I'd lost my boots. Had I been wearing them in the cell? It was too exhausting to think about.

We came out beneath an enormous chariot, which was more like a desert ship. It was made of spun gold and some light metal. Long, solid strands, nearly as wide as I was, wound around each other, branching out at the back of the chariot into fine points in all directions. In the space between the metallic strands were gemstones even my family couldn't afford. Red, green, and blue, they were the size of a single chariot each and sparkled gently in the predawn light. The light that confirmed my fears—it was time for the Procession.

The first Grey was led toward the chariot. Another woman, more slender than the one I'd become acquainted with, started up a ladder on the chariot's side. That meant our whole line was moving forward. The other six were on the opposite side of the chariot, likely proceeding up a ladder there. One by one, we followed forward and finally upward.

Walking was hard, but climbing was harder. I kept fading in the hot sun and slipping downward, pulling the Grey ahead of me back toward the edge. I tried to apologize—which would be the second time I'd apologized to a Grey—but I couldn't get any words out. Sick of me slowing them down, the guard shouted something, and the next thing I knew, my line was pulling me over onto the chariot's deck.

"You will now head back to Centrisle," Jiyorga said. I couldn't see him, but he was projecting his voice, using the same artifact he did for the Drawing. He could be anywhere nearby. "Follow instructions, and you'll make this as easy on yourselves as possible."

From the first pull it was obvious this arrangement wasn't going to work. We weren't about to fall *off*, since the woven metal rose in high walls around us and curved up over our heads. But there were holes between some of the weaves, and the deck we stood on gave lots of room for us to topple around, with nothing to hold but one another. With each movement, we swayed.

To think that before all of this I was trodding through festival tents and buying scarves for Westalyn. I wondered how she'd spent the feast. I'd somehow make this up to her. I couldn't tell if my latest wave of nausea was coming from whatever sickness the contessa had blessed me with or from imagining what she and my mother might have discussed in my absence.

I found my footing and looked forward with as much focus as I could muster. With the partial glances I got through the bars, it looked like we were in the hands of the same set of slugs that had brought us to the palace. Two regular armored slugs were pulling the guards in their personal chariots, and I had to guess that it would take at least the enormous one to pull us. I still couldn't spot Jiyorga or the contessa, though I knew they'd be in attendance for the Procession.

I kept slipping every time the slug lurched. The Grey weren't doing any better, which was a small comfort. I tried to reposition myself to the side for better footing when it stopped suddenly, toppling us all sideways. Since I was at the back, that meant I ended up on the floor with my side scraped up and the whole line of Grey on top of me.

"*Get off!*" I shouted, panicking. I'd never felt the weight of another person before, and the Grey were coated in unbathed filth. I could smell it on their robes. Greasy strands of hair were brushing over my exposed arm. My nausea was back in full swing.

Everyone knew that if you happened to touch a Grey, you needed to wash immediately, and I should have bathed already after the journey yesterday. I just had to hope the Grey stench didn't get into my robes.

They were slow beings, most built thick and stout. Since we'd all fallen in a heap, my feeble attempts to push at them were futile. I groaned.

I did a lot of yelling after that, too. Any time it lurched forward or slowed down, we'd be flung toward one of the ends of the chariot. When we stopped I'd be scraped and bruised and buried, and when we started I'd trip into them. If I had any paint left on my face, it was definitely peeling now.

You'd think we'd get better at catching ourselves, but when your own footing is dependent on five other people who have no disposition for learning, and you're drugged with something magical from the Planetary Palace, you aren't exactly in peak physical condition. One of the following stops was so sudden, those of us at the back were flung into the air. One of the Grey ahead of me hit his head on a light-metal strand, then hit the floor unconscious. I managed to block my own impact with my shoulder, stiffening my whole arm. On top of losing my paint I was going to be discolored there, too. What a way to greet the people.

The Drawing Ceremony was the biggest celebration of the festival, and the Procession was the grand finale. No one missed it. It was the only event the contessa attended personally. In previous years I'd watched the Grey walk on the high platform over the festival grounds, on display for our satisfaction. They had always looked more tattered than usual up there, and now I knew why. And the damage was only going to become more severe once we took to the platform. I was starting to shake.

When the grounds came into view, I was scraped all over and my skin was leaking fluid. I'd never seen a grown Lumen injured before. It hurt. My heart was racing uncontrollably in my chest as we slowed outside the large tent where I'd taken Westalyn to the show the day before. All of the Centrisle population and thousands of visitors from the other stretches of Palunia would be on the other side, ready to use me for their entertainment.

I wasn't going to let that happen. I couldn't. I drew in a deep breath and gripped the nearest piece of the metal piping. I wouldn't go. I was a Lumen and, beyond that, a lord of house Ju Demma. A few words and a ballot in amber weren't going to take that away from me. I outranked these guards and it was about time they learned it.

"Hey!" I shouted to the Grey in front of me. The chariot was slowing down. They didn't turn to face me. "*Grey*, you will obey me."

They spun around and actually looked conflicted. Like they were starting to see me as an equal. I fumed and wondered what my face looked like. With a rush of anxious anger, I scanned the vessel around me. We were beneath one of those gemstones, next to a gaping hole in the side of the chariot. I tugged on the length of chain between myself and the Grey I'd been shouting at—*hard*. They toppled toward me. I didn't stop there, pulling continuously until they came to me on their own.

Should be enough, I decided. I was dripping liquid under the hot sun but couldn't secure my hood properly with my arms chained. We were coming to a stop. There was no time left.

I climbed onto the lowest metal tube. One upside to lacking shoes was that I stuck to it, but it was hot. I let it burn me; this would be worth it. I scrambled upward, grabbing hold of the next piece and pulling myself up. Just a little more and I'd be able to wrap myself around the outside. I reached forward with my arm, leaning in to reach the next one, when the chain went taut.

"Come up here!" I called down to the Grey. They didn't move at first. I gave the best tug upward I could. "You do this or, so help me, I will make sure you end up in a cell instead of a ship."

They looked up at me. They either understood my words or my tone, because they lifted themselves—slowly—up the first woven tube.

It gave me the slack to get over. I started to climb out when I noticed a red guard coming up the ladder on the other side. He didn't see me. I kicked off the side of the chariot wall with a grunt.

It wasn't enough. As my body swung back toward the vessel, I put both feet in front of me, knees bent. This time I kicked hard. On pure momentum I swung up over the bar, looping my chain around it and suspending the Grey above the ground on the other side. I heard the clink of the chain sticking and waited, wondering if I should have brought a Grey down with me. I forced myself to look up, where the morning sun was coming toward center sky, hotter and brighter by the minute. My plan was in motion.

I'd gotten to the other side of the large red gem—a fire gem. It was said that they could light anything that wasn't blessed by the wizards, as long as they could absorb enough light. I waited, hoping and pleading with any wizards who might take my side.

I was preparing to hang my head and weep when I caught sight of something. Smoke. The links supporting me were starting to smoke all around the gem. I watched them distort and melt until they snapped. I fell.

There's no feeling quite like coughing up a mouthful of burning sand. My hood had come off entirely, leaving my hairless head exposed. The guards would be up there now, observing the mess I left behind and noticing me gone. I scrambled to my feet to break into a run when a sudden burst of pain seared in my right shoulder, the same one I'd already injured, causing me to fall onto my face.

They yanked me up, tearing at my wound. I was nauseated all over again, and my eyes couldn't focus. I glanced over to see what was wrong with me. A long, dark object had gone through my shoulder. They'd speared me. I couldn't keep the sickness down anymore.

When they rechained me to the group and forced us to walk, I was a mess. We were being herded into the tent from the back, and I still had a spear through my shoulder. All I'd done was expedite my fate of bodily harm by jumping down here of my own accord. *Just don't look*, I kept repeating to myself, preparing for my walk. *Don't look at them.* I heard cheering and Jiyorga's voice calling out over the crowd. I'd done everything I could. I wasn't going to get out of this.

The cheering turned to cries of celebration when the first Grey left the tent and entered the public eye. The Procession was a walk across a suspended bridge, which had been set up during the feast the night before. The festival grounds would be largely empty now to make room for the hundreds of thousands of people that wouldn't miss this for the world.

The walk was an hour long. Each of the twelve were subject to the most direct and severe humiliation. Which, for a Grey, wasn't much different from the rest of their days. For me though . . . it was going to be painful. While I hoped they'd recognize me for the Lumen I was and reserve their impulse to mock me, it was going to be mockery enough walking the length of that bridge. The only thing I could say for sure was that this would be recorded in the history tomes.

One after the other, we entered. And with each chug of the chain, my shoulder throbbed, my chest tightened, and my breath shortened. Ten more. Nine. *I can't do this. I can't. No, no, no.*

"Guards, are you sure you want to make this mark on Lumenkind?" I asked, hoping I appeared a lot calmer than I felt. I'd learned plenty of theory about diplomacy, but it wasn't something I'd ever had to practice.

One of the red cloaks looked at me, then wiggled the spear in my shoulder. I fell to the ground, jerking the line of Grey back toward me and letting the fluids from my would spill all over myself. I was seething with rage and agony. I could pull the spear out and . . . and swing my untrained arm at a guard while the other stood and watched? I could leak to death with my wound exposed?

Grunting, I pushed myself up with my unwounded arm and somehow got back on my feet. I gritted my teeth and stepped forward, joining the line.

Three . . . two . . . It was my turn. I could hear them. I could see them. The ones nearest to the tent could see me, too, and they were pointing and whispering with whomever they were standing nearest. The Grey kept on going though. And the force of five of them overpowered even my best stance. They tugged at my footing and I let them. I could at least walk with what little pride I had remaining.

I took my first step out onto the bridge. The cheering began to quiet as two guards came and clipped my chains. At first I saw nothing, shocked by the sudden brightness of morning light. I'd forgotten to pull my hood back on. As I scrambled for it with my cramped, unspeared arm, I felt their stares, their judgment, their mockery. I had nothing left to do but take it.

Hundreds of thousands of Lumen in all directions watched me. Patches of Grey gathered, too—some to document the event in paintings, while others joined as part of the crowd. It was the only public event in which Grey and Lumen weren't segregated. And no one seemed to mind. They were all too busy watching me.

There were several crossings along the way, where two guards stood ready to force you along if you grew too tired or tried to escape. After about ten minutes of walking, the first one came into view. When I got close enough to see their faces, I caught one of the red cloaks giving me a look, his eyes dancing from mine to the spear in my shoulder. I forced a wide smile and waved erratically with my other hand. As I passed between them, they tore at my gem-covered cloak, stopping me in my tracks while they ripped it to shreds, tossing the morsels into the crowd.

Naked, I continued down the bridge with my head down. Insults and awful noises boomed and echoed around me, but it was like they were coming from somewhere far away. I was lost in my own thoughts, though I couldn't put words to any of them. The noise kept intensifying, though, until it forced my concentration.

I glanced up for just a moment. The contessa's Grey were marching behind me with their dreaded instruments. That was about the only thing that could make this worse. My face twisted, and I dared to look out into the crowd. Extravagant lights, oversized jewelry displays, and celebratory banners were everywhere. *Yes, what a wonderful, blessed day this is.* Celebrating the fact that I was being actively humiliated and was about to be sent off to die. Didn't they see how wrong this was? But then, until this moment, I'd been just like them.

After the next checkpoint, the throwing began. Throwing stones was tradition. "Gives the Grey a bit of color to remember us by," Jiyorga had told me as a child. Now the thought made me sick. I watched them hurl rocks of various sizes at the two Grey ahead of me. A mix of simple desert stone and cheap, sharp gems. I wondered if my people would actually throw them at me.

I didn't have long to wait. They pelted us without discrimination. Or maybe I got the brunt of it. I was the last, so I was getting whatever was left in their hands. I thought I saw some people hesitating, but they quickly joined their friends in whipping them at my body. They hit me everywhere, and I had nothing to cover myself with. At best I deflected a few with my spear, which was so excruciating I fell over a few times. But somehow I stayed on the bridge, and somehow I kept getting up.

Ahead of me a particularly large and fast-moving stone hit one of the Grey men, knocking him to the ground. He leaked red fluids and stopped moving. Guards rushed over from behind me to remove him. He'd probably be replaced. Maybe they could kill me here, too. I paused. I considered just stopping and facing the crowd, but I was a coward.

The rest happened in a fog, but I made it to the end. I trembled and stumbled a lot of the way, worse off than many of the Grey since they'd already passed the finish and didn't have a spear in their shoulder. I was handed crew robes, but I was too broken to examine them. My head was throbbing, my skin was burnt, I was dehydrated, and I was covered in wounds. How I was still alive was beyond me. I collapsed then onto the staircase leading away from the bridge.

I opened my eyes a moment later as several guards placed their hands on me. I expected to be lifted, to be carried to a healing center. As many held me in place, one of them placed his boot on my back and dug in hard. He then yanked the spear.

I yelled and cursed over the sounds of celebration. The crowd couldn't see me here. I was entirely in the guards' control. Around me dark blue fluids leaked and began to drip down the stairs.

CHAPTER 6

I WAS STARTING to miss my cell from the palace. It at least had that terrifying floor to look at. This place had a whole lot of nothing.

Now the only separation I had from the Grey were a few black steel bars, which were admittedly preferable to chains. We were arranged side by side in our individual boxes, with bars on three walls and a yellowstone wall behind us. Across from our row of cells was another yellowstone wall with a couple of small windows nearly as high as the ceiling.

The Grey were struggling to walk in their new uniforms, which didn't seem to consider their body shape very well. They were based on ancient designs. All my clothing at home was made to stay cool in the sun—loose-fitting and made of fine, simple fabrics. These uniforms were made to fit tight on our bodies and were designed in two pieces: one for the torso and arms, and one for the waist and legs. It was absurd by all fashion standards. I wasn't really sure what the point of a special

suit was, given the ships were supposed to have natural planetary compression chambers.

I was lying on the cot in my cell when I heard a *clunking*
noise in the distance. The stone cot was one improvement over
the palace cell, I guess. Except my body was still throbbing with
pain. It was a three-day wait while the ship was prepared, and
there was one more to go. Lumen didn't often need medicat-
ing, but when we did we got it promptly and it was fast-acting.
They'd taken half a day to get me enough not to die, and it was
clearly an old supply since I was still in pain.

As a Lumen I'd also never had to consider what happened
after the Procession. Usually the Grey were carted off and we
went for our ceremonial days of rest following the festival.
Occasionally we would see the ship heading out, but since
there were no more festivities to take part in, it wasn't such a
big deal. Then occasionally there'd be reports from the ship,
but that had never really interested me either. At least not since
I was a kid. You learned not to put too much stock into a ship
that would eventually go off the radar and be destroyed.

I watched the two Grey in the cell next to me. They'd
paired all of them but left me alone. I guess maybe they'd put
one with me if they found another Grey to replace the man
who had died. I really wasn't so different from them anymore
by society's standards. My nearest cellmates were an older man
and what looked like a young boy. They were both pacing the
perimeter of their cell. It hadn't really occurred to me that some
of the travelers would be children.

Clunk, clunk. I let out a sigh and set my gaze instead at the
windows. It wasn't that I had a particularly active life, but being
forced to sit still without sun was not to my liking. Grains
of sand occasionally trickled in through the windows, which
meant we were underground. Two guards sat in cushioned
chairs against the far wall, silently observing us.

The *clunk* turned to a *whirring* noise as a third guard appeared, pulling a wooden cart behind him. There was a cloth strewn over the top, concealing unidentifiable objects beneath it. The wheels slowed and clicked into place on the hard, dusty stone. The new guard motioned to the other two to join him. When all three were standing in line behind the cart, facing us in our pathetic excuses for domiciles, the one in the center pulled back the cloth. I gasped.

There were breads and fruit. Actual fruit. We hadn't seen natural food at our most esteemed feasts since I was a child. Then my eyes set on the jug next to the fruit. "Is that—" I began, my throat growing hoarser every second I spent wondering. I couldn't say the word.

The jug was clear, and so was the liquid inside. There was a cup along with it, which one of the guards poured half full before starting toward the cages. He decided to start at the end farthest from me, with the Grey. Of course. Though to be fair, if it was what I thought, Grey needed it to survive.

"Hey, red cloak!" I muttered, growing dizzy. I kept imagining the refreshing liquid on my tongue.

Then the door by the stairs creaked open again and someone entered. I strained, pressing my face to the bars, but I couldn't see who it was. Someone tall, in a long, trailing cloak. *Of course.* The contessa.

Supposedly she rarely left the palace. I'd certainly never seen her except during major events and, I guess, the visits I'd paid. I braced myself, my eyes darting from her to the drinking vessel that was making its way down the line of cells.

"Travelers," the contessa said. She wore no headpiece this time, and she came painted white with accents of all colors on the edges of her face. "Our fate depends on you. It's now that I'll reveal to you the truth of your mission." She motioned for the guards to move the cart away. They complied. Again her eyes were covered, but she turned her head to face each of our cells before continuing.

She pulled a chain out of her robes. It hung around her neck, and there were two objects on it. I couldn't see them clearly. But when she removed one I recognized its light. It was the key she'd used to access my secrets. An artifact of light that seemed to take on whatever form she needed it to.

She held it up and focused its light on the back wall, beyond the cart and the guards. The projection shone and distorted itself into shapes and mixtures of colors, like a painting come to life.

"You know the story of Lumen ancestry," she said. I had to hold back laughter. Unless she was giving this presentation solely for my benefit, her audience certainly did not know Lumen history. "We had to flee our homeland, Lor Annaius, when we could no longer defend ourselves from the creatures of Draconia. They burned our crops, our vegetation, and nearly all our population. We fled in what ships we could secure with little notice, with little time, and with little consideration.

"What was lost that day of departure, so many thousands of years ago, was our dignity, our identity, and our lifesource. The water reaching your lips now"—It *was* water. Three more Grey to go—"we all know this to be a lifesource for the Grey. While we don't have the luxury to provide you with fresh, pure water such as this in daily life, we make sure you to give you what you need to survive. Rainwater, and what we've managed to harvest from the Southern Pits, though tainted, diluted, and mixed with your bread, is enough.

"But we Lumen, we do not need to consume to survive." I saw the old Grey man in the cell adjacent to me glaring in my direction. The cup was coming around to him and the boy. *What did I do wrong now?* "No, we need only to be in the presence of amber. To have its substance in our air and beneath our feet. But as this planet cannot create its own source, our supply in diminishing. The Amber Tower was an invention of our settlers, who drained what they could back home and placed all that their ships could carry into our planetary vial. They tried to get the planet to accept it, to rebuild the supply, but their efforts were futile. Still, by the grace of the good wizards, we've survived this long. But our good fortune is coming to an end."

The light projection then took the form of the Amber Tower. Except there was no amber in its chamber.

"It remains to be seen how the planet will respond," the contessa said. My eyes were locked on the image, and it seemed the guards' were, too. "But the Lumen lives will not last. We used the last of the amber to draw your names from the Cup."

"*What?*" The word jumped out of my throat before I could consider my manners. "You knew we were on the brink of death, and you chose to fill the *Cup*? When forty thousand Grey volunteered anyway? You could have skipped the antics and just asked!" Fury had overtaken me. This was the most ridiculous thing I'd ever heard.

The contessa pointed the key at me and the image behind her faded. My body began to feel heavy again. Speaking would take too much energy, so I held back. I sat on the cot and observed. She returned the light to the wall and continued, explaining what would happen to the Lumen if we didn't make it back alive, as though guilting us would make our chances any better.

"Wait," I managed to choke out. I tried to hold eye contact with her, as uneasy as her unobstructed gaze made me feel. "If Lumen need to be around amber to survive, you knew you were sending me to die either way. Should I be grateful that I get to go out with a bang?"

"That is where this crew is needed," she said, largely ignoring my commentary. A new image formed behind her, this time full of color. First a backdrop of deep blues and violets, then bright, shining stars. A planet formed next, but it was dark. Black itself, save for a small mass of fire burning up what remained of its surface. *Draconia*, I thought, remembering my history teachings. "This is what remains of Lor Annaius."

I stiffened. *This has to be a mistake.* Lor Annaius was always depicted as a vegetation wonderland.

"When the dragons took our planet, they claimed it as their own, burning up every plant on its surface. But what their fires can't destroy is the planet's core and its remaining amber, which holds our old world together. Here on Palunia, amber evaporates if it's left on the surface, and it will never truly bind with the winds or the core. But on our home planet, it is the bringer of life.

"We believe that if you, our travelers, are able to retrieve even a vial of amber directly from the source—from the core of the planet itself—it will serve as a new source here on Palunia for centuries to come. Of course, we hope you can collect much more than that.

"You are charged with this mission, travelers: take our ships, reach what remains of Lor Annaius, and bring our amber back. The ship's fluid chamber filled, and a vial from the core, could mean we never face this crisis again."

She reattached the key to the chain around her neck. I strained to try to see what the other object was, but she wrapped her hand around it too quickly and tucked the chain into her robe. "Chosen eleven of Palunia—travelers competing with every crew before you for the Cup and the riches it bears—do you accept your mission?"

The Grey cheered and shook the bars in agreement. I wondered what would happen if I said no, but I didn't have the energy to keep fighting. The guards gave the cup of water to the Grey in the cell next to me before returning it to the table. I didn't even have the will to complain.

"You'll leave by the predawn light," the contessa said.

She approached the guard who'd been attending to the Grey. I was close enough to hear. "I'm staying above. Have them bathe and get the injured ones treated properly. If this crew dies, we might not make it long enough for another one."

When she left, the guard handed pieces of fruit and bread through the bars. They skipped over me entirely, which didn't surprise me at this point. I couldn't help staring as the Grey took deep bites of juicy, fleshy fruit.

The old man ate, but he let the child have his pick first. There were round blue fruit, red fruit of many angles, and soft, yellow heart-shaped ones. The bread looked surprisingly moist, too. After surveying their meal, I snapped out of my fixation and found the old man looking my way. I glanced away but still felt his eyes on me. He raised a hand forward, placing it between the bars. I gaped.

"For me?" I'd never been offered food by a Grey. I'd been prepared food by a Grey, but we would never eat off the same plate, let alone directly from the hand. It felt dirty. But, looking at myself, I was dirtier. I approached cautiously. My body was so weak.

He dropped a few of the small blue fruit into my open palm, then gave me what was left of their bread. "You sure?" I asked stupidly. The child was smiling. I gave a weak smile back and ate.

I woke up later to my shoulder aching. I was on the floor; I must have rolled off the cot in my sleep. It was dark outside now, according to the slits on the ceiling, but this room was lit by torches so the guards could keep an active eye on us. I tried to move my arm, but it felt like my shoulder would shatter if I managed to. Wincing, I forced myself back onto the other one and rolled over anyway, gasping in pain.

Then I heard a rustling outside my cell. I strained to see what was approaching from across the room. Guards, with another chair—this one smaller and collapsible. And following them . . .

"Mother!" I gasped, getting up and letting myself fall dizzily toward the bars. I gripped them as she ran to me.

"Damaus," she said, placing her hand on mine.

"What are you doing here?" *Is this another hallucination?*

"I convinced the guards to allow me visitation," she said. "It isn't right to keep a prisoner from his loved ones. I think you've got enough to deal with already."

There was a tone in her voice I hadn't heard before. I squeezed her hand. "Mother, I'm sorry for those words. I didn't mean—it was only something I remembered—"

"Shh, Damaus." She squeezed back. "You gave me a start, and Jiyorga may never forgive you. But no one knows you as well as I do. And right now I care a lot more about the fact that I may never see you again than about a few thoughtless words."

My face began to swell. I hoped she couldn't see in the low light. "Where . . . where is Westalyn?"

She didn't move and kept my hand held tight. "You just focus on yourself for now. If there's any chance of you coming back home, you need to put your survival first."

She didn't know what the contessa had told us. No one did. But I couldn't tell her. My mother was too high-ranked for that burden; it would do nothing but throw the planet into panic. "I am," I lied. "I'm fine. But, please, tell Westalyn to come. I need to speak with her."

"Damaus," my mother said. She was serious, with her eyes locked on mine. "Maybe the reason the crews never succeeded before was because you weren't a part of them. Maybe we were foolish to send . . . the others. Whatever this treasure is, it's important to the contessa, and she is counting on you to get it. If you can, try to take this on with honor. Come home with the treasure, claim the damn Cup, and go down in history as the bravest Lumen who ever lived."

"That's time!" A guard approached her with a vibrant torch. I shielded my eyes but didn't release my mother's hand.

"Please just ask her to come! And Jona! And Roeni, if you can find him. Please, Mother!"

"High Empress Quisala Ju Demma, your escort is awaiting you outside." The guard stood over her. She released my hand.

"With honor, Damaus," she repeated before taking her leave. I watched her walk away, feeling worse than before. I didn't ask her how Jona was doing. I forgot to tell her I ate fruit.

I was ready to curl up on the floor when my cell slid open. The guard had returned with a torch in hand. He stood aside.

"What?" I gasped. "I'm free to go?"

"Your bath," he grunted, and I thought I heard a few curses under his breath. He led me out of the prison chamber to a wooden door at the end of the room. Behind it was a crumbling staircase. We took it round and round and came out at ground level. There, through a row of bars, I felt the cool night air on my skin. I wanted to stay, to appreciate it one last time. I wanted Westalyn to be there. But there was nothing and no one. We continued down a long, dark corridor. At the end we reached another wooden door and, behind it, a warm chamber.

The many rows of bath curtains were drawn, but by the smell I could tell this was a salt-oil bath. Someone had left their robes out here with another guard. I blinked to be sure my eyes weren't deceiving me. Draped over the bench weren't tattered grey robes, but the robes the *contessa* had been wearing.

I sat. This bench was at least cushioned. In shared bath-houses it was expected that you didn't say a word. The guards kept their greeting to a curt nod, though that wasn't out of the ordinary for them. It was hard to imagine that the contessa could need a bath. Or that she didn't bathe in some mystical space dust. I knew she was supposed to be as mortal as the rest of us, but she didn't look much older than me, even though the difference in our ages was hundreds of years. That said, it was easy to hide your true features when you painted your face solid gold.

I studied the pattern on today's robe. It was black yet slightly reflective, with sparse gold lines drawn around it like rings of various sizes. It was a fitted robe that I remembered she wore tightly, buttoned from the collar to her ankles where the fabric stopped, and tied with a red sash. Between the folded layers of fabric, I caught a silver glimmer.

Did she really leave it behind? The bath was guarded, and it wasn't like you'd want to bring a piece of jewelry into the salt bath to be tarnished. I wanted to reach for it and get a glimpse of the key. I wanted to see what else was on the chain, but with two guards in the room it wasn't going to be easy.

I sat for an hour, with salt on the floor to entertain me. I swished the hard pink crystals around a layer of oil on stone with the bottom of my foot. The guards were mostly ignoring me, signaling messages to each other with their eyes as best they could.

When I was sure they weren't paying attention to me, I extended my clean foot to where the robe was hanging and gave a gentle tug. The fabric gave a little, but it bounced back without revealing any more of the chain. I glanced back at the guards, who still weren't looking my way. I took a deep breath and tugged again. This time the robe fell halfway to the floor. I dislodged my foot quickly and pretended not to notice.

One of the guards turned to me, paused a moment, then went back to his companion. Slowly, I turned my head toward the robe. The fabric was open now, giving me a clear picture of what was inside. What I saw caused such anger—such *fury*—that I had to bite my own lip to contain myself. There was the key, its gem light out, next to a tiny vial. A vial filled with amber.

CHAPTER 7

I ROCKED ON the cot in my cell when I'd finished my bath, dressed in the absurd travel uniform, and took another healing injection. We'd been told far too many times to get a good night's sleep, but that was the last thing I wanted. My mind was racing through any exhaustion I had left. I watched the Grey go for their baths one by one and contemplated what to do.

Not only did she waste the supposed last helping of amber on the Drawing, but she was hoarding a private supply for herself. My friends and family were going to slowly die, and she was to blame for it. And there was nothing I could do but fulfill her stupid mission. I wanted nothing to do with it. I shouldn't have been here. But maybe my mother wasn't entirely wrong. Maybe I could make a difference. I was clearly more intelligent than the Grey, even if I knew nothing about space travel or how to infiltrate a planet overtaken by dragons. I sighed.

The only thing that could have distracted me even a little would have been another visitor. Westalyn, Jona, Roeni . . . even Quorian or Masus would do. Anyone I could have a decent conversation with. But they never came. I watched the slits of windows near the high ceiling and tried to guess how much longer we had as the sky changed color. It was both the longest and shortest night of my life.

I woke up unsure if I'd slept at all. There were times when my eyes were closed, but my mind refused to let go of the reality that I was about to leave everything behind. That I was really being sentenced to death. Except before the actual dying part I'd have to sit awkwardly in a ship full of Grey until we were pulverized or ran out of resources.

The guards yanked us from our cells and lined us up, this time without chains. And we didn't really need them. As far as I could tell, they were never really in danger of the Grey running off, since they seemed legitimately interested in this death quest. But when they no longer needed the chains around my wrists, it meant they knew they'd worn me down. And they were right.

We climbed several sets of yellowstone stairs before coming out at ground level. We were still in Centrisle. I hoped to see a crowd, and to see my friends and family at the front of it, but there was no one there. Not a single Lumen. I knew they'd be exhausted, but all of them choosing sleep over bidding me goodbye was what made me accept my leaving.

Head hung, I followed behind the others. I was barely aware of the fact that I was climbing the ladder back into the megachariot. Without chains to pull us in six directions at once, I leaned myself against one of the sides, looking out between the golden tubes. A few Grey shifted away from me and focused on whatever was ahead of us. *Great*. I was even scaring Grey off.

I don't know how long I stood there, stuck in my own head. For the first time in maybe my entire life, I wasn't worried about impressing anyone. I didn't recognize my own pale hands, hardly blue at all in the morning light. It was strange to be outside without paint, without a cloak, and without any gems, but it was freeing in a way, too. I'd never felt so insecure, but I was coming to care less and less about it.

I wondered where Westalyn was. Had she stayed at our palace anyway? I wasn't doing a great job of holding in my emotions, but I really thought she'd come. I thought there was something special forming between us, and I couldn't stand the idea that she'd just forget about me when I was going through the worst times of my life—the end of my life.

The Grey were all huddled at the front of the chariot now, leaning out between the glimmering tubes, making their strange Grey noises. Without thinking I trotted over, too, lighter on my feet in my uniform boots than I was used to. When I reached the back of the group, I had to nudge a couple of them over to get a glimpse of what they were looking at. I shuddered as my uniform touched the others' and then gasped.

I thought our chariot was big, but the one in front of ours was even bigger. It was matte black with gold trim around all of its plating. It looked like a war vessel. I couldn't find a single gem on it, and by the way it was moving through the sand, it didn't seem to be pulled by a slug. I knew at once who it belonged to, and I found my fingers curling into a fist just thinking about her.

It wasn't fair. It wasn't fair that the contessa had so many more riches, all the secrets, and all the ancient artifacts to herself. It especially wasn't fair that the Lumen people were nearly as doomed as I was, while she held her own personal life stash. Not only was I about to be expelled from my own planet, but I'd have to wonder if my loved ones were still alive the whole time. I'd run out of chances to fight though. She was going to get away with this. She'd be the last Lumen in existence, and that would be okay with her.

Our chariot followed the black one, surrounded by slug-pulled guards. I just kept oscillating between dozing off and scowling, all while standing behind a close-knit group of smiling Grey. I probably should have embraced it at this point.

We slipped farther and farther from the city, and I knew where we were going. Northeast. To a place I hadn't been in at least a few years now. When I was a young kid, my father would take me every so often to see the open shipyard, where wings, cockpits, and consoles were scattered and strewn like food waste at the festival. It was hard to remember him now. I remember that we'd found a ship mostly intact. That he'd sat me on his lap and taught me how to change altitude and how to choose my direction. Of course none of it actually worked, but I wondered if I'd retained those skills enough to put any of them to use on the journey.

There were full-size, functional ships, too, of course, but they were behind enormous locked gates and protected by official palace representatives. Letting children run loose on military-grade spacecrafts wasn't in the planet's best interest, it turned out. And yet sending twelve unqualified crew members after ancient minerals was a surefire strategy for success.

It was an hour or two before we reached the yard, but we saw it coming a long ways away. The military ships were like old silver palaces on the horizon. They were huge, and I could only imagine how complex they'd be to fly and maintain. Unless the Grey were trained in mechanics and flying, it was going to be all on me to figure out how the thing worked. Me, a young Lumen who had spent his days lounging, bathing, and drinking wine. I wondered if there would be wine on board.

We reached the outer circle first—the junkyard. As we drove through on our oversized chariots, considerably more slowly than we'd just darted through the desert, I glanced down at the broken pieces of ships. Some were still in the places they'd been since I was a child—either they were too heavy to move or no one had bothered with them. I had the urge to jump down and inspect a few trinkets one last time, but we didn't stop. We kept going toward the inner circle, where a gate taller than our chariot wrapped all around the actual ships.

We reached one of the great doors to the gate, where two guards stood. I couldn't see well enough to witness their exchange with the contessa, if there was one. All I knew was that we stopped for all of about a minute before the gate opened and we continued through.

The ships were narrow, but so tall. Like box-shaped beacons to the sky. Some had pods resting next to them, too. And not all ships were alike. They were different in their shades of silver, black, and grey. They had different insignia painted onto their sides. Some had rounded edges, while others were clear-cut plates of armor. Antennae reached out from all directions on some, while others didn't seem to have them at all. It was hard to believe these had all come from Lor Annaius so long ago. I wondered how many of them were left in working order.

One of the ships was stationed away from the rest, toward the opposite edge of the circle from where we'd come in. There were more guards at its base, as well as a couple of raggedly dressed Lumen. *Mechanics*, I realized. A job given to lower-born Lumen from outside the cities. We approached the monolithic vessel, which was dark grey in color, its outer panels forming many flat edges. It had one long antenna coming from its side, and sitting next to it was what looked like a spinning top, which was about the size of our chariot.

We slowed in front of it and came to a stop behind the contessa's chariot. Somehow my feet had betrayed me, and I found myself nearly sandwiched between two Grey trying to peer ahead. We waited and watched but couldn't see what was happening. I should have been happy for any time I had left on Palunia, but I found myself more interested in exploring the ship. I wondered if the Grey felt it, too—if this was what compelled them to put their names in the Cup.

I studied the one closest to me—the woman I'd helped settle into her chariot on our first ride together. She was staring straight ahead, plain-faced as usual, but her expression was serious. Almost nervous. I turned to the Grey on my other side, who was making a similar face.

"Are you guys okay?" I asked, looking at each of the Grey, who didn't move. "This is what you wanted, right?"

I gave it a few more tries before sighing and giving up. I wasn't going to get conversation out of the Grey. I was just desperate for someone to talk to, and they were the only people on the planet who had a shot at understanding what I was going through. I looked back every so often, hoping for a chariot carrying Westalyn or Jona, but I saw nothing beyond the junkyard but endless desert.

Enough time passed for me to pace around the deck of our less interesting sand-ship about a hundred times. The uniform had, thankfully, come with a helm that I used to shield my head from the blazing sun. Before long I'd have hair to cover my head, assuming there were no head-blades on the ship to shave with. I'd have actual strands of grease-carrying hair, just like the Grey. I wondered if mine would be dark like theirs or white like Westalyn's. She was a lot braver than I was when it came to testing the limits of Lumen fashion.

Morning turned to midday, which broke into evening. It was great, really, having all that extra time to hope for friends and family and seeing no one. I considered antagonizing the guards just to relieve my boredom when two emerged from the ladders on the sides of the chariot.

One of the guards beckoned, silently motioning us toward him with his hand. I started over from my position midpace across the deck and joined the back of the line that was forming, followed by the second guard. We shuffled one at a time down the ladder until we were all on the sand. It was thicker and fresher here than in the city—almost like the open desert. I supposed not a lot of people walked through the gated-off shipyard. I dragged my new boots through it, taking my time as the guard led us toward the spacecraft.

It was like looking at a palace tower but uglier. This thing didn't have a gem on its surface. Just many metal plates. I'd never really gotten a feeling for the size of an entire functional ship. It was many times longer than the great chariot and at least three levels deep. It wasn't quite the size of the Ju Demma palace, but it may have been larger than Quorian's. A ramp led to an opening at the base, which was too dark to see into clearly. Where the sun did shine in, I could see what looked like scarves hanging from the walls and ceiling.

Standing in front of the entrance were two mechanics, two more guards, and the contessa herself. She was smiling at us. If that was meant to be charming or inviting, it had the opposite effect with today's light metallic blue paint on her face. She looked almost like a ship herself. Maybe she was part machine; it would explain her coldness. The mysticism surrounding her had been replaced in my mind with a burning hatred.

When we reached the base, she began to speak, her quiet voice carrying over the yard. "The moment has come, travelers. You've been given your quest, and you know what to do. Please save our people. Please provide us with a new life where we don't have to suffer. I don't know how long we have, so it's safe to consider you the last viable crew. It's imperative then that you take this journey with pride and dignity—that you forget what you may miss here on Palunia and focus on what need we have of you.

"This ship is ready for you to board. The moment the last of you steps into the entrance chamber, it will be sealed and you will be sent onward to your journey. Please, do not let us down."

No one moved. I'd expected more of a speech than that. Maybe some gifts. Some instructions would have been nice. Were we supposed to just figure out how the ship worked? Was she controlling it with her mind? With her fancy light key? I had too many questions running through my head to do more than gape at her. But we were moving.

I looked over to find three Grey had already entered, and the fourth was on her way. Five, six, seven. They weren't wasting any time. If I stayed, would the ship stay, too? How did it know when the last man would enter? None of this made sense.

And the contessa's speech was infuriating not only for its lack of content, but because I knew she was keeping the only amber for herself. That she would make my mother and Jona and Westalyn and Roeni and every Lumen suffer while she lived forever. That we were being sent to die, on the off chance that we made it back to preserve life here on Palunia. Eight, nine, ten. I'd made my decision.

With the other Grey on board, I started my walk to the ship ramp. The guards smirked at me, evidently expecting me to fight them. But I didn't. I walked slowly, calmly, toward the ship.

Then, before they could try to stop me, I changed course, powering toward her. The contessa jumped, startled by my advance, and I saw it. I gripped the chain around her neck and pulled until it came loose. She shrieked. The guards ran for me with their spears drawn as I bolted for the ramp and rolled into the ship. I looked up to see a spear barreling toward me.

The ramp door raised, deflecting it, and then locked closed. Low lighting filled the chamber from pods on the floor as the ship rumbled and shook in place. I slipped the chain into my pocket.

I waited, expecting that door to open any minute and for me to be killed on the spot. They'd tell my family I died on the journey, after I was subject to their malicious, vindictive, lying hands. But the door remained closed.

The rumbling changed to violent shaking. I saw the Grey fastening themselves into fixtures on the wall. They were belts, not scarves. I scrambled to copy them, wrapping fasteners around my body in whatever pattern I could make sense of. I clicked everything in place as best I could, and the next thing I knew, we were being ripped from the comfort of the ground, shot into the heights of the planet's atmosphere.

ACT TWO

CHAPTER 8

EVENTUALLY THE VIOLENT propulsion ended and the ship stabilized as much as I figured it was going to. I examined the ten Grey, still fastened to the walls of the entrance bay. I couldn't see the expressions behind their helms, but most of them were actually looking at one another. It was a change from the blank-faced stares and lack of eye contact I was used to. But this was an experience unlike any other by a long shot.

We were in space. In actual space. No more Mother, no more Jona, no more friends. No more Lumen at all. I certainly wouldn't miss Jiyorga or the contessa. No guards either, thankfully. But up here, without any paint, with all of us in the same uniforms, there wasn't much point in differentiating Lumen from Grey.

I decided I may as well unclasp my belts and start figuring this ship out. The Grey had locked themselves in much more neatly than I had. I undid one of the buckles and then had to unravel a couple of the belts to be able to access the next. Four buckles in all. When I let the last one go, I tried to set my foot on the floor, but I couldn't. I was suspended completely in the air of the entryway. It wasn't even clear where the floor was. It had been beneath me, but now I thought maybe I'd been tied to it. I tried to remember the direction the plating had faced outside.

It took a little while, but I figured out how to use the air to glide toward the access door, which led to the rest of the ship. When I got within about arm's reach, it slid open automatically, its plates spiraling back into the wall around it. I went on, leaving the Grey behind.

First there was a tunnel. It didn't seem to be straight, exactly, but I had lost too much of my sense of direction to know if it was inclining or turning. It wasn't long before I came to a three-pronged fork. The tunnel continued ahead, but it also went up and down. I took a deep breath of the air inside my helm and pushed myself up by the upper tunnel walls, ignoring the ladder that ran alongside its opening.

I came out into a large, open space. I forced my foot down onto the floor and felt it sink slightly beneath me. Looking down, I saw the blue tile glow faintly where I stood. It was made of synthese, like all spacecraft from our ancestors' era. Then immediately my body began floating again.

On one side there was what looked like a kitchen and dining area, with casual tables and chairs bolted into the ground, the chairs bearing more strap-in belts. Most of the space was taken by what looked like an observation deck in the center of the open room, filled with about thirty cushioned chairs, all equipped with belts. In front of the chairs, a few paces away, was a large dome-shaped window. My eyes caught the darkness outside and the glimmer of lights in the distance. *Stars*, I realized. My father had told me about stars, but I'd never believed they were real.

I swam over as best I could and placed my hand on the dome. Like everything else, it was made of synthese and bent slightly at my touch. Down near the bottom of the dome, growing more and more distant, was a yellow-green planet. I watched it slipping farther and farther away with all of my loved ones. I stayed a moment after it had gone out of sight, taking deep breaths from my oxygen supply.

Then, to my left, I saw the captain's console. I knew it at a glance. I had used one as a child, though it was only a portion of the size of this one. This was a semicircular desk filled with slots, that I guessed were screen emitters, and small surfaces where command panels could be illuminated. There were even a few physical buttons, which I'd never seen before. A couple were labeled: one said, "Regulator" and another, "Airflow."

I tried Airflow first. I didn't feel it right away, but after a moment the ship seemed warmer. I didn't realize how cold I'd become until I removed my gloves. Now it was pleasant inside, like the temperatures back home. I could feel bursts of air flowing around my fingers. I took another deep breath and removed my helm. I tried letting out a bit of air and letting some back in from the room around me. It was oxygen. I was breathing normally again.

Regulator. It wasn't very descriptive. I wasn't sure what was left to regulate. It could be that the flow of air was inconsistent throughout the ship. It could have something to do with the engine or the speed we were traveling. A little training would have gone a long way. I shrugged and gave it a push.

I promptly fell to the floor, hitting my wrist against the console surface on my way down. Wincing, I nodded to myself. *Gravity regulation.* Couldn't have had that one on by default.

I stood and walked easily back to the dome window. My legs were fine at least. Palunia was long gone, but there were stars everywhere. I barely noticed when the Grey found their way up behind me.

Before any of *them* could mess with things, I sprinted over to the console, my wrist still aching, and placed a hand where the command panel should be. Light emerged from my fingers onto the console, forming outlines of buttons with text and symbols on them. One of the symbols was a series of dots connected by thick lines. I pressed it.

Light rose up from the slot in the desk, forming a translucent display in front of me. It was curved and huge—extending for most of the width of the desk—and showed a projection of the constellations around us. I motioned from the bottom-left corner, which pulled the visual top-right, exposing more of the systems around us.

All we could ever see from Palunia was the atmosphere-masked sun. We'd missed out on so much of the endless universe around us. The map projection showed a green fog all around our home system and nothing but countless stars here. We were approaching a system called Daeru. For a system of its own, it didn't look like there was much in it. Just wide open space to sail for the next few weeks.

"Any of you want to do that thing with your voices?" I muttered, my eyes drawn back to the stars. Amazing as this was, I could already feel boredom setting in. I tried to see the shapes in the stars that my father had talked about, but they were all just specks of light to me. My enthrallment with space was going to get old soon.

"You mean sing?"

Startled, I turned from the projection surface, knocking my helm off the side of the console. It toppled on the synthese floor without a sound, causing the floor tiles to faintly glow with the contact of each edge before landing safely. I scanned the room for the speaker, but the observation chamber still held just a room full of Grey.

"Who said that?" Maybe there was a communicator enabled with someone from home. There was no indication light coming from the console though.

"You expect so little of us, don't you?"

Then my gaze caught hers again. I forgot the stars and the time and the distance, and even the words she'd said, and found myself staring into those deep black pools. "You . . . ?"

She stood in place, still hunched over, still looking ragged and colorless. It was her expression that threw me. It was calm, as Grey were always calm, but her lip curled upward and her brow lowered. The others raised their heads and looked up to her, too. I suddenly found it difficult to speak or move.

Before I had a chance to come up with a response, everything around me started to glow bright blue. There was a high-pitched ringing that seemed to continually bounce in and out of my curled ears. I grabbed my head, which was searing with pain. *What kind of sorcery is this? Have they been a cult of sorcerers all along, waiting for a chance to lure one of us out and kill us? Maybe they made sure my name was in that Cup. Is this what death feels like?*

And then the light faded and the ringing remained only in my ears. Each time I blinked I saw nothing but white and blue splotches of light over my field of vision. The room around me was darker than I remembered. "What did you do to me?" I muttered.

They were quiet, and I couldn't make out their faces. Not that I'd be able to tell them apart.

"Was that your sorry attempt to blind me?" I tried to let out a laugh. "You plan to take me hostage out here? Because the joke's on you." I stumbled over to the locking seat behind the console, too shaky and disoriented to strap myself in.

"They sent me expecting me to die with the rest of you. How great is that? I'd ask you to make us a celebration wine, but I'm guessing all we get is stale water here. Though you love that stuff, don't you? You've been treated like royalty while I've been a prisoner."

I leaned back, searching for a position I could rest my head in where it would stop throbbing, not daring to open my eyes again. At least this was a hell of a lot more interesting than wandering an empty galaxy.

As the pain and pressure decreased, I started to think clearly again. I'd come up the tunnel. There was another floor below. That meant there was likely an armory on this thing. If I could figure out an excuse to head down there for a while, I could protect myself from *them*. Hell, when had a Lumen ever needed an excuse for the things he did? Launching us into space didn't change the pecking order. If they were using sorcery, though . . . conventional weapons may not work. Even without it, I didn't know the first thing about wielding a spear.

I got up too quickly. The room started to spin around me, forcing me to grab the wall near the window for balance. I hobbled toward the back of the room, toward the ladder, when one of the Grey actually stepped in front of me. "What is that?"

"You're going to have to learn a few more words if you want to communicate effectively," I snapped. "Now, if you'll let me by—"

"Pulse dragon," came a voice behind me. I turned to see the group of them piling themselves at the dome window.

"Of course," the one who'd blocked my path said, rushing to join the others.

"*Pulse dragon?*" I shouted at them. "How do you even know what that is? They're a relic of ancient history, passed down in children's stories. You can't actually—"

Then the blue glow returned. If the Grey were setting it off, it must have been with their minds, because they were all practically pressing themselves to that window. What was more, it seemed the light was coming from outside. Blocked for the most part by the rest of the crew, it hardly fazed me this time. Then the Grey at the front fell backward into the arms of the others, knocking most of them to the floor.

I couldn't help smirking, glad not to be the only one affected by the light, when my eyes were drawn back to the stars. I *could* see a shape now. It was moving. It was coming toward us.

Gaping, I took a few cautious steps toward the clear synthese pane and looked. "By the ancient wizards, that is a pulse dragon."

Its body was made of bone. Historians recorded that the flesh of a pulse dragon burned up as it left the mountains and fiery atmosphere of Draconia. They turned from red-fleshed volcanic lizards to oversized skeletal beasts. Many died on their ascent, but the few who made it were said to be immortal. They were the scouts of the dragon race, with their unique ability to reach systems multitudes of light-years away from their home. Once a pulse dragon left the nest, it was said never to return.

The creature in front of us had large gaping holes where most creatures had eyes, and its mouth was nothing more than intertwined teeth, nearly as sharp and long as its ribs. The ribs themselves bent inward, and at the center of the hollow beast was a glowing blue orb. The orb danced around, reminding me of the colored spheres that lit the sky fire at the Planetary Palace. Extending from this fearsome creature's body were wings of bone three times its size in each direction, and a long, spike-covered tale.

Its mouth opened and the orb inside began to vibrate, increasing in size and spilling light between its thick, curved ribs. It was staring right at us.

CHAPTER 9

I BRACED FOR IMPACT, wondering if we'd be the earliest ship to lose signal with our home planet. Not much else went through my mind, unlike the many of the great stories would have you believe about Lumen facing their deaths. I was just dumbstruck, waiting for the ship to explode and my life to end.

But nothing happened.

I snuck a peek between my fingers to find the Grey exuding their own light. They stood hand in hand, emitting white rays.

"What?" I croaked, getting shakily onto my feet. I dared a glance out the dome window, expecting to see the dragon resisting, ready to annihilate us. But it was completely still. Even the stars were no longer glimmering. Some were on while others were off. "Did you . . . stop time?"

"In a way," the woman from the chariot said, her face strained and focused outside the ship. "We won't hold for long."

I didn't have a plan, but I ran to the console. *Any lasers of my own on this thing? It is military.* Only problem was, I didn't know how to fight a space dragon. I also didn't know if they traveled alone or in packs of hundreds. I scoured the controls for anything that might help.

"By not long," I said, scanning for anything useful and wondering how half the inputs worked, "do you mean seconds or minutes?"

They didn't respond, but I saw the light beginning to flicker and fade around them. I had to focus to actually read what was on the buttons. *Exhaust? Engine Preserve? Signal?* None of this was going to stop a pulse dragon. Then I spotted *Jump*. I sucked in a quick breath of air and gave it a go.

I felt nothing. I expected it to jump in place at the very least, or to rattle the crew inside. I was just starting to look for another button when I felt us pull back in the direction we'd come from, only to be flung so forcibly forward we all lost our footing. The last thing I remembered before passing out was the light going out around the Grey.

I woke up dizzy and disoriented sometime later, in a stiff heap on the floor under the dome window. I winced, then remembered we'd moved. I opened one eye and began to survey the open space around us. The dragon appeared to be gone.

I lifted myself up on one elbow, realizing there was chatter behind me. Most of the Grey were sitting around the tables, while two of them prepared something at the kitchen station. *Food.* I realized I hadn't eaten since the night before. That had to be a full day ago by now. I sat up, still too nauseated to stand.

"Good initiative, crew," I said, realizing these folks might be more useful than I thought. One or two looked in my direction, and no one spoke. "And good work stalling things back there. I couldn't have gotten us away without your help. Let's eat and then take a look at the galaxy map, shall we?"

They were all looking away now. Some were having whispered conversations with one another.

"You can't feign incompetence again after all that," I reminded them. I stumbled onto my feet and joined them at one of the tables. It felt strange to think of dining with a Grey, but I didn't have much choice. "And speaking of, I have about a million questions. Starting with, what the hell happened back there?"

"We don't answer to you, Lume," an androgynous Grey replied without looking at me.

"Like hell you don't," I snapped. "The hierarchy here hasn't changed just because we're away from home. I didn't see any of you operating the console. Without me, you'd have been dragon dust. I resolved myself to be your captain, and that's what I'm going to do."

I was almost convinced at that point that this whole thing had been a nightmare or hallucination. A Lumen being drawn from the Cup and humiliated in front of all of Centrisle? Being imprisoned at the contessa's palace? Being shown magical boxes containing supposed secrets? And now, blasted into space with *intelligent* and *stubborn* Grey? I tried to snap myself out of it, but I kept opening my eyes to the same bizarre reality.

One of the Grey removed a covered pan from a metal cooking contraption built into the wall. She turned, and I saw it was that woman. She lifted the lid and set the whole pan in the center of one of the tables. The one who'd been helping—a man around my age—withdrew a second pan for the other table where I was sitting. It looked awful—like a cross between bread and gruel—and covered in dark spices and dried plants.

"Thank you, Marlithan," said the old man who'd been in the cell next to me the day before. The woman nodded and sat down next to him. *Marlithan.* It was difficult to pronounce, even in my head. The rest of the Grey murmured their thanks.

I stared at the pan while the others at my table began to take portions by the handful. If I'd had any appetite for the brown-grey mush, it was quickly fading. Everyone sharing from the same dish—and directly with their hands—it made me feel ill to watch. I glanced over at Marlithan, who was staring directly at me. I darted my eyes past her, back to the stars beyond the dome. By the look of it, we were in the Daeru system, because even the stars seemed far away.

I slouched into my chair and slid my hands into the tight pockets of my uniform pants. I was still waiting to wake up from the dream—to start Drawing Day over properly. If I had a chance to do it again, I wouldn't have put my name in the damn Cup. I may not have even left my garden bath. I slid back further, dragging my boots against the malleable synthese. Then I felt something cool around my finger.

I had almost forgotten about it. I pulled out the chain holding the key and vial of amber from my pocket. There probably wasn't any other amber on the ship. Without it I'd die within, what, a few months? A year if I were lucky? At least on Palunia some still remained in the ground, but who knew how long the Lumen had. I frowned, studying the tiny vial, hating the contessa.

I glanced up and froze. Every pair of Grey eyes were on me. Or, more specifically, on the object in my hand. I turned it over, spinning it between my fingers, and their gazes followed.

"Yes?" I met their eyes with mine. They were giving me the creeps.

"The Omnilight," one of the youngest said.

"You can take a breath," I said. Even their gaping stares were somehow expressionless. Maybe Grey didn't have feelings.

"It's really . . . the Omnilight?" It was Marlithan this time. She stood in place.

"You're going to need to ask better questions," I said, trying not to let my nerves show. "What's an Omnilight? The key?"

I dangled it in front of me, and all ten Grey jumped in my direction. I snatched it back and kicked my chair away from them, sliding into the cooking station. "*Hey!*" I spat. "You wouldn't dare attack me!"

"Your disrespect knows no bounds, you fool," Marlithan said, her voice stiff with disappointment.

"Well, that's rude," I scoffed. "After I helped you with the chariot? After I gave you all gravity and air to breathe? After I rescued us from that pulse dragon? And between you and me, I don't think the contessa or her toys deserve much in the way of respect. She's a vile woman deep down."

"Yes, she is," Marlithan agreed. "But the Omnilight you hold now is far bigger than she, or you, will ever be."

"Is this your way of trying to knock me down a peg?" I asked. "Look, the last thing I wanted was to spend the rest of my life locked up in here with you guys. I had plenty better things to do back home. But this"—I dangled the chain with the key and vial again, much to their fury—"this is the last few drops of what my people need to live. Your friends don't get enough water, but they get by. Mine will soon be out of their life source. *Capisce.* Gone. And so, while it would be fun to wander the galaxy, this is starting to matter to me. I'm really not okay with my friends dying, so I resolved to captain this ship and bring it as damned close to Lor Annaius as I can get it. You guys keep failing horribly—not you in particular, but you know what I mean—and I figure you can let someone with a bit more brainpower take a shot at it. So I won't be talked down to. I won't be *attacked*, and I won't be lectured about *respect*. You are my crew. Got it?"

They didn't respond in words. It seemed I'd lost most of them before I even finished. Marlithan had stayed, but the look she was giving me was ice-cold. There was plenty of emotion there. I opened my mouth, tried to come up with something else to say, but she walked away.

I sighed, still twirling the key and vial in my hand. I took another look at the abandoned gruel on the table in front of me and firmly decided I wanted nothing to do with it. I got up and opened the nearest cupboard, shuffling around airtight containers of ingredients, looking for anything immediately edible. Mush, mush, and more mush. Frustrated, I figured I could go look in the lower level. There had to be more food stored somewhere on this thing.

I set my boot on the first rung of the tube's thin metal ladder, and none of them looked my way. I descended, feeling heavier than usual. I wasn't sure if that was just my suit or if the gravity system was set too high. I was going to have to figure out how to check that later. I was going to have to figure out a lot of things if I wanted to prove to them that I was their captain.

The tunnels hadn't seemed as long when I floated between them. I'd have to explore the rest of the ship later, but I continued past the tunnel where I'd entered and headed toward whatever was below. I had a good feeling anything being stored was going to be in crates at the bottom of this thing.

My father had once told me there was no up and down in space. That everything in the galaxy was just floating in its own made-up orientation. I started to wonder, based on that assumption, if I could change the way the gravity worked. If I could have us walk on the ceilings. It might be worth trying out if I got bored or they got too annoying.

The tunnel ended, but the ladder continued down into the room. I looked behind me as I descended. This was a storage space, but it was enormous and it was filled with oversized crates. They were arranged in seemingly no order, painted a huge variety of colors, with some stacked one way and some another, often crossing on top of one another. There was clearly a lot more exploring to be done upstairs, because this room was at least four times the size of the open area.

It was almost too much to take in. I wanted to scurry back up the tunnel, maybe explore that middle floor or figure out what else was on the observation level. But I also wanted to stay. One distinction between Lumen and Grey was that we Lumen thrived alone in open spaces. Community was something to be enjoyed sparingly. If we'd had the riches for it, we'd have our own individual palaces instead of towers of a shared palace among my family. That was how Jiyorga's side of the family did it, and that was how those closer to the contessa lived, too. The Grey could enjoy every moment of being huddled in the same room, but not me. I lived for this.

Part of what had enthralled me with the junkyard as a kid was the idea of exploring something. When you grew up in a pretty palace filled with pretty things, even if it was spacious enough, it was still your home. Deserts were no good for walking in, so no one did that—you'd likely end up buried before you'd get anywhere. Having a ship to myself though—that was fascinating. *And a galaxy, too,* I thought, but brushed that aside. I was going to start small. All I had to do was choose a crate to open.

I scanned the room, looking for something that stood out. High and low, near and far. Orange, blue, red, white, black. On Palunia we valued colors in the forms of gems and fashion, but those were based on yearly palettes. Not this. This was a room full of contrasts so stark they made me feel uneasy. As I walked around the room I started to notice more detail about the crates, too—how they were made of a metal I'd never seen before and how they were all damaged in their own way. They were old. Maybe from another planet.

The early Lumen had foraged nearby planets in the Palunia system for the supplies they needed when they landed. I supposed crates could have been among those things. Or maybe they came with the ship. Maybe these were filled with artifacts from Lor Annaius.

Then I saw the crate I wanted. It was high up, though not the highest, but it was going to make this difficult. It was painted white, but there was another insignia that looked to be sprayed across one of its plates in a deep red. The symbol was like the face of an animal I hadn't seen before. Angry, with spikes around its head and claws on its hands. I noticed after that some others had been vandalized as well, but none quite so elegantly. That crate was going to be mine.

I jogged past it to a stack of only two crates. Even this one stood far above my head. I took a deep breath as I backed away from it. Then, carefully assessing how high I'd have to go, I ran forward with my hands outstretched and jumped. I barely reached the top of the bottom crate.

Each crate alone was taller than I was by a long shot. I walked around the stack's exposed sides to confirm that the two were locked into one another. That meant there wouldn't be a place to stand on the bottom one even if I found a way to get that high. What I needed was a ladder. *Of course.*

I walked back to the tunnel, surveying the room again, seeing it from a new perspective. I gripped the suspended ladder and squinted upward. As I had hoped, it wasn't all one piece. The hanging segment was hooked into the one inside the tunnel. I lifted it and it slid out of place. It was taller than me—a good starting point.

I carried the ladder to the two-crate stack and leaned it up again them. It was about a crate and a half high. That would do. The ladder was thin and flimsy, but it had already held me once.

I took a step and it wobbled to the right. Instinctively, I leaned to the left, balancing it again. All my years of riding slug-chariots hadn't been for nothing. Slowly and carefully I approached the top. I stopped when my hands reached the last rung, not ready to take them off. I looked down. I wasn't that far yet. If I fell from here, I'd probably land on my feet. I exhaled, lifting one hand and setting my palm against the upper crate. Then I did the same with the other, taking another step up.

The ladder shook, but I managed to steady it. Another step, another wobble . . . and then it stabilized. Two more rungs to go. I lifted my right leg first, balancing on my left. But my legs wouldn't stop shaking. I tried to calm myself, but my body's ridiculous physical state was acting of its own accord, independent of my thoughts.

My left knee jerked. The ladder slipped and fell backward. Scrambling, I managed to clasp the tips of my fingers over the upper lip of the crate. I let out an expletive my mother wouldn't approve of.

If I kicked off against the crate, I could propel myself upward. Though, that would require turning in midair to make sure I ended up facing the crate again. If I tried to just pull myself up, it would be less risky, but I doubted I'd be successful. Maybe some combination of the two would work.

I bent my right knee and set my foot flat against the crate. I could barely feel its enormous grooves with the uniform boots. I pushed with my toes, attempting to boost myself upward. My grip went from fingertips to knuckle. It was a start. I squirmed, inching my way up a joint at a time. I got my hands and then somehow my forearm over. I took a deep breath and gave a hard kick up, tugging all the weight of my body up with my untrained arms. My abdomen reached the edge, and I buckled over on top. It took the wind out of me. I held there until I could get my footing again to shimmy myself the rest of the way. At last I was lying in a pathetic heap on top of the crate. I was going to get to the others, but for now I decided a rest was in order.

Lying there was not only satisfying but relaxing. I ended up dozing a bit, and when I opened my eyes, my body began to feel lighter. Then the room began to look farther away. I looked down to see that I was *floating*. I scrambled in midair, trying to get back to the solid surface of the crate. My toes scratched against it, but I couldn't land. I cursed as I floated up toward the faraway ceiling.

My back slammed into another stack of crates. I winced, then waited until I started to pass the top of that stack and gripped hard onto the side of it, throwing the rest of my body across it. I was just too short to hook my feet over the other side. I didn't know how long I'd be able to hold on with my already-worn fingers.

"Is that better?" a voice asked. I couldn't turn to see who it was, but I had an idea.

"Marlithan?" I butchered her name, but it was close.

She floated into view, gripping the same crate, her hands too close to mine for comfort. Facing me she shook her head. "You Lumen are stubborn."

"You're assuming because I climbed a crate that every Lumen is stubborn? What did you do?"

"No," she replied. Her voice was deep, maybe deeper than mine. "You may think you have a variety of features and abilities, but to a Grey, all Lumes are the same. And all stubborn. You refuse to open your mind. You refuse any perspective that isn't your own."

I frowned. "Even if that were true, you Grey are all the same. You all have the same robes. You act like mute fools in our presence, which is its own kind of stubborn. You're worse, because you hide whatever it is you really are."

"If that's true, it's because your people made it the case," she responded. She wasn't angry. Her tone never changed. She stated it like fact. I found I didn't know how to respond to that.

"What did you do?" I repeated. I'd figured it out now, but I wanted her to admit it.

"I switched off the regulator," she replied. "It looked like you were having difficulty."

"You spied on me, and then took over *my* console?" These fools had no respect.

"Damaus, was it?" She raised a hairy brow.

I nearly choked. "Did you just use my personal name?"

"Damaus," she pressed. "You are in a common, though unexpected, area of our ship. *Our* ship. We Grey were selected as you were, and we have the right to use this ship as we please."

I was actually being talked down to by a Grey. And she was talking circles around me. I was as shocked as I was angry.

"Listen," I snarled. "If what you want is free reign of this ship, you can at least leave me alone. But don't forget your place, *Grey*. This might have been your idea of a little . . . predeath playground before I was drawn, but I *was* drawn, and I'm not going to be bossed around by you either."

"You fail to see the irony in your claims, Damaus," she said, and I could swear she slowed down on my name, enunciating every letter as further insult. "Now, which crate were you hoping to reach?"

I glared at her. "It's none of your business." I was only a stack away now, but it was third from the top. Then I noticed something that caused me to momentarily forget my anger. "Why didn't the crates move?"

"Magnets," she answered simply.

I stared. "What did you say? What does that mean?"

"An old technology of ours," Marlithan said. "It binds objects together. These crates are bound both to one another and to the floor that holds them."

"Is that some kind of sorcery?" I asked, thinking of the contessa's ancient artifact collection. I was still struggling with the idea that this Grey woman had anything to teach me. "You know what, nevermind."

"It isn't sorcery," she continued anyway. "Well, in a way it is. It's manufactured sorcery, from a time before you stole our planet."

Manufactured sorcery. I'd heard that term somewhere before. "I didn't steal your planet, Grey. Our ancestors escaped their death—some of them, anyway—and sought refuge on Palunia. All the histories say you were too basic a race to have your own customs—probably because you pretend to be mute—so it was little more than a lifeless planet. I know that when we gave you serving jobs, you were grateful. That you're just as happy bringing a Lumen a flute of wine as making those singing noises. Just admit that you're grateful."

"History has a way of being biased to its writer, or to its intended audience," Marlithan said. Again, her tone didn't change. It wasn't unkind. But it annoyed me. It annoyed me that she had a tone at all.

"I'm not about to pretend everything in our texts is some fabrication," I retorted. "Lumen historians are some of the most respectable men and women our society has ever produced. I should know—the Ju Demma family has had a few over the generations. It was a life path I was considering for myself. Except for the water crisis you all created that was going to get me stuck in the pits. And, of course, except for this stupid Cup."

"If you think that we are responsible for the water crisis, then you really ought to read some alternative history," Marlithan said. She let go of my crate and floated up to another, on top of the white one. It was faded blue in color, with some form of lettering stenciled around the top perimeter. "Since you seem to want to distance yourself from the rest of us, you could make use of the time and learn something."

She gripped the crate, then dug into her uniform jacket pocket. She pulled out some kind of thick round disc and set it on the corner. Then three more, placing them carefully, one by one on each of the corners. She also withdrew a device I didn't recognize. It was flat and matte black in color. When she placed it in her open hand, it began to emit an image above, much like the console.

"What is that?" I asked. "Where did you get that?"

"From my room," she said, focusing on the light projection.

"We have our own rooms?" I asked. I had a lot of exploring to do. She didn't respond. "What are you doing, Grey?"

"Did you know," she said, not bothering to look at me, "that we don't prefer that term, *Grey*? That it was something you Lumen invented to reduce us to our appearance? An appearance, I might add, you cloaked us with?"

"No," I said, frowning. "That doesn't make sense."

"I know," she replied. She swiped something and touched the projection with her finger. I heard a clicking noise. Then she kicked herself and the projector away from the crate before selecting something else from it. There was a distant humming in the room suddenly. I looked around, searching for the source, but I couldn't find it. Marlithan was watching the crate.

Suddenly, in a quick flash, the lid of the crate slammed up to the ceiling, which I now noticed was the same matte black material rather than synthese like the tunnels and other rooms.

When the echoes of the collision subsided, I let go of the surface I was on and let myself float up to join Marlithan, who was kicking her way back toward the crate.

"What—" I began, but my attention went to the sight in front of me. Peering over the edge, I saw that the crate was filled with smaller boxes, and each of those was filled with old tomes, big and small, made of paper. Actual paper. I thought I'd been lucky to touch what little I had as a relative of Jiyorga, but I had never seen this much in one place. It seemed wasteful and, yet, historic. It had a distinct smell, which was old, foul, and somehow enticing. "Did you steal these?"

Her expression changed this time. She glared at me, making me feel half the size I usually did around the Grey. "We are the protectors of our history. Of our world as it was. It would serve you well to learn about the people you walk all over before you accuse them of stealing something that's rightfully theirs, that has rightfully been theirs from the beginning of time."

"Okay, okay," I groaned. "Sorry." Another apology to a Grey. "Hey, where are you going?" She was hovering toward the tunnel.

"To make sure we're on course and to see if any of the crew need anything." I opened my mouth to speak, but she continued, grabbing the ladder from below before I could get a word out. "Don't worry, *Captain*. I've got this covered for you, so go ahead and read."

CHAPTER 10

I COULD HAVE followed her out. I could have taken my rightful seat in the captain's chair behind the console. I could have gone to find my private room or explored the rest of that middle tunnel, but for some reason I stayed in that crate. Also, for some reason, the boxes and the books within them stayed in place and the lid remained in its spot above me. I managed to wedge myself between two boxes, which mostly did the trick. Every time I started to float, I dug myself a little deeper. These had to be stacked at least a few boxes high.

I picked up the first book that stood out. It was small, bound in a rough sort of material. The title was written in a language similar to ours, but with some characters I didn't understand. *The*—something—*of Yesterday's . . . Spirit?* I wasn't sure. I flipped through it, and found only pages filled with words. That would be a struggle.

I spotted one below it that caught my eye. It was bound in green fibers. It had gold text on the spine that I was pretty sure said *The Beginning of Time*. I pulled it out to find that it was huge and for some reason had a weight to it. It would probably be even heavier with gravity on. Come to think of it, all of these books had enough weight to remain in their crate somehow. I wedged the corners of the cover between my nested legs and scanned the first page. It was a drawing of a sun far over a blue planet. I wondered just whose beginning this was. The planet in question reminded me a bit of the early stories of Lor Annaius.

The author was Thorelian Rhyanar, which sounded Grey to me. The language was easier to understand in this one, but there were still words I wasn't familiar with. Maybe my father had just never taught them to me. I kept flipping to the pages with pictures. The next one had a woman with a dark face wearing a stark white gown, with beams of golden light glowing around her head. It spoke about an old race that had gone, I think, into hiding.

"The . . . *something* . . . people would hide outside the cities, in caves or abandoned houses or in reserves underground, building communities there until they got too big. Then they would separate into smaller groups and travel carefully so as not to be detected. Those who survived would start all over again. The . . . po—por?" I couldn't make out the word. "The *something* would have any they found executed." *Executed? On the spot? Just for being alive?* I shook my head. This stuff was never mentioned in our books.

Another page showed majestic creatures. Some had fur, some horns, some wings, and some combinations of the above. They were as ferocious-looking as they were beautiful. "The ancient animals of our land once ruled the planet." This was fantasy. I set that book in place and picked up another.

This one was hardly bound at all, with just a slightly tougher paper on the outside. It was unlabeled and tied with ribbon, and an old ink stick was looped into its binding. I flipped through and found that all the pages were blank. This was for writing. Out of curiosity I loosened the ink stick from its noose and scribbled on the page. Nothing came out. I moved it to the opposite corner and continued scratching until, finally, a faint black line appeared on the page. It thickened, soon dripping ink a bit too carelessly onto the paper. I placed the small writing pad in my uniform pocket, then picked up another book.

With each book I picked up, I took a few notes. I don't know why. They weren't related to one another in any way I could really connect, but they piqued my curiosity. They made me want to know more. I wrote down book names and page numbers, with descriptions of the covers to reference later. I wrote out entire quotes, like, "What happened to the machines?" and my own questions and summarizations that I may not even understand later. It was a disjointed mess, but I guess that's what thoughts are when you don't know where you're going.

The book that captured my attention for the most time down there in that crate was called *Inside Ourselves*, and it was filled with words similar to the first one I'd tried. This one was a little easier to read, and it did have very occasional sketches inside, but my thirst had grown. My desire—no, my *need*—for information drove me. I wanted to read the words, and if I found that first book again, I might want to read it, too. I was even starting to get meaning out of words I didn't know from their context.

I almost didn't notice when Marlithan joined me again. She sat across from me as I finished scanning the last paragraph of the fourteenth chapter. I looked up at her, gaping.

"I wondered if you'd find any in that series," she said.

"I don't believe it though," I pointed out. "You mean to say it happened this whole time? Hundreds of years? Before you were even born, this *muting* started? You, and your ancestors, had to pretend, all your life, whenever you were in the presence of Lumen?"

She nodded. "Yes. That's the way it is."

"This . . . contraption here?" I asked, turning the open book to her and pointing at one of the ink sketches inside. It was a person-sized box filled with holes, hung from a chain. The box was surrounded on three sides by walls filled with spikes of varying lengths and thicknesses.

"The contessa," she said. I wasn't surprised, exactly, but I stiffened at the confirmation. I sat silently and waited for her to continue. "When a Lumen admitted to hearing a Grey speak or to witnessing one of us behave in any way nonsubservient, she would do two things. For the Lumen and those they told, she would wipe their minds. Make them forget what they knew. With us . . . well, she'd make sure we never spoke again. She burned our people's vocal cords and would use this with any who put up a fight."

I was numb. I thought back to that Grey I quoted. He was dead now, somewhat thankfully. Sent out here to die instead of being given that treatment. Though we'd spent a night at the contessa's palace, too . . .

"Marlithan." I stumbled over her name. I thought I saw her smile in response. "Let's say I believe you. Did anything like this happen to you?"

"I'm still speaking, aren't I?" she said. "No, I've never been the cause of a contessa visit."

"But the night of the Drawing? What happened to you guys?"

"Much better than what happened to you," she said. "You sat in a cage while we ate fresh fruit and made music. While we slept in newly laced cots."

I nodded, remembering the cold floor below me, remembering the embers dancing around its surface. Then I remembered my dream. "You *were* there. You came up to the room that night. But how? Why?"

"Curiosity," she replied simply. "I'd never seen a Lumen foolish enough to put his name into the Traveler's Cup."

"Well, forty thousand of you do it," I said, smirking. "That seems pretty foolish, too."

She smiled back. "It is a bit. But it's better than being slaves in our own home. Better than being tortured for speaking, for existing outside our politically useful functions. There's more for us here. And a night of being treated like people at the contessa's palace is worthwhile, too."

"But you know we're going to die, don't you?" I said. "I mean, I don't want to. I'm going to do everything I can to stop that from happening, because my family . . . they need the amber. Everyone I know is dying, but it's going to be slow and painful for them if I don't get to Lor Annaius and back. I know our chances are slim. No one survives this. Even if we somehow make it to Lor Annaius, even if we manage to get to the planet's core, there's a sleeping demon in there."

"You sound conflicted," Marlithan noted. "Damaus, sometimes there are fates worse than death."

"I don't know about that," I said, wishing she would just listen, but I scribbled the phrase down in my notebook anyway. "So why did you come back down?"

"To make sure you didn't get crushed to death when I turned the regulator back on," she replied.

"Hmm?" I looked up to see that the crate lid was still attached to the ceiling. I lifted my right leg, which was stiff from being buried for so long, and found that it moved normally. "How long has the regulator been on? And why wasn't I crushed?"

"A couple hours now," she said. "If you'd checked the storage cabins before climbing crates you'd have found the magnet pads. And if you'd surveyed this room, you'd have found the ceiling controls. You have a lot to learn, Damaus."

"Teach me then," I said. Marlithan raised a thick eyebrow at me. "I'm serious. Look." I flashed her my open notebook but pulled it away before she could see what I'd scrawled in it. "I don't know what to believe yet, but I'm open to learning. Clearly there's more to you all than I thought. I'm trying. I'm getting faster, but I'm slow, and I doubt we'll survive long enough for me to get through this entire crate. Help me choose what to learn. I admit that maybe I wasn't raised with the most . . . well-rounded view of history."

"Damaus," she said. "We both know that the moment it gets hard or you read something you disagree with, you're going to give this up and start bossing us all around again. Don't we?"

I frowned. "I mean, I'd try not to."

"I'll help coach your learning if you extend it beyond the histories."

"Are each of these crates filled with different subjects then?" I asked. "I was always interested in science. And sorcery. I could learn how to do some maintenance around the ship."

"I don't care what you learn in books," she said. "And Welsia's already picked up every ship manual for herself. But I do care how you treat the other members of this crew. If you think you can learn from me, I'm here to tell you that you can learn from them, too. All of us who you call Grey are individuals, with individual strengths, stories, and ambitions. You will learn our way of life—our *real* life, not forced servitude—and you will start to see things the way we do."

I sighed. This wasn't at all what I was trying to sign up for. "Do I have to eat out of your communal space dishes, too?"

Marlithan seemed to consider that for a moment. "Yes," she replied, most expression gone from her face.

I sighed more loudly. "I'll think about it."

"We're having a meal to end the day now. Join me?"

I remembered then that I was craving food badly. That I'd come down here to find food. I'd been so engrossed in climbing, and then in reading, that I'd completely lost my appetite. "Yeah, sure," I said, wobbling to my feet. I picked up the book I was reading and my notes. "But, uh, how do we get down with the regulator on? I'm not jumping from here."

"With magnet pads in the future but, for now, with me," she said, grabbing me by the arm. I jerked, shocked to have anyone touch me, let alone a Grey. She brought us to the edge. "You will jump. We both will."

"Uh, no," I said. "That's not happening."

"Learn to trust, Damaus," she said. "Consider this your first lesson."

"I'm not—"

But she was stronger than I was. She held tight as she let herself go, and I was too concerned about holding on to my books to pull her back up. We were flying downward, and I was going to crush my face into the floor. I pressed my eyes closed, and then we slowed to a stop. I opened them to see that she was glowing again. And so was I. Our feet gently came to the floor and the glow faded.

"What are you people?" I asked, bewildered.

"You just used up your free lesson," she said. "If I decide to help you, it's not because you deserve it. Come have a proper meal with us and we'll see what I let you in on next."

CHAPTER 11

AFTER THE GREY were kind enough to let me take my own portion of the food first, and after about an hour's attempt at conversation that wasn't as awful as I imagined, the youngest of them—Rodiger—showed me to my room.

It was on the same floor as the lookout, though it was farther down the corridor than everyone else's. I supposed that was what happened when you were last to select a room. The door slid open as we approached.

"Well . . . good night!" Rodiger said. The young Grey was actually smiling a big, toothy grin. If it hadn't been going on for so long, I really would have thought I were dreaming.

"Uhh, you too," I mumbled. "Thank you."

The room was larger than I expected. The lights inside gave off a slight yellow hue, which I supposed was to help us feel more at home. There was a bed in one corner, admittedly smaller and less extravagant than both my beds in the palace, and a cushioned hammock hung in front of a smaller dome window. In the center of the room was a circular table, where my projection device sat, and a couple of chairs, all bolted to the floor. Lock-in straps hung from the chairs. They were on the bed, too, and some hung from a cushioned wall on the opposite side of the room. *For emergencies*, I guessed. In one corner was an enclosed washing station.

I set my books on the table and immediately sat down. I was still reeling from all the information I'd taken in earlier. I didn't know how much of these histories could be trusted, but I also needed some explanation for the sudden awakening of these Grey.

I wondered if Jiyorga knew, as he was calling the names, that he'd be freeing these people from slavery. I wondered if he knew these were the best days they'd ever have. Did he know they were competent? That they could speak our language? *Or was it their language?* How much of their culture did we claim as our own when we set foot on Palunia? And what did it take to make an entire species of people so subservient?

I wondered if my mother knew. She remembered that I interacted with a Grey. So why wasn't that memory erased? Was it because he spoke in front of all of Centrisle with his final words? It would be hard to wipe everyone's minds.

I also wanted to know how the contessa did it. I wanted to know what abilities these Grey had, too. I was going to have to find books on sorcery next.

I powered through my exhaustion, fueled by the most intense curiosity I'd ever experienced. Young Lumen were taught lessons as a formality, but we weren't taught to *learn*. We weren't taught that there was any value in knowledge. If I was going to die in a week, a month, or a year, I wanted to make use of the time I had. I only wished I had a way to inform my friends and family before they died, too. I swore that if I did make it, I'd make the contessa answer for herself.

My door buzzed halfway through chapter twenty-three as I was jotting down another thought. My notebook now held several pages of unintelligible scrawl.

"What?" I called. There was nothing. Frowning, I got up, and the door opened in front of me. It was Marlithan.

"We're eating momentarily," she said.

"Again?" I asked. "Do you usually have a meal in the middle of the night?"

"No such thing as night or day here," she replied. "However, we just had an extended sleep. If you look at your projector you'll see that seven hours have passed since we went to bed."

"Seven hours?" I started. "I . . . sorry, I haven't slept, or used that thing yet. I'll skip this one."

She nodded and walked away without any further questions. Now well aware of my exhaustion, I turned from the door and it closed. I noticed a row of dotted lines above the door change from red to green. Assuming that meant the pressure was okay, I kicked off my boots and the rest of my uniform and pulled the blankets of my bed over me. I don't even remember closing my eyes.

On some level I knew I was dreaming, as images of the Planetary Palace came into view. Those floating bridge-corridors moving and crossing one another. I walked along one but couldn't reach the end. It just kept expanding, growing longer in the nothingness.

"She isn't here," someone said. I turned around and saw a familiar-looking Grey man.

"You're the one who died at the Procession," I realized.

"You're going the wrong way," he insisted, taking my hand and pulling me back the way I came. I looked over my shoulder, conflicted. I was so sure that I had to go that way.

"But what about the secrets?" I demanded as we started running.

"You need to see your brother." We kept on running. The bridge got narrower as we did, but we pushed on until my knee gave way. I jerked in place and toppled over the side, falling hard and fast.

I opened my eyes to find myself on the floor of my room. The tiles were flexible, but I wouldn't recommend falling onto them. I cradled the arm that had taken most of the blow. It wasn't badly damaged, but it was sore. Dazed, I looked out my room's smaller dome window in the darkness of my room to see that, of course, it was still night. Space was just endless night. I was going to have to get used to that.

As I got to my feet, the light automatically came on. I trudged my stiff body to the corner of the room, where the washing station was. To one side was a standing shower, and to the other was a sink and mirror with various supplies. No paint though. Not that it would matter at this point.

I stepped into the shower, and immediately warm liquid began to spray on my body. Startled, I jumped back out, soaking the floor. It wasn't oil. I looked at the drops now cooling on my arms. It was clear, with no smell—not even perfume. *Water*, I realized. They must have filled our ship with water. *How much did that take away from the other Grey?* I wondered.

I'd never cleaned myself with water. It wasn't moisturizing at all. It didn't make me shine. It made me sort of fade. There were tubes inside, attached to various dispensers. I tried lathering some of those onto my body. Some burned, and none would stay on with all the water pummeling me. Mildly frustrated, I got out. I stood there with a puddle at my feet because there was, of course, no sun to dry myself under. A large, dry piece of fabric hung nearby. I grabbed it and began dabbing at myself, now shivering with the change in temperature.

When I got each drop off, I took a white undersuit from the wash station shelving, which was of course too large, and put my uniform back on. I looked at myself in the mirror, not recognizing my own features. I was so pale I was almost Grey myself. On top of my head, short, rough hairs were starting to emerge. I thought they may have been blue in color, but it was still hard to tell. I looked for something to shave them with but found nothing. Soon the Grey and I would be indistinguishable.

I came out to find a few of them in the chairs on the observation deck, chatting and looking out at the stars. They were a lot like regular people with no other Lumen around. Marlithan was nowhere in sight, but Rodiger was exclaiming something in an excited conversation with the old man.

"Good morning," I addressed the group. They looked over at me, and a couple passed their own whispered half-greetings. They hadn't all forgiven me for, first of all, being Lumen and, second, being an ass the day before. It was understandable.

I approached the console, running my hand, which was dry from the water-shower, over the smooth black surface of the station. The light projection appeared, and on it was information about the ship. Its name was Quotient, and it was . . . *four thousand years old.* I couldn't really wrap my mind around how old that was. It originated from a system called Terr and had been maintained on Palunia. *It must have been traded to the early Lumen at some point,* I guessed. There was a huge list of features I didn't understand, but on that list was the *magnetism* Marlithan had introduced me to. I also saw *running water, gravity regulation,* and *light jump.* There was an image of the ship on the bottom-right of the projection. I expanded it.

Now I was looking at a map. This would have been useful the day before. The main level, of course, held the console, observation deck, kitchen, passenger quarters, and a few areas marked *communal zone.* I'd have to check those out later, too. The level below this was empty on one side, with the narrow tunnel to the ship doors. Apparently it was narrow because that's where the engines were. On the other side, though, underneath our quarters, were a couple of storage spaces, something called a *pod room*, an *arsenal*, and a *communications chamber*, whatever those were.

The level below that, which I had thought was the bottom, was of course the giant storehouse of crates. There was nothing else on that floor. But there was a fourth level below—a smaller chamber—labeled *substance storage*. That was where the amber would go if we managed to strike a big enough source, I guessed.

I took out my notebook and copied each level's map into it. I intended to do some exploring once I verified we were on track on the galaxy map. I was about to switch views when the door separating the open area from the personal rooms opened and Marlithan entered. She first went to the group in the chairs, whispering something to them. Then she came to me.

"You know," I said, "if you want me to act like one of you, it doesn't do you a lot of good to leave me out of conversations."

"You've left yourself out by sleeping the day away," she noted, but again, she didn't seem upset. "Also, Damaus, as you're learning to trust us, we're observing whether or not we *can* trust you."

I started to protest, but she took a step away. "Do you still want to learn?"

I left the console unattended and followed her back toward the personal rooms. "Trust goes both ways . . . Marlithan." I almost called her *Grey*. That was going to take some getting used to.

"We use different phrases, but we're saying the same thing," she said. She was still kind, but I thought her patience was wearing. I walked behind her through the corridor. I couldn't remember the exact path to my room, but I thought it was to the right. We took the first turn left, walking in a straight line until we got to an open room. It wasn't much of a room at all. Instead of a door, there was just a large opening without a wall. An interior window was cut into one of the other walls, making it easy for anyone walking by to see the people inside. Here there were several round tables and chairs. There was a shelf filled with books and small boxes, a mini kitchen station where I saw a nice collection of tea leaves, and a couple of lounging chairs. This must have been one of those communal spaces.

Marlithan sat at a table that had a few books on it already. "I got these for you," she said, motioning for me to sit with her. I reluctantly followed her instruction. "But before we get to that, let's talk about your social progress."

"Social progress?" I asked. "Look, I was reading late. I'm probably not going to make every meal on this ship. I might even spend time down in the crates, or in any of the other rooms I can escape to for a little while. I wasn't raised like you, spending all your waking hours together, sharing food and singing, and whatever else it is you do. Lumen bask in space and time alone."

"Damaus, I was going to tell you that you've made progress," Marlithan said, ignoring my defense. "The others have noticed, too. Young Rodiger is particularly interested in you, as their opinion of Lumen has had less time to form. You're innocent as far as they're concerned."

"So you don't mind if I only emerge for a meal a day? If I only say hello?" I felt myself breathing freely again.

"I'm hoping we can add more depth to the conversations," she admitted. "But, Damaus, just as you don't want to be left out, I don't want to be the messenger. Spend time with the others, if they allow it. Get to know their names and something about them. Let's make that your first test."

If they allow it. That would take getting used to. I shrugged. "Fine." With my notebook I was a lot more confident when it came to memorization.

"Now, how far did you get in *Inside Ourselves*?" She pointed to the book.

"I finished it," I said. She raised an eyebrow, as was her usual response. "I did, really. I stayed up as late as I could reading. Then, this morning, or whenever I woke up, I finished the last few chapters."

"And?"

"And . . . it's a lot to take in," I admitted. "But I don't know if I should believe everything or just think of it as some kind of alternate explanation. Is there another book that combines Lumen and Grey historians? Something that bridges them together? They're way too different."

She shook her head. "No, Damaus, and this is an important lesson in itself. There has never been such a thing, because we have never been equal in society. We have never been collaborators. Your people invaded our planet and stripped our historians of their rights. We had many more books than this, but most of them were destroyed. We tried to make copies and to rewrite what we knew from memory. In our communes we store what we can. And whenever we could, we would bring extras to the shipyard storage crates."

"*You* put them in the crates? Why?"

"Because they're durable. Because despite whatever weather happened to touch Palunia, they would be protected. Because if they discovered our communes and had us executed or banished, the texts would be safe. Because the worst that could happen would be that they would go to space." *Space seems kind of bad*, I thought. I sensed there was more but didn't push it.

"And you knew just from looking at the crate that it had your books in it? But who loaded it onto this ship? How did you know?"

"Working men," she replied. I remembered the mechanics who'd prepared the ship for us. "They're the closest we have to an in-between race. They've been mistreated by your people, too, so they're happy to help us out, especially with something so minor. Most of the crates are filled with weaponry or are left empty to receive additional goods from our destination. But some contain important artifacts of our identity. And we know by the serial codes. The letters in those codes each hold meaning regarding the contents inside."

I nodded. "I always assumed the lowborn Lumen knew their place."

She glared at me. "Their *place*? Have you learned nothing?"

"Sorry!" I threw my hands up, running one over my now-bristly head. "I didn't mean it that way. Just . . . I thought they were content."

"Your intent is irrelevant, Damaus," she said. "Because you are a highborn Lumen, you do not see the problems of others. You do not see the fact that these social *places* exist at all as a fundamental flaw of Palunia's system and society."

"Can we talk about books?" I asked, hoping to calm her down.

She paused a moment, then picked up *Inside Ourselves*, flipping through its pages as though to refresh herself. I wondered if she'd read it. I wondered how many of the books in that crate she and the others had studied.

"What did you find most surprising?"

I opened my notebook. I'd taken in so much that ranking it all in my head was going to be a difficult task. "The public executions, for a start," I said.

Marlithan nodded. "When your ancestors took government? Tell me, Damaus, what does Lumen history say about that time?"

"That you all had no one to rule you," I said. "That you were too simple, like wild, unintelligible creatures. Since we came from dignified society, we thrived with governance. We found that it stabilized our societies, according to one of my old uncles. He said that when we arrived we lowered a ship into the ground where the Planetary Palace is now. That the great king of that time took on his position out of duty and created civilization."

"And does that sound like the Lumen you know?" She was baiting me.

"Sure, it does," I said. "Well, maybe I have less respect for the founding family. But regular Lumen are great people. All my loved ones are Lumen. Everyone I've ever respected has been Lumen."

"The same Lumen who hold a planetwide celebration about shipping us into space? Who ogle and cheer as we're beaten naked in front of them?"

I frowned. "Okay, I was angry when they did it to me."

"And if it hadn't been you? What would you have been doing while we walked, Damaus?"

I didn't answer. I suddenly wanted to go sleep some more.

"Your people are brutal," she said. "You don't have to believe our account of things past, but you can't deny what you've witnessed firsthand. You've seen our people beaten and slaughtered in front of you. You've seen shoppers throw their coins and old clothing at us. You've seen countless Lumen steal from us. You yourself have, in all likelihood, bossed a Palunian around in your own home. Maybe you've never executed one, but if you were honest, would you count our lives as valuable as your own?"

I was squirming in my seat. I didn't like this one bit. Things were making both more and less sense. It was hurting my head. "Stop it," I muttered.

"How many times do you think we wanted to say that?" she asked, staring at me.

I looked up into her eyes and then something just broke me down. I lost control, shoving my face into my arm on the table. How *had* I been okay with any of this? How could I have viewed it as normal? Why did no one tell me that Grey were intelligent? That they had feelings? Were these flaws instilled in us by the contessa, or was it just who we were? I hated the contessa. I hated myself. I hated my mother, and Jona, and Westalyn, and Roeni, and Masus, and Quorian. I still hated Jiyorga, too, of course. My chest ached as I thought of these people I had loved and respected, that somehow I *still* loved but could no longer respect.

I felt the chair across from me send a ripple through the floor as Marlithan stood over me. She stepped away, leaving me with all the conflicting thoughts that ran through my mind.

CHAPTER 12

I READ ANOTHER twelve books over what I thought was a few weeks. It would be hard enough to tell how much time was passing even if I had the sun to judge, with all the strange hours I'd been sleeping. But out here there was nothing but a clock on the console. And I was still awful at timekeeping, especially with the ancient numerical system that thing used. It turned out it didn't matter though. Timekeeping now was as useless to me as it had been at the palace. Only instead of lazing around in the sun, I was cooped up in a ship traversing the galaxy. Both had their perks.

I had to admit now that the Grey history books filled a lot of gaps the Lumen teachings had left. Where the two contradicted each other, the Grey text came out stronger. Helragizan, the old man, had taught me to analyze text. It turned out he was a historian himself and had written a couple of books that were stored only in Grey communes. I had managed to make some headway with a few of the crew members, but many still regarded me with disdain. I supposed now I could see why.

"What are they like?" I asked Helragizen, as I set a pan of dinner on the table. The remaining Grey, or *Palunians*, who had been hanging around the console and the lookout wandered over. "And where are they?"

"The communes?" He grinned. When Helragizan spoke, he did so one slow syllable at a time. "The point of them is to keep Lumen away."

"Well I can't exactly go and visit now, can I?" I pointed out.

He nodded, relenting. "Yes, yes, that's true. Well, I can tell you they're small. Only about ten to twelve of us in each one. Centrisle has about a hundred of 'em."

"A *hundred*? How? I've lived there my entire life and I've never seen any suspicious Grey. I—I mean, Palunians."

"That's the point," a large, brooding man responded. I believe his name was Gonian. "If we all scurry off in different directions, y'all won't know the difference. We were meeting right under yer noses for centuries."

"Think underground burrows, nooks in old abandoned palaces, the boring tents of festival grounds," Hel added. "Those nasty guards caught wind of us once in a while, but we always managed to outsmart them. Rodiger and I were part of the same commune, along with his mother. I promised to look after the kid for her."

"And you stored books in there?" I asked.

"Yap!" Gonian said. "Though in mine we didn't place them all out in the open. If they came down and found a few Palunians hangin' out, they'd probably beat us a little, but the texts are sacred. We buried our books. Had to bring a magnet with us to find 'em again."

"How would a magnet help you find books?" I asked, confused.

"Our books all have a metal page," he said. "Didn't you notice? Since your kind don't bother with magnets, we use them to locate and safely store our books. Take a magnet to it, and they'll turn right up."

"That's how they stayed in the crate," I realized. "Marlithan turned the regulator off, but the books didn't move, even with the lid attached to the ceiling."

Gonian nodded triumphantly. A few of them were always so pleased when I learned something. More of the crew joined us around the two tables and started to take portions of food with their hands. I did the same, dropping a piece of the vegetable loaf I'd made onto my plate. Things had changed, and I found that after a while I didn't mind it as much as I had planned to.

"I have another book for you, Damaus," Marlithan said as she sat down across from me. "I left it in our meeting room."

"It's always a mystery with you, Marl," I joked. "Not even a hint?"

"Only that I think you'll find it more interesting than the others." She took a huge mouthful of food. It wasn't a coincidence that I was the thinnest member of our crew. I'd been slowly loosening the compression on my suit over the last couple weeks though.

"Then I'm in for a heck of a ride," I said. "Or is that just your way of getting me to spend a month on a giant tome?"

"It's fifty pages," she said. "Fifty very important pages."

"Pardon my lateness." Welsia, a woman who was *nearly* as thin as I was, emerged from the tunnel. "I think you'll be interested in what I found."

She walked over with a box. It was orange in color and labeled *Tangerine*. Sounded like a Grey word. "What is that?" I asked, as the others broke into giddy laughter.

"The Lume's never seen a box of the stuff!" Gonian exclaimed, seeming to find that hilarious. "He's only had us, his *rightful servants*, pour it in his glass."

"It's wine, Damaus," Marlithan said, rolling her eyes.

"It isn't my fault I didn't know!" I scoffed. "Come on, I don't think of you guys that way anymore."

"Don't pretend it's vanished from your head, lad," Gonian croaked. "You deserve every bit of our laughing at your expense. You've laughed at our friends and relatives taking a beating in public, remember."

"Fine," I muttered, hating that he was right. "How about I serve you all a glass if we drop the subject?"

The crew cheered, and I found myself smiling again. At first I'd been caught off guard that they were so intelligent and formal. Now I saw they were as ridiculous as my friends and me once they got going. I didn't know which was more surprising, but I liked this better.

Welsia helped me find a tool to cut the box, and Gonian found some glass mugs that were good enough for me. Inside the box was a giant, sealed bag. I cut off the tip as Welsia supported the end of the box, and together we poured.

When we were all seated again, Hel began to emit a low noise. The young one, Rodiger, added his own voice. I still didn't understand why they did this, but I found, with some reluctance, that the two noises complemented one another. As they held the sound, Marlithan began to sing over it.

Ensaya, great leader of men
Bringer of peace, enlightenment
No challenge at your feet too great
Nothing too small to contemplate

After a verse the others joined in, blending their voices together. What had always seemed like just noise to me was now somehow beautiful.

You climbed the mountaintops to know
What life was like for us below
None insignificant to you
Nothing for us you wouldn't do

You were a bold and noble soul
Inspired all you came to know
Each day a pleasure in your rule
Unjustly ended, sad and cruel

They took your head without a thought
Left your accomplishments to rot
With your last words you wished us peace
But on that day our spirits ceased

For what is peace in dire times
When we must pick up arms and fight
Two ideals strictly opposed
Inevitably disposed

"Wow," I said when they stopped. "That was beautiful."

"Didn't you refer to our music as *noise?*" Gonian quipped.

"I did, and it is," I replied. "But it's good noise."

They all laughed, and soon I joined in. "Okay then, teach me one. Something easier to learn."

With some difficulty, I sang. It sounded awful, I'm sure, but they all worked to coach me, and we were soon drunk enough that it didn't matter. We went late into the night, or whatever time of day it was, singing, drinking, laughing, and telling stories.

Marlithan even went to get one of those boxes from our meeting room, which turned out to be some kind of game. We pushed the tables together and I tried my best to follow the arbitrary rules, and their relationship between the cards and game pieces—without much luck. But it didn't matter. Every mistake I made was great entertainment for them.

I lost count of the amount of mugsful I'd had. At some point it was decided that between the eleven of us we had to finish the box, and a box poured about forty flutes. Safe to say I was feeling at least as good as I had during the festival, and I had about as difficult a time hobbling to my room. I remembered as I passed the fork in the hallway that Marlithan had left her mysterious, all-important book in wait.

Holding the wall, I stumbled toward the common room. The light turned on as I entered, and I saw it lying on the table. It was hardly more than a leaflet of paper, and the cover was simple black. The title was printed in thin white text, and there was no author listed. It simply said, *The Omnilight*.

I sat down and flipped the book around in my hand. I hadn't even touched the key and vial since the first day here. It was locked away in a drawer in my room. There was no writing on the back of the book either. The last page was indeed made of metal. The first page had one phrase on it. I nearly dropped the book as my eyes skimmed over the words.

Let the fire of your sleeping god rain on me.

Part of me wanted to shove it closed. I didn't exactly feel ready for whatever this was going to be. *Marlithan was preparing me for this*, I realized. Slowly convincing me of their history, having me buy into the Palunian struggles. I knew before reading any more that I needed some amount of their perspective to understand this text properly. If she left it for me, it was because she thought it was time for me to handle a few secrets.

But what I found inside wasn't what I expected at all. It was short and light, with illustrations on every page. It was practically a children's story.

Before people, before kings and queens, before lands and planets, day and night, there were only the Seven. They bore the weight of the universe on their shoulders, bringing balance to all. The universe begins and ends with the Seven Sorcerers alone.

The first sorcerer controls the stars, rising and setting suns so that planets may have both light and darkness, and his name is Sayun.

The second sorcerer controls life and death. He grows the planets from the dust left across the universe, fills them with flora, gives them breath, and sets his creatures in motion. He is called Jarozen.

The third sorcerer paints the objects the light touches, which Jarozen created. He fills the skies with reds, blues, and greens, and colors each creature according to his vision, and his name is Aelia.

Fourth is the sorcerer of spirits, who puts in each creature a greater purpose—passion and fervor for a world better than the one they know, to keep improving on the canvas Aelia painted. He is known as Yelizan.

The fifth sorcerer knows all things. He has no power to impact the universe he sees, but has tracked all of history from the beginning of time. He is known only as the Observer.

The sixth sorcerer defends the balance. He, and he alone, can move along the thread that keeps all of creation from falling in on itself. His name is Lesani.

The seventh sorcerer is said to be the most powerful of all, and none know his name or his true purpose.

I read this over several times, and each time I found myself focusing on something new. Each sorcerer mentioned also had a colored symbol by its name. And whatever seemed plain at a glance was frustratingly vague or open to new interpretation with every passing. Of course the writer was talking about the Great Wizards, but they were wrong, according to Lumen tradition. What about the Wizards of Thought and Chance? The first sorcerer sounded like the Wizard of Light but with way more to do.

I had been starting to trust the Grey text, but this changed things. I had to be careful here, because this wasn't purely historical. This wasn't just knowledge or new information; it was the essence of *creation* I was studying. Maybe I hadn't been the most devout practitioner of wizard worship, but it was what our society—and all societies of the universe—were built on. I suppose it made sense that cultures would interpret them differently. I'd just never had my version of them challenged before, and it made me extremely uncomfortable.

I chuckled a bit to myself, realizing how scholarly my own thoughts sounded. Marlithan was doing a good job with me.

I opened my notebook to an unused page and drew a vertical line down its center, separating it into two columns. On one side I listed the sorcerers from the book. *Light and Darkness, Life and Death, Color, Spirits, Knowledge, Balance, Unknown.* In the second column I tried to match the ones I knew. I started with the first one, penning *Light* next to *Light and Darkness.* We had *Thought,* so I wrote that one next to *Knowledge.* Six and seven were completely new to me; I'd only learned five. That left *Life and Death,* which might have been *Chance,* and *Spirits,* which could also have been *Thought,* if I included spiritual thought, and if I remembered my own teachings well enough. For the final sorcerer-wizard pairing, I ended up with *Color* and *Healing,* which weren't a great match.

Sighing, I closed my notebook. I'd come back to this puzzle later. I flipped the page in the book and continued on.

No one knows Seven's true form, but the legends say he encompasses all things, including all six of the other wizards.

Great. That made perfect sense. I rubbed my eyes and kept going.

Seven may have come before the universe itself. It's said that his power is greater than the others' combined and that he knows all things before they happen. That he, in the blink of an eye, could create a universe exactly like the one we live in. He is the most powerful being that's ever existed in that he created the notion of existence himself.

I chose the wrong book to read while intoxicated. I must have read that paragraph five times without gaining any new understanding. But despite the urge to ditch the books and go to bed, I kept on again.

No one has ever seen Seven. It's said that his power resides not as a tangible, mortal being, but as a light source some-where deep in his universe. He is a changer of forms. He is interested not in channeling good or evil, but in constantly observing and affecting his creation with great pride. Some claim they've seen him, but none know his name.

Only one account of Seven has been particularly con-vincing. It's rumored that a child from Freyana, a min-er's daughter named Valia, found a gem. It both was and wasn't a proper gem; it was light embodied in stone. The object was transparent in color, unlike any gems the planet of Freyana had produced before.

The girl told of visions placed in her mind while holding this gem that no one could explain. She knew of events before they occurred. She knew the way to heal sick townsfolk without priests or medicine. She made time pass quickly and slowly on separate occasions, and she changed the color of their sun.

The girl died shortly after these unexplainable events—the scholars assume from trying to wield a power beyond her ability. The people of Freyana responded in two ways to her death. Many believed it was too much for her, that she had made a grave mistake. They lived in fear of a power like that ever returning to their planet. Others believed it was not the gem but the girl herself who held arcane abilities. They chose to worship her, and so among them, Seven was named Valia.

Those who have studied the Sorcerers lean mostly in favor of Seven working through the girl, Valia, with no innate abilities of her own. No one knows where Seven went after her passing, but it's believed that his power was stored inside of that gem, which we now, by legend, call the Omnilight.

This was some kind of scholarly fairytale. Marlithan and I hadn't even discussed the wizards. Until now, I'd have been surprised if she believed in them. First, because the Palunians didn't receive our religious education, and second, because she was so . . . analytical. I just finished reading a book on her recommendation that attempted to explain all of sorcery with science, like they were one and the same. *That doesn't mean they aren't equally valid explanations though.* My thoughts were starting to sound more like her than myself.

I made a tea to try to draw out some of the alcohol and to keep me awake a bit longer. As much as I wanted to put it down, I had to finish this book.

The rest contained a lot of theories about where the Omnilight had gone. There was a map showing a record of places people claimed to see it. Our system wasn't even pictured there. Either the book was too old or no one knew it had been taken to Palunia.

All we Lumen knew was that the contessa was the keeper of artifacts. The gem I'd taken, though, if it was this *Omnilight*, wasn't just some ancient tool. I wondered if even she knew its real power. Had she intentionally withheld information about the Omnilight from us? Were there secrets about it stored in her palace? It wouldn't surprise me.

It seemed ridiculous now that I was always so unconcerned. That I followed her and all our Lumen tradition so blindly. I hated to even think of how I'd treated the Palunians, knowing now that they were probably more intelligent and capable than I was. Of course they hid their abilities. Our people would have beaten them out of them.

Only the contessa knew they were competent, but did she know just how smart they were? What would our world have looked like if the Palunians could just live as themselves? If their culture had been maintained all these years?

I reached the last chapter within a couple of hours. The tone shifted. It was no longer about sorcerers—this was purely scholarly, like the tens of other books I'd read since boarding this ship. The language was simple, but the content hooked me with every word.

After a thousand years of no reported activity, the Omnilight was largely forgotten and considered by many who did know of it to be a tall tale. Worshippers of the sorcerers stopped including Seven in their texts and tellings, citing that since he encompassed the others, they might also be equal to him. That maybe Seven was never a unique being at all.

And so modern worshippers focused on the initial six and other variations of the great sorcerers as new societies grew and developed. Seven's identity was not entirely forgotten, but was changed and shifted over the millennia. His reputation grew the most vile in a young region that never knew the original sorcerers: the region known as Saritee.

I flipped the page over and found a map. There it was. To the bottom left was the home I'd always known, and mid-right, stretching a hundred light-years, was Lor Annaius. Bottom-right was Draconia. I'd guess we'd only traveled maybe an eighth of the way so far, though admittedly I'd let Welsia take over the console weeks ago.

Looking at Palunia as a sketch on a page, I let out a sigh. I missed my friends and family, but I felt differently now. I didn't feel like I *belonged* there anymore. The regret and panic I'd had about joining this crew was more than unwarranted; I'd have been giving up a part of myself I didn't know existed. I'd just be another "Lume in a cloak," as Gonian called us. I didn't think I'd ever be able to live in a palace again.

I took another look at the map before continuing to the next page.

Saritee's version of Seven is not the neutral creator, but the most powerful force of evil that's ever existed in space and time. The Saritean story claims that the keeper of Seven, known to them as Ulric the Slayer, had his power locked away by the ancient King Lumina. As the story goes, the great king sealed him in the planet's core.

I paused. I didn't have to read the next part. Ulric being locked away was what drew the dragons. The planet couldn't sustain its natural defenses with something so vile encrusted inside it. He was, in Lumen history, credited with the destruction of our home.

> *According to Saritean sages and their texts, it's said that Ulric was after a gem more pure than the brightest sun—the "first partical" of the universe—and that it may be located on Lor Annaius. A Palunian sage by the name of Naheizan Regalin, through her research into many texts of old, was the first to tie this back to the Seven Sorcerers and the Omnilight. She saw a truth that only the Palunian people were willing to accept: Ulric the Slayer was not a simple beast, but was in possession of the Creator himself. She concluded that the people of Lor Annaius had taken something that was not rightfully theirs, trading his watchful reign for one of terror and control. Naheizan urged this message across Saritee, starting with the Palunian star system.*
>
> *The king of that time, King Lumina XXXVII, soon supposedly decided that the threat of Draconia was too great to remain on Lor Annaius. After the immigration of Lumenkind, publications and writings from Naheizan ceased. The last known document of hers is this letter:*

I turned the page to find a letter written in what at first looked like unintelligible scrawl. I rotated it until I could start to make out words. It was in that old Palunian dialect. I wrote out a translated copy in my notebook as I read.

> *If this letter is found it means that I am dead.*
>
> *I uncovered one more piece of information last night, in an old text imported from the Rakus system. It talked of alliances between King Lumen and the Mother of*

Draconia. It was written by a lone Lumen who witnessed a deal—an offering between dragonkind and Lumenkind. If we're to believe the account of that man, we will soon see the end of Lor Annaius. A gem for a planet.

If that account can be believed it means the Lumen mean to seek a new home, and I believe I know which land they'll seek it on. And I believe this is how I will die.

They will use religion as an excuse. But I can tell you, I worship the same sorcerers, and their motives are not based on any teachings of old. They will use religion not only as an excuse to take my head but to take our planet and our voice. Do not let them— I beg it. Resist them.

They will resist us with force and sorcery, but I beg you to resist them only with words until the time comes when we must fight. As they have abandoned their principles in fear of us, we must show them who we are. We will not give up on our beliefs as they have.

There was one more page before the metal insert, and on it was one small paragraph.

Naheizan was found leading an underground rebellion fifty years later, after Palunia was taken under Lumen rule. As an old woman, she was beheaded during the tri-annual Killing Cup, where all insubordinate Palunians were publically executed. Given the opportunity for last words, she said this: "May the fire of your sleeping god reign on me."

CHAPTER 13

I MUST HAVE sat for half an hour just processing what I'd read. I think to some extent it shocked me sober. When I'd calmed myself enough to function, I got up, snatched up the books, and bolted for Marlithan's door.

I knocked on it a few times and was ready to knock again when she appeared in a bed robe. I didn't care. "Come," I instructed her, and started down the hall. Then I realized what I was doing and spun back around. "Sorry. I mean, please come with me, if you don't mind."

She smiled. "I didn't figure you'd flaunt your *rightful leader* attitude near me again."

"Only to tell you that I need someone smarter than me."

She smirked and we went to my room. I locked the door as she took a seat at the table. Then I dropped the book in front of her.

"How much of this is true?" I asked. "I believe you, okay? Everything you've given me has been convincing, but this . . .

this changes everything. I'm asking you as a friend—how much?"

"It's hard to say exactly . . ." She trailed off, then looked into my eyes. I knew I was staring and standing over her, but this was important. "Damaus, it depends on what you accept as truth. Do you believe in the sorcerers?"

"The wizards, yes," I said. "Though now I don't know which version."

"If you believe the sorcerers, or wizards, exist and you accept that most of this book is speculation, then I can tell you it's at least 80 percent valid by Palunian standards. Speaking as a friend, *I* believe it to be true."

"Fair," I said, sitting across from her. "Can we talk about Naheizan Regalin without speculation?"

She nodded. "Naheizan's work is everywhere in our community. It's historical, traceable, and as factual as anything old can be. Her research has been verified as well as we can from within the communes."

"She was really executed?" I pressed. Marlithan nodded. "And the festival . . . It was really that blatant? About killing Palunians?"

She nodded again. "After a while the Lumes began to find it dull. They knew anyone arrested or wanted would be killed eventually. They wanted something more entertaining, more appetizing and worthy of feasting. At some point they realized they had no need for warships anymore. So the Drawing element was brought in. And it became the only way for us to escape."

"And the destruction of Lor Annaius," I began.

"Planned," she answered. "The Lumen king made a deal with the devil. When he realized the Omnilight had been in Draconia all along, he offered them the entire planet for it, promising two-thirds of his population to feast on. He took all hope from his people."

"Like a *sleeping god*?" I murmured.

"Kings were gods in those days," Marlithan said. "Believed to be the only path between the Lumen people and the sorcerers, according to the religious histories."

I nodded, my mind still handling too much to speak anymore. I leaned back in my chair, my thoughts fluctuating from deep analysis to nothing at all.

"You know, Marl, I think I've realized the Lumens' biggest problem after reading this text." She raised a brow. "We were never taught to think for ourselves. Makes us pretty easy to fool."

I stretched, realizing again how tired I was. Then I felt a slight rumble below my feet.

"What was that?" I asked. A larger rumble came next. "Something in the crate room? An issue with the magnets?"

Marlithan looked concerned, too. "I don't know, Damaus."

The next rumble shook me off my feet, sending me flying across the floor of my room, my shoulders crashing into the wash station. The ship had changed angles.

"Pulse dragon!" I hissed, pulling myself up and running for the door. Marlithan raced behind me as I headed out of the room toward the console. We were thrust into the wall of the corridor along the way.

"*Fasten your bedbelts!*" I called out, hoping the others could hear me through their doors. Then I kept on running.

I couldn't see anything through the dome, and I hadn't thought to inspect from my personal window. *This can't be how we die.* The course was still set for our destination. Welsia had been the one to set up the coordinates and program our jump controller. We only traveled with jump during set hours of the day, but this was going to be the exception. I flipped off the regulator and hoped they'd heard me.

I brought my hand up to the projection and selected *Jump*. The ship engine roared from below the console. A bar slowly filled across the top of the desk, from red to orange to yellow to green to blue. It was time. I locked myself in and watched as Marlithan did the same from an observation seat. *Charge* changed to *Engage* on the screen and I selected it again.

I would never really get used to the feeling of being hurled into space at half a light-year an hour, but at least we managed to flee intact. Pulse dragons were slow, so we probably lost it in the first five seconds, but I let it go longer. I wondered if Ulric the Slayer really was inside the planet's core, assuming we'd make it that far. I stopped the ship after about ten minutes and left the regulator off.

I'd gotten more used to floating around down in the crates, and there was something enjoyable about it. I really felt like I was in space when I wasn't stuck to the ground. I pushed over to the dome and looked out, wondering where we were now.

A glimmer of light caught my eye around the outside of my view. I pressed my face to the window, trying to get a better look, when I felt another rumble.

"They *followed* us?" I gasped, looking back at Marlithan, who'd unbuckled herself from the seat. "They can do that?"

She shook her head, joining me. "I don't think it's a dragon, Damaus." I started to head back to the console, but she grabbed my arm and pulled me back. "Look!"

Something was coming toward us, but it wasn't a pulse dragon. It wasn't a space creature at all. It was another ship.

"*Do something!*" I shouted at her. She just stared back. "*Sorry!*" I yelled louder. It hadn't occurred to me that other ship-operating races would be the end of us. Interplanetary battle was outlawed in our system, but I didn't know anything about the laws outside. I didn't even know where we were.

I struggled my way back to the console chair to try to find something to do. "This is a military ship," I mumbled. "Do we have . . . blasters or something? A laser—or seven?" I started searching through menus. I'd learned a bit about ships but nothing about their military uses. "Marlithan, can you go look for anything big in the armory?"

"It's too far without the regulator. By the time we get anything, it'll be too late to equip and program it."

"Then I'll turn the damn regulator on!" My palm was hovering over the button when she reached over and grabbed my hand.

"While we're being *attacked*? Do you want people attempting to walk? Do you want to disable our chance of escape? Jump-travel again, Damaus!"

"But they'll just follow us again!" Despite knowing that, I hit *Charge* as another series of rumbles took over the ship. *Red . . . Orange . . . BANG!*

The lights flickered and then went out. The console went dark. I swung my hand around until I found Marlithan's and gripped it tight. We huddled under the console desk together to keep from floating away and waited to die.

There was no other *bang* or *rumble*, but there were noises below us.

"Someone's here?" I whispered, though I didn't need an answer. A moment later the ship grew cold. That meant whatever crew this was had made it past the entrance bay, through the tunnel door, and were on their way up.

"Marlithan," I whispered, squeezing her hand, "thank you for everything. I'm . . . I'm sorry for what we did to you and the others. I'm sorry I didn't do anything about it, either."

"Apology accepted," she whispered back. Though we couldn't see each other, I smiled. And we waited. I thought they'd be up in no time, but no one approached for several minutes.

Then, after a few more anxious, silent moments, there was a *clink, clink* noise. I immediately flashed back to being locked into a chariot by the red cloaks. But this was someone on the ladder. In the eerie quiet of the powered-down ship I overheard breathing. They were catching their breath. Didn't they know we'd be out of oxygen soon with the system down?

"Damaus?"

I froze. I knew the voice. "Westalyn?"

CHAPTER 14

I COULDN'T TELL where she was, but I let go of Marlithan and pulled myself out from beneath the desk. My eyes were slowly adjusting to the dark. We weren't close enough to a star to get any useful light.

"I'm here," I called, hoping to touch her.

"Damaus Ju Demma," she said, and I thought I heard her sigh. "In the name of the contessa, I command you to return the object which you stole from Her Fairness. Failure to comply will end in your immediate execution."

A blue light appeared across the room, near the tunnel opening. She was armed.

"Westalyn, I have a lot to explain to you," I said, praying to the wizards, whoever they were, that she wouldn't shoot. "Please—"

"Who's there?" Her weapon pointed the other way. The crew must have come out to see what was going on. "Stay back, Grey!"

"Hey!" I yelled. "Don't call them that!"

I was starting to see better now. She kept her weapon extended but turned back to face me. Her suit was tight like mine, but it was darker in color. She could probably see me just fine. I remembered then that I had the personal projector. I reached into my pocket and pulled it out, flicking on its light.

It was so strange to look at her again. Even in the suit, she'd painted her face as beautiful as she always had. Her gems were simpler, but they were there. And still that lock of hair fell over her ear. Her head was exposed without her helm on, and she was beautiful. Compared to the rest of us, she looked like a goddess.

"What did you say to me?" she asked, as I set the projector down on one of the observation chairs, leaving a faint glow throughout the room.

I looked over toward the corridor and saw that Welsia had come out on her own. She was an incredible mechanic, probably on her way to sort out the power failure. Except now she was cowering and silent, just like they'd been on Palunia.

"Westalyn." I gritted my teeth in an attempt to tell her nicely. "You're scaring her."

"What does that matter?" She frowned. "Besides, I only have a problem with *them* if they get in my way. Hand over the vial and the contessa's artifact."

"I can't," I said, hating to disappoint her. "Please, let me explain."

"She's offered your return in exchange."

"*What?*" Instinctively I looked over to Marlithan, who was still under the desk. But she didn't return my gaze.

"Bring the items back personally, and you'll rejoin Lumen society," Westalyn explained. "When you left, the contessa paid a visit to your mother. It was a deal they worked out. And they sent me as bait."

"Is my mother okay? Did anyone else come with you?"

"She's fine for now, but your family will pay for this if you don't return it. My ship's a quick-travel pod, just large enough for forward blasters to slow you down. I came alone."

"Can we go somewhere to discuss this?" I asked. There was my room, but the key and vial were lying in the open after speaking with Marlithan. I knew I could trust Westalyn once I spoke with her, but it might be a bad idea to dangle that in her face so soon. There were the crates though. "I know a place."

She shrugged. "It's not like I have anything else to do until you decide to come with me."

I picked up my projector and used it to light the way ahead of us. "Down here," I said, using one hand to push myself down the tunnel. I kept going lower and lower until we reached the opening to the enormous storage space.

"Where are we?" Westalyn asked, her voice suddenly filled with wonder. "And just how big is this thing?"

"I've been here, what, a couple months now? And I haven't seen it all yet," I said. I took her hand, and she immediately yanked it away. "Sorry," I mumbled.

"Have you completely forgotten your manners?" she asked, though I didn't sense much bitterness in her tone.

The light from my projector didn't illuminate the whole room, but it was enough to find my way to the latest crate I'd explored with Marlithan. "Make sure to hold on to any crates you pass, or you'll end up on the ceiling," I warned. Holding hands would have simplified things, but Westalyn wasn't a woman I wanted to defy. I reached the stack and then let myself float up to the top, gripping the ledge. I waited for her to join me. "We're gonna force ourselves into this and bury ourselves in books. Got it?"

"What?"

I decided showing her was better than explaining, and I flipped over, then tucked myself in. She hesitated but followed, holding on tightly to the edge as she let her body float over the crate.

"Help me, Damaus," she instructed with gritted teeth.

"With what?" I found that I was smiling.

"Oh, for—just pull me down!" she exclaimed. I laughed and did as she instructed, gripping her torso and pulling her back toward me. I tossed a few books on her for good measure. "It's not funny," she muttered. "You aren't supposed to touch me yet."

"Yet?" I asked.

"I assumed that when you came back you'd want to . . . pick up where we left off," she said. She looked at me, and my chest tightened.

"Westalyn, I have a lot to say," I began. She held my gaze, but I looked away. It was only now occurring to me how different her perspective of things had to be. I'd had months to process, to analyze, to come to conclusions. "First, do you trust me?"

"Hardly," she said, laughing a bit herself. "I had to chase you down in another star system, Damaus. You have great qualities, but I wouldn't praise you for reliability."

"Fair." I shrugged. "But I've learned some things here. Really important things. Things about the Palunians, and about us, about the contessa, about our homeland."

"What, are you some kind of scholar now? I suppose you haven't had much else to do."

"Something like that," I admitted. "Look, did you ever feel back home like there was something wrong with the way we lived? With how much we relied on the Palace for information, or how we so willingly enslaved an entire race for our own benefit?"

"Enslaved? You sound like one of those new-age preachers from the water pits. The Grey are happy to serve us. What else would they do? And where else would we get information? The Palace is the political center for a reason. What is all of this, Damaus?"

"Did the contessa tell you what you were coming to retrieve?" I asked.

Westalyn nodded. "A vial of amber along with a *precious artifact*. I didn't exactly ask questions. She's the contessa. If I said no I'd probably be sent to dig water or end up locked in a sinking cell."

"You told me something on the day of the Drawing," I reminded her. "You suggested that we might have been running out of amber. Do you remember?"

She nodded. "It wasn't the first time the thought occurred to me."

"You were right," I said. "You were completely right, and I should have listened to you. That's what this whole thing is about. Below this room is another compartment just as tall and nearly as wide, and if we can, we're meant to fill it with amber from the lakes and core of Lor Annaius. You aren't *running* out—you *are* out."

"What?" The lighting was low, but I could have sworn I saw her face go pale.

"Whatever's in the ground and atmosphere now is all you have left. Once it's processed the Lumen will start to die. I'm so glad to see you, because I don't just have *a* vial of amber but the *last* vial."

Her expression changed from shock to anger. "You took it for *yourself*? You left us to die while you roamed around reading books?"

"No!" I exclaimed, caught off guard. "I didn't take it *for* me; I took it *from* her! She wasn't going to share it with you. She was the one hoarding it around her neck, along with the Omnilight."

"How do you know what her intentions were?" Westalyn was shouting now. "How can you sit there and accuse the contessa? What's happened to you, Damaus? And what the hell is an Omnilight?" She tried to stand up but quickly forced herself back down as the lack of gravity took over.

"There's more." I tried to stay calm. I reminded myself that I would have acted the same way not long ago.

"You left us to die and took the only thing that could save us, and you expect me to care about anything else you have to say? We would have *suffered and died*, Damaus. Your mother and brother. Do you care about them at all? We'd be living shells on a planet ruled by Grey until we died!"

"Would be a nice change," I retorted.

Suddenly the lights went on. I squinted, then slowly opened my eyes all the way. Westalyn was staring at me, stone-faced. "What did you say?"

"I didn't mean it exactly," I rescinded. "But the Palunians aren't what you think."

"They've changed you," she said, as though she had some kind of revelation. "You have empathy for them. You *care* about them. Hell, you're even starting to *look* like them!"

My hair had grown in dark and was getting shaggy on top. I forgot what paint even felt like. And I'd forgotten to be ashamed of my appearance until now.

"They're smart, Westalyn," I said. "And, dammit, I do care. They aren't just servants and documentors. They're historians, scholars, artists, mechanics, and smarter than you or I could ever be. They only submit to Lumenkind because we forced it on them when we stole their planet. What we grew up learning was wrong. We've celebrated all the wrong things. The Palunians deserve more than that. And the ones on this ship are the greatest friends I've ever had. But of course I still care about you, and Mother, and Jona, and my friends back home."

"Then why have you abandoned your journey?" she asked quietly. "Why have you chosen not to save us?"

"I haven't, and I will," I said. "I had to take that vial from the contessa, but I'm doing everything I can to get that amber. I just need to hold it over the contessa's head long enough to make some changes."

Westalyn stiffened and stared into my eyes. "Are you joking?"

I shook my head. "No, I'm serious. This thing with the Palunians is important, but I'm not going to let you all die over it. I need your help, actually."

"No, Damaus." She clutched my arm tightly, this time taking me aback. "You're going in the *wrong direction*. I got one of the mechanics and your brother to help me get a signal on you in my pod, and you're going the opposite way. You have been for weeks. Did you set this course yourself?"

"I . . . did . . ." I stammered, panicking. "I set it for Lor Annaius, I swear. But the last time I checked . . ."

She let out a long sigh. "This is why we can't trust them."

CHAPTER 15

"TIME TO GO," I told Westalyn. My head was spinning with conflicting thoughts, each bouncing off one another and leading nowhere. I undid my uniform jacket and withdrew two magnet pads with handles from the inside pocket.

"How?" she demanded. "The gravity's back on."

I didn't have it all worked out. I only had two grippable pads. But if they could hold Marlithan, who was tall, broad, and packed more weight than me, I could bank on it holding the two of us.

"Let me get over the edge first," I instructed, setting the pads on the side of the crate and gripping them as I swung my body over. I hung suspended by the handles. "Now I want you to climb onto my back."

"*What?*" she exclaimed. "You go! Turn the gravity back off or get a ladder."

"I need to find out what's going on. Please. This is the fastest way."

She didn't look happy, but she obliged. Thankfully the magnets held their place as she climbed over the side and slipped her hands over my shoulders. It was true that I'd gotten more accustomed to physical contact since joining the crew, but it was another thing entirely to feel the weight and form of Westalyn Chi Soha against my back.

I lifted the right pad, and my left began to shake with all the weight. I took a deep breath and set that one lower, then lifted the left. It took some time, but we descended the four-crate stack successfully. When Westalyn hopped off, I returned the pads to my uniform and led the way to the entrance ladder.

Maybe she was lying. *She didn't look like she was lying* But there's no way Marlithan and the others would betray me. Maybe Welsia did this on her own. I climbed up fast. There was no use speculating; I needed an answer.

I only noticed my arms were aching when I got to the top and pulled myself into the main room. Welsia sat at the console, and the entire group of Palunians had buckled themselves into the observation chairs. Something was going on.

I couldn't figure out which words to start with until Westalyn met me with a nudge. *Answers.*

"Welsia," I called over, without bothering to approach. She and the others all looked at me. It wasn't the most polite method, but this was serious, and if she couldn't tell me, someone else could. "Which star system are we in currently?"

"New Aneth," she replied simply, returning to focus on the projection in front of her. Westalyn gasped. I forgot she'd never heard a Palunian speak.

"And how far is New Aneth from the target system?"

"Approximately a hundred . . . sixty," she replied, not taking her eyes from the image.

Stunned, I looked from her to Marlithan to Westalyn. "And Welsia . . . why are we farther from Lor Annaius than when we started?"

She didn't answer. She flicked a switch under the console. A panel with buttons and a control stick folded out of the desk, enabling manual controls. She buckled herself into the captain's chair. "I suggest you two take a seat before I turn the regulator off and charge this thing."

"Dammit, Welsia!" I shouted. "Marlithan?"

"Damaus," Marlithan acknowledged, motioning to a seat beside her. "I'll explain once we land."

"Land?" My throat went dry. "*Land!* Where exactly do you plan on *landing* if our destination is on the other side of the galaxy?"

"That's time," Welsia noted, her hand motioning toward the *Regulator* button. "Crew, prepare for descent."

I scrambled for the seat next to Marlithan, pulling Westalyn behind me. We both sat down as Welsia disengaged the switch. As we started to rise off our seats, I leaned over Westalyn, holding her in place and buckling her in. I hooked my feet under the row of seats ahead of me. Marlithan grabbed my left arm and Westalyn my right, helping me down into my own chair. I buckled in and mumbled thanks to them.

We lurched forward with a painful jolt. That never got easier. I looked over at Westalyn, who seemed to take it better than me. I somehow managed not to be sick as we hurled through New Aneth.

"This is ridiculous," I said to Marlithan, not caring who overheard. "After all we've been through? I *trusted* you. Now, because of you—*all of you*—my family, and all of Lumenkind, are going to die."

"The Pilgrimage is more important, Damaus," Marlithan began.

"And why do you get to decide that?"

"Oh, shut yer face," Gonian groaned from the front row. I winced like I'd been slapped. "The Lumes deserve whatever fate they've created. Turns out you're an all right guy, Damaus, but it took isolating you with nothing to do for a month before you cared what we had to say. It isn't on us to educate them. They had their chance."

"*Excuse me, Grey?*" Westalyn snapped.

"Don't call them that!" I hissed. "Sorry. Gonian, you don't have to educate them," I sputtered, wanting to respond to everything he said at once. "I will. Westalyn will help me."

"Damaus!" she scowled. "I'm not turning against my own people for whatever righteous cause you're toting."

I ignored her and continued. "I had a plan! To start a movement from within. To bring the amber, but to hold it until the contessa admitted to her crimes. To allow Lumen access only when they renounced their ways and apologized."

"You don't know Lumes like we do." Gonian sighed. "They'd lie to get what they wanted and discard their loyalty the moment something more appetizing came along."

"I thought we were friends!" I blurted, losing track of my argument. I sure wasn't going to impress Marlithan this way. But my studies were suddenly less important. "How would you feel if your family were left to die?"

He turned and locked eyes with me. His, like all Palunians, were dark, but I'd never seen any this angry. "My family was sent off in a ship like this six years ago. My life-love and my daughter were sent to die for your Lumen games. So don't tell me I don't know how it feels. Every one of us in this room knows what it's like to be, or have their loved ones, ripped from the family. I thought you were becoming less of a self-centered twit, but I guess we overestimated you."

I was out of words. I sat, fuming, not able to look at any of them. I'd failed Westalyn and she was here to witness it. And these supposed friends of mine had failed me. The fact that they weren't beyond leaving my people to die . . . I should have seen it sooner.

My knuckles had gone white where I gripped the arms of the chair on both sides of me. On my left Marlithan placed a delicate hand on mine, but I shook her off, glaring at her. She frowned, and I thought I saw hurt in her eyes. *Good*, I thought, fairly certain my anger was misplaced but finding it hard to care.

"Time to land," Welsia announced. We slowed to regular speed for a minute. Then our trajectory changed as we began to nosedive. In front of us, a huge, beautiful planet appeared in the dome. From outside its atmosphere it was lush yellow-green and blue. I didn't see any desert or rock mountains. The atmosphere itself had a faint yellow glow, and it was somehow inviting.

I should have taken control from her and fought her if I needed to, I thought. But it was too late, and my curiosity was getting the better of me. We were descending through cream-colored clouds, which wisped easily out of our way as we pushed against the wind.

When we passed through the atmosphere, I saw water. Endless turquoise water, stretching to distant masses of land. As we lowered, we approached great green hills filled with vegetation. Connecting the water and hills was a strip of sand, but much smaller and much more welcoming than the deserts back home.

"What is this place?" Westalyn asked aloud. She was as stunned as I was by its beauty.

"It's our home," Marlithan said.

CHAPTER 16

"YOUR WHAT?" I asked.

We descended over the hillside and came upon a valley. I gasped. There was an obvious landing pad, but behind it were ships. Many ships. Hundreds at least, and they looked like the ones in our shipyard back home.

We lowered close to the ground. "Brace yourselves!" Welsia called. "I've gotten pretty good at flying, but this'll be the first time I've landed one of these things."

I gripped the seat hard again as we flipped upright toward the sky, our backs to the ground. Then we started to tilt even further, tipping upside-down.

"Welsia!" I yelled out, but she gained control.

"Sorry about that!" she blurted, straightening the vessel and cutting out the engine a little at a time. We jerked downward over and over. This time I thought I would be sick. There had to be a better way to land. If we hit the ground at the wrong angle—

"I did it!" Welsia cried. The jerking stopped. We'd landed on solid ground. The crew cheered her on as they unclasped themselves, floating freely around the room.

"What now?" Westalyn hissed at me.

"I guess we go out," I said. "Wait here though. I need to get something."

I'm pretty sure she protested, but I wasn't about to leave the Omnilight or my notebook behind. I may have lost my home, but at least I had something new to believe in. I floated to the corridor entrance, then swam through the air to my room. To my relief the items were floating but still there, near the table.

What did you think, that Marlithan would steal them? I didn't know what to think anymore, but in spite of everything, I couldn't harbor that much doubt in her. First I grabbed my helm. Then I placed both the book and chain in my jacket, along with the magnet pads, and pushed toward the door.

The crew was already making their way down to the middle level. Westalyn had unbuckled herself and was gripping one of the bolted-down chairs to ground her. I nodded to her, and we started down together at the back of the line.

I hadn't even approached the entrance since we left. Of course I'd imagined our arrival on another planet, but it hadn't been this one. And even then, I'd accepted that the ship might be the last thing I ever saw. So much for that.

But I had another idea forming in my mind. "Westalyn," I whispered before putting on my helm. She looked at me. "I have a plan."

She slowed, making sure we kept our distance from the others. A glance told me Welsia hadn't yet figured out how to open the door.

"We'll go out," I began. "We'll see what this place is about. I have a few more questions for Marlithan if I can bear talking to her. But tonight—assuming the sun ever sets on this planet—I'm coming back. I'm going to get that amber, and I'd like you to do it with me."

"I didn't sign up for that," she noted. "I parked my pod in your landing bay though, so I would appreciate a ride up there."

I nodded. "If you change your mind, let me know."

She gave me a pained look. "You're really going to go alone? Damaus, if you just bring back that vial and artifact—"

I shook my head and put on my helm. The door was opening.

The first thing I noticed was a sort of singing in the distance. The second thing was a wonderful warmth on my body. The crew left the ship in pairs, and I noticed none of them wore helms. They breathed in whatever air was on this planet like they hadn't breathed properly in their entire lives.

I removed my helm and led Westalyn out with me. I had never felt something so wonderful. It was like the cold breezes over the desert at night, but it was filled with a light mist and warmed by an enormous sun. I took a deep breath myself. I couldn't tell if it was just that I'd gotten used to the stale oxygen of the ship or if compared to Palunia this was some kind of paradise.

I set my gaze on the hillside and froze. There were *people* approaching. The crew looked at them with excitement, but Westalyn and I exchanged anxious glances. When they got closer, I could start to make out features.

They were Palunians—hundreds, if not thousands, of them. They wore many colorful patterned layers instead of grey robes, but their hair and bodies were unmistakable. They were cheering and *running* toward us. They beamed at the crew. But when they saw me, their clapping slowed. I may have fooled a few at a glance with my hair and lack of paint, but Westalyn . . .

She pulled off her helm and the crowd went silent. She was plainly Lumen. Some began cursing, others booing. I went to put a hand on her shoulder to comfort her, but she reached into a holster on the back of her uniform. I'd forgotten she was armed.

"Westalyn, *no!*" I cried, stepping in front of her. "I need you to trust me enough not to harm anyone here. If you care about the people back home, please."

She relented, reholstering her weapon, but I could see the fury in her eyes. I looked down to the crew, who were busy embracing and speaking with many of the Palunians here. Or . . . whatever they were called on this planet. I sat on the ramp to make myself less visible for a while and invited Westalyn to do the same.

"Gonian!" a voice called. Two women—one middle-aged and one around my age—were running with arms linked toward the front of the crowd, where the gruff Palunian stumbled to his knees and started sobbing. He forced himself up with one hand and wiped various fluids from his face with the other. He ran full tilt and wrapped the two in his arms. Their faces were lost to me with the distance, but they were obviously shaking. I felt a lump in my throat.

Welsia bolted into the crowd to hug and kiss one of the women. Most of the crew had friends and family members come forward. They were separating into the sea of grey faces. All except Marlithan, Hel, and Rodiger, who seemed most content with one another.

I glanced at Westalyn, who was staring out into the crowd with her mouth hanging open.

"You okay?" I asked. Seeing her reaction made the lump grow bigger somehow.

"It's . . . beautiful," she said, and left it at that. I nodded and watched with her.

After the crowd started to thin, Marlithan came and stood next to us. "There's a feast starting in the Community Square soon—a whole celebration. Come along and hear me out?"

I frowned. "Do they want us there?" The friendliest among them were staring at us with caution, but most gave Westalyn and me dirty looks before leaving the landing site.

"Probably not," Marlithan admitted. "But I need to be there, and the least we can do is make sure you're fed. Besides, you're going to want to make a good impression here eventually, assuming you'll give it a chance."

I glanced at Westalyn, who shrugged. She was still looking past me toward the dwindling crowd.

I wanted to know what was going on, and what was on Marlithan's mind, too. I was still angry, of course, but this whole thing was starting to make a lot more sense. Being away from their loved ones for several years, not knowing if they had lived, was a lot more difficult than the couple months I'd had to deal with. And though I knew it would disappoint her, I couldn't stay here.

We walked alongside Marlithan and Hel, followed by Rodiger, who kept pointing at the nature around us.

"What is that stuff?" he asked of the green hills.

"Grass," Hel replied. "It grew on Palunia once, before the water dried up and the deserts set in."

"And that?"

"A tree."

This went on the whole way to the town. Honestly, I had the same questions Rodiger did. I'd read about the natural state of Palunia before the Lumen invasion, but at most I'd had ink sketches as a reference, and they really didn't do the fully formed plants justice.

"I wonder if this planet has amber," I whispered to Westalyn.

"Why, you want to live on it?" she asked.

"Who wouldn't? It's so warm but in a pleasant way. Don't even need to cover our heads. The water looks beautiful, too. Hell, I want to roll around on this grass. And if they have plants, they're bound to have natural food meals with real fruit and vegetation. We never had these luxuries back home."

"Yes, but it's *home*," she pressed. "What happened to not abandoning them? I thought you were going to get the amber no matter what?"

"I am, I am." I sighed. "It's just that I've never seen this much beauty in one place before. I'd have traded my entire gem collection to spend time in a place like this."

She nodded. She felt the allure, too, I guess—the appeal of a life on a new and inviting world. The appeal of a life away from the palaces and politics of our broken society.

We reached the top of the hill, facing another valley. Below us was a small, circular town filled with beautiful wooden houses. In the center was a huge wooden table that ran the length of the town. It must have been able to seat a thousand people. It was so simple but so grand. The singing on the wind grew louder, too, though I couldn't find any singers.

I started to descend, but the three crew members didn't move.

"I can't believe it," Marlithan said. "We're finally home."

"Aye," Hel agreed, putting one hand on her shoulder and another on the boy's. "We can start all over."

They joined me a moment later, and Rodiger kept asking questions all the way down that none of us had the answers to. It didn't seem like Marlithan had done much research on this place, because she was as wide-eyed as I was. Most of the wooden houses closest to the town center appeared to be shops of some kind. They served food and beverages, provided clothing and antidotes and all sorts of things. I noticed a stand with a man giving away wooden instruments, too.

Everything was wood. Palunia hadn't seen a living tree in centuries. Only a few small structures and artifacts remained back home, and they were carefully preserved from the elements and stored in viewing palaces. Here the wood had a natural, exposed sort of beauty that our great palaces lacked.

That was really one of the fundamental differences in our culture, I realized. Lumen, and the cities we built, were completely artificial. We got our beauty from gems and paints on our skin, but most of the time we failed to see what was in front of us. I wondered briefly what Westalyn would look like without paint, then flushed. I'd have a lot of adjusting to do if I made it back to Lumen society.

We sat together on one of the benches at the long communal table. I didn't see anyone else from the crew. We ended up next to some older Palunians and a handful of children. They all stared at Westalyn and me—the children with curiosity, and the old folks with animosity.

I glanced at Westalyn, who was looking down at the table. If I didn't have a barrage of questions to ask, I'd probably have gone to eat air-packed food on the ship.

"So, shall we start with what the hell this place is?" I whispered to Marlithan.

"Aneth," she replied.

I stared, then motioned for her to continue.

"A few hundred years ago Palunians gathered to research livable planets with the goal to escape Lumen slavery. They studied many systems from the books available in those days and found this one. It was described as being lucious and vegetative, with a breathable atmosphere.

"It is true that the Lumen were getting bored with the Killing Cup, and that they'd need more amber eventually. But it was one of our own who nudged the idea into Lumen culture. The crew that boarded the ship during the first Traveler's

Cup was given instructions to reach this place. Once they left the Palunia system they'd bust up the radar feeder signaling the Planetary Palace, leaving the Lumen thinking they'd died. In reality they made it here and became the founders, and every three years the growing community has welcomed more and more of us."

I gaped at her. "Why didn't you tell me any of this when I was reading all that history? You lied to me."

She shook her head, but didn't look at me. "I . . . simplified."

"So that's it then? You're going to stay here? Just ditch everyone back home?" I exclaimed. "And you, Hel? The boy's mother can just rot unless she happens to get picked next time?" They both stared at me with narrow eyes, but I'd heard enough. "You know, for a group that's had it as rough as you all have, I'm frankly impressed at how selfish you can be."

I stood and hopped over the bench, storming away from the festivities toward some nearby hills. When I got to the base of one, I ran up toward its crest.

I felt so *sure* about what I'd learned from Marlithan. But then, I hadn't learned from her directly. I learned under her guidance through books from scholars and historians throughout Palunian history. The betrayal was unforgivable, but it didn't make the facts less true. It just meant I believed in them more than they did. I also hated that I was now my own voice of reason even in my anger.

From the top of the hill, I saw smaller hills and, beyond them, water. I could still hear the distant sounds of singing; they seemed to carry themselves on the wind without a single point of origin. I breathed the fresh air in and found another scent in it. The smell of water, I guessed. I grinned and started the trek downward.

I was going to enjoy a day on this planet, and then I was going to go. Knowing now that the Palunians were giving up on their own kind reinforced that I had to get the amber to save mine. It wasn't going to be easy on my own, or even with Westalyn's help, but I'd rather die trying than senselessly kill a planet full of people.

I thought of my mother and Jona, and I wondered what the contessa had done with them. Had she threatened them to give her information? Had she already harmed them for my crimes? Would my mother even be able to forgive me? I had just continually let her down. But even if I disappointed and worried her, I was going to do everything in my power to save her life. I had to.

I slid down the last hill and found myself on sand. It wasn't tough and dry like the desert; it was powder-soft. Surprised, I undid the bottom section of my uniform, removing the trousers and boots. I slid my toe around and felt that the sand was cool here. It felt refreshing between my toes. I removed my jacket, too, setting it cautiously under the lip of the hill. Then I stepped out of the hill's shade.

Suddenly everything was warm. The sand on my feet, the sun on my head, shoulders, and legs. It felt amazing. It wasn't burning so much as comforting. I sighed and approached the the shining turquoise water.

"Damaus!"

I looked up behind me, shielding my eyes from the sunlight. Westalyn stood at the top of the hill.

"I've been chasing you the whole time!" She gasped for air.

I smiled at her, which was as much as I could muster, then turned back to the water. It extended beyond what I could see. They could drink from this for the rest of their lives. They really had it all here. I stuck a toe in pulled it back out. It was cold.

I closed my eyes and sighed, trying to force the tension out of my body. I took a few steps in the brisk water and tossed the top half of my uniform to the sand behind me. It got continually deeper. Each time it lapped over a new area of my skin a shiver went down my back, but I found I didn't mind. In a way it made me feel more alive. It was somehow the opposite of home. It was what home could have been, if only Lumenkind had done the right thing before the planet was destroyed.

I took a deep breath and dove forward, immersing myself in it from head to toe. I stayed there, holding my breath as long as I could, letting go of my thoughts and just *being*. Lazing around in the garden bath wasn't a lifestyle I wanted to go back to, but right now I longed for the peace it provided me. Whenever I had troubles before—and they were trivial—a soak in the oil would always clear my mind. The water was having the same effect.

I rose when I couldn't hold my air in any longer and turned around. Westalyn was standing at the water's edge. "What are you doing?" she cried.

"Come in here!" I invited her, smiling.

"Into *water?*" she shrieked. "That stuff is awful for your skin. And my paint—"

"Westalyn." I approached her with a hand extended. "You do know you're the only person on this *planet* who cares about paint."

She stared at me with wide eyes. "But . . . in front of you? I . . . I always imagined how this moment would play out." She turned her head away from me as she spoke.

"Hey," I said, taking her hand. She took mine in return, squeezing it back. "I'm not gonna make you. But all these traditions we have are just that, Westalyn. You can wear paint if you want, but you shouldn't need to hide behind it. Especially not in front of me. I mean, have you seen my face? My hair? I look ridiculous."

She looked back into my eyes then and laughed, covering her mouth apologetically. I moved her hand away, holding both of them in mine. "So what do you want?"

"I want half the courage you have," she admitted.

"You're kidding, right?" I said. "You just flew *solo* across space and time into an unknown galaxy over some guy with a vial. I did none of the work to get here. In fact, I thought I was going the other way."

We both laughed, looking into each other's eyes. "So, Westalyn," I said, "are you going to jump into this water?"

She looked at it and then at me. "I think I might, Damaus. And I think I might swim twice as far as you did." She separated her hands from mine and stripped herself of her uniform, tossing it onto the sand, and ran. She ran until she couldn't run any more and then disappeared under the surface.

Grinning, I followed after her. She rose up out of the water to breathe and then darted away from me. I chased her, but she outswam me easily. This continued until we were both too tired to move. We sat together in the shallow water watching the sun move toward the hills.

"This must be overwhelming for you, too, huh?" I asked, breaking the silence that had lingered since we sat. "I'm sorry. I can be a self-centered dolt."

She shook her head. "It's the opposite, Damaus. You're just worried about too many people."

I sighed. "Maybe you're right. Maybe I need to dial it back a little. If I can save the Lumen, it'll be a start. I'll just have to get them to treat the Palunians better in time."

"You really care for them," she noted.

"I'm not so sure anymore." I scowled, placing my head in my hands. "I thought they were different, you know? Marlithan taught me so much about how we were the selfish ones, but they're content to just stay here while the others rot. I don't understand how."

"You understand them better than I do," she said. "And by the way, you could have started by giving me a heads-up that they can talk."

"I forgot!" I groaned. "I mean, I forgot you didn't know. My life changed up there, Westalyn. My definition of normal changed. Even now it's hard for me to share the Lumen perspective like I used to."

"Tell me again."

"Tell you what?" I asked.

"I know you're going to do what's right somehow, Damaus. Earlier I was just so angry that I couldn't listen to you," she said. "But you were right about the Grey. They aren't what I thought. So tell me about them. Tell me why all of this is so important to you."

"First, they prefer to be called Palunians," I said, smiling. She nodded. "*Grey* is a name we gave them and reinforced with the robes we made them wear. Most of their present culture was entirely dictated by customs Lumen chose for them.

"And they're smart, Westalyn. Smarter than we are, even. They have a whole underground library of books they've written over centuries. A lot of them are on our ship right now, which is how I came to learn so much. They aren't only historians and scholars, though. They're also clever and committed. You know how back home there was only one Palunian in our lifetime who used our words?"

She nodded.

"Well, the rest have just been suppressing their language. And that's the best part! It's *their* language, Westalyn. Not ours. The ancient texts are written in Palunian. You know how we learned growing up that it was a language our early scholars invented because it was superior to Annaian? It was actually taught to them by the ancient rulers of the planet. Yes, *rulers*. They had a whole government. A whole structured society. And their planet looked a lot like this one.

"We moved in, learned what we needed to, and immediately executed those rulers. We gave them a choice: surrender or die. And they fought back. We killed *thousands* of Palunians who resisted. Then, sick of seeing their friends and family die, they played along. All while meeting in secret communes under the cities."

"Secret communes?" she asked.

"Like little underground burrows or abandoned palaces. Maybe scraps in the shipyard, too. They're like families. Some, like Gonian's, really were families. And Rodiger—their mother was left behind in one. But everyone puts their name in for the Cup because anything is a better life than what they have."

"Though this life isn't just marginally better," I muttered. "This is luxury."

I could tell Westalyn was studying me, but I just kept watching the setting sun reflecting on the top of the water, the patches of light rays dancing around carelessly. The sun was changing from yellow to orange behind the hillside.

"It is fair, though," she said, after a minute.

I looked up at her. "What is?"

"With everything you've told me . . . Can you really blame them for being tired, Damaus?" she asked. "They spent their whole lives fighting just to stay alive. I know my family's beaten our live-in Grey—*Palunians*—on more than one occasion. This crew, and everyone here, deserved the out they got. They escaped. That's the dream, right? Not to return and start fighting all over again."

"Hmm," I murmured, processing the idea. I was still bitter, but I had nothing. "You might be right."

"I'll help you," she said. I looked up at her again, quizzically. "I'll come get the amber, and dammit, I guess I'll confront the contessa, too."

CHAPTER 17

WE GOT BACK to the feast as it was ending. It took a surprising amount of time to find our place at the table. The town center had filled to the brim in the time we'd been gone. There was a stage set up near the head of the table where a group of singers and percussionists were performing, and I found I didn't mind it.

I finally spotted Marlithan, but the room on the bench next to her had been taken. I approached, setting a hand on her shoulder. "I'm sorry," I told her.

She nodded and nudged over, shoving Hel and Rodiger into the next group of people, who didn't seem too bothered. Westalyn and I squeezed in quickly, before the group on our other side got any ideas. Though our friends were no longer eating, there was still food spread the whole way down the table, and it looked *magnificent*. Brightly colored food grown from plants in all shapes and sizes, soft-looking bread, some kind of spiced oil, and tall wooden cups filled to the brim with water.

"I won't hold it against you as long as you drop the subject," Marlithan said. "How's that?"

Sullen, I gave her a stiff nod. I thought about telling her we were leaving but decided against it. I didn't want to be talked out of the plan. Also, on some level, I think she knew. "Why aren't you singing?" I asked instead.

"Because I'm a guest!" she beamed. "This group is Aneth's finest—the *Tonians*. Music has changed a lot here. They've developed all new genres for us to observe and learn."

I didn't get it, but I let her go on about the group. She was practically glowing. I had never seen a Palunian look as happy as she—and come to think of it, everyone on this planet—did. Westalyn was right. Who would want to go back to Palunia after having a shot at this?

"Damaus?" Hel motioned me over with a finger behind Marlithan's back. I leaned in as Marlithan kept talking about music with a less enthusiastic Westalyn. "Tonight's gonna go on too late, but tomorrow I'd like to pick your brain about something. Walk at dawn with me?"

"Oh, I—well, all right," I said. He smiled at me so genuinely it made me consider staying for a moment. But now the decision was made, and I knew it was the right one. "Hel, I'm really sorry for what I said earlier."

He responded with a wink and a nod and went back to speaking with Rodiger.

Westalyn and I tried everything on the table in front of us.

"This one's . . . interesting." She laughed as she chewed on a small, round purple thing. She handed one to me, and I cautiously placed it in my mouth, then chewed. It sprayed sweet water everywhere. I covered my mouth in embarrassment and saw that the Palunians sitting across from us were laughing with, or at least *at*, me.

There was every flavor from sweet to spicy, and the colors didn't seem to indicate anything. We were having so much fun eating that I filled up fast. I let out a satisfied moan and rubbed my ever-expanding belly.

"Are you two done? Most groups have cleared their sections already," Marlithan said. It was true. Most of the enormous table, as far as I could see, had been stripped of the dinner and replaced with some kind of white cloth.

"Who takes care of that?" Westalyn asked.

Our whole section laughed except for me.

"Oh, what were you expecting from a Lume?" Hel said to the group. He turned to Westalyn. "We look after ourselves and work in teams. Help me carry the leftover food to the meal barrels?"

She looked uncomfortable, but she didn't hesitate. The two of them picked up most of it, and I took the rest, following Hel back toward one of the shops. It had a sign in front labeled *Free Farm* in burnt lettering on wood.

"What happens with this?" Westalyn asked, as we distributed the leftovers across several small barrels. There were probably twenty sitting outside, and many times more inside the building. They were pretty evenly filled, most a little over halfway.

"They stay here for households to take," Hel explained. "We'll bring one back tonight."

"So we'll all stay together, then?" I asked, hoping to sound convincing enough not to raise a discussion.

"There's been a house built for us, yes, somewhere in the outer ring. Welsia, Gonian, and some of the others will likely go to their loved ones though. And I suppose it's possible they might displace some folks over to ours if they prefer."

When we got back to the table a white sheet had been thrown over it. We took our seats and noticed that the crowd had grown quiet. The musicians had left the stage, and a Palunian (or was *Anethan* now?) stood at its center. All eyes were on them.

"Welcome, newcomers!" they said, and the table burst into applause, cheering and even singing. Despite my bitterness, their enthusiasm was contagious, if a little jarring, and it went on for several minutes. During it many people came to our seat and embraced Marlithan, Hel, and Rodiger. A few even embraced Westalyn and me. She was too shocked to know how to refuse anyone, so I took a few extra hugs on her behalf. Eventually the people settled again.

"You, like many others here, reached Aneth by travel. This means that you spent your life suffering the perils of life under Lumen rule. And for that we are deeply sorry. We hope that we can make it up to you by sharing all we have with you in this time of needed comfort.

"You who put your names in to leave your rightful home have shown true bravery—bravery like I have never needed in my life. I was just informed that one of your crew was killed before you even left the planet. We mourn the death of Militaw Throzen, senselessly beaten for entertainment in front of his friends and family."

There was a murmur of agreement and disgust among the crowd. The image flashed back into my mind of that man, only steps ahead of me, being struck with a rock big and fast enough to knock him down. I recalled how they'd removed him like trash and how I'd had to step around the red water that had spilled from his body. It was beyond infuriating.

The speaker continued when the conversation paused. "Here you are free. Your only responsibility is to support this community. To do your part in farming, in building, and in listening to one another. We aim for a society built on understanding and empathy. Those of us who were born here long to learn from you. And we look forward to sharing in more creative skills—to write more books, create more art, and expand on our music today. Because it's only when we work together that we move forward."

This person was so unlike Jiyorga, who owned the stage with power. It was clear that they had earned the respect of their people by being one of them and not by shining far above them. This wasn't a place for palaces or rulers. I was sure this person lived in a wooden house, too, and I was willing to bet they shared it with others outside their family.

"Before the great mural begins, I just want to introduce myself. My name is Fendaza Vheren. This month, and each month for the last eleven years, this community has granted me the honor of Council Leader. It's a title I hold dearly. These people are everything I have, and I am forever indebted to what they continually do for me. I trust that those of you joining us today will feel the same welcome that we share.

"Now, if you'll just get your paints from the supply shop, where Derrikas has prepared a palette for each of you, we can let the mural begin."

"The what?" I asked, but Marlithan had already risen. She sprinted excitedly toward a shop a few houses from us, along with several others. "Should we go, too?" I asked a shrugging Westalyn.

Those across from us shook their heads. "One per section," the woman there said.

"We're painting?" Westalyn asked.

"A shared painting," the woman replied. "Each time a new ship arrives we hold this ceremony and we paint as a way of reforming our community. Combining our spirits onto a single canvas. When it dries some will stay behind to attach it all together. Then it will be hung above the table where these lights are now."

She pointed up to where calming yellow and orange orbs were glowing, attached to various interwoven strings. I hadn't realized how late it was getting. There was no trace of the sun in the sky now, and it had gotten considerably cooler.

Marlithan then returned with a palette and several brushes and placed it between our side and the others.

"So . . . what do we paint?" I asked.

"They're already going," Westalyn whispered, nodding to her other side, where children and some adults were doing everything from handprints to calligraphy.

"Whatever is in your heart," the woman across from us said, and took one of the brushes. As she focused on the canvas I noticed Marlithan roll her eyes, and I had to keep from laughing aloud.

So I took up the brush and dipped it into the first color I saw. It was a sort of violet. I added red, blue, green, and yellow. It came out in a sort of grey-brown. I kept smushing it around, not really knowing where I was going but enjoying the feeling it brought. When my mind was this focused on the paint, it was like everything else went away. A bit like reading those books but more relaxing. Like I could escape and ponder new thoughts, or ones I'd been avoiding.

I kept stroking the paint around on the surface. I smiled as I saw something new in it—a familiar face. I made lighter shades with white paint and darker shades with black. An hour must have passed before I thought to look up again.

Marlithan was letting hers dry and watching mine. Nervous, I froze. I couldn't think of an explanation to get around the embarrassment I'd felt at painting someone sitting next to me.

"What is it?" she asked.

I opened my mouth to protest in offense but realized I'd been given an out. I laughed instead. "I have no idea. I don't have that natural Palunian talent."

"This one does, though," the woman across from us said, nodding at Westalyn. I looked over and gasped. She'd chosen to paint the plants and had done an amazing job. Flowers and fruit in vibrant colors swirled in the most unique style.

"Where did you learn to do that?" I asked.

"I just tried," she mumbled, averting her eyes from any of us and focusing on the details.

I glanced around at what everyone had done then. Marlithan's was a familiar-looking symbol. Hel had done something with words. Rodiger had painted several people. I got up and looked from behind him.

"It's the crew," he said. "This one's me, and that's Hel, and that one is you!"

I was surprised to see how much I looked like everyone else in his painting. Shorter hair, but even my skin color wasn't as discernible as I would have painted it. We were all holding glasses and smiling, by the look of it. His skills weren't as developed as most of the others, but it made me smile.

"It was a special night, wasn't it?" I asked.

He nodded. "It reminded me of my house. If you ever go back, you should visit them."

I smiled. "Sure thing."

As I stepped back to my place on the bench, I got a better look at Marlithan's painting. It took a few seconds for me to recognize it. "That's one of the sorcerers?" I asked.

She nodded. "Yelizan." His symbol was a light greyish-blue, which she'd outlined in a rainbow of other colors. It was a horizontal line that looped on one side, crossed with a vertical line that curved slightly, almost like a *J*.

"Sorcerer of spirits, right?" I had read the book several times now, but I couldn't remember what that particular sorcerer was responsible for. "Why'd you choose that one?"

"A spirit is a force of change," she said. "A source of power, too. I've been reflecting a lot on it since my name was drawn, I suppose. I'm wondering if I've fulfilled some kind of great purpose by coming here."

No, but you would by coming to Palunia with me. I didn't say it. She was finally happy, and I'd just have to accept that if I cared about her. "Maybe your great purpose was managing to educate a Lumen," I said instead.

"It wasn't easy," she admitted with a smile. "And you have a long way to go yet. You'll likely never get there."

"I know," I admitted.

When we'd all finished our parts of the painting—mine an indistinguishable blob among masterpieces—we rose from the table. The woman and her group across from us insisted on embracing us goodnight, and everyone but Westalyn complied.

"I don't touch other people," she explained, hoping that would suffice. It made the woman frown, but they left soon after without asking any questions, wishing us the best. I noticed the other strangers still weren't so friendly in the way they eyed us.

"This way to the house, if I understand correctly," Hel said, leading us around to the other side of the table and over the hill. I lingered to look at what the other groups had done, struck by the beauty of it in a way I never had been back home. *Paint doesn't compare to gems,* I would have said. And that was true. Neither compared to the other. Gems were just things—colorful stones that happened to be split into shapes that captured light. A painting was like a person's own story spilled out in color.

"You can see the mural tomorrow, Damaus!" Hel called, beckoning me to join them. I nodded and rushed over.

It took us longer than I expected to walk to our supposed new home. There were occasional posts with more of those dim light orbs hanging from their tops, but their glow didn't carry very far. We walked about ten rows back and then started down one of the circular paths to the left.

The houses here were built close together. That was what struck me as the most unusual. The shops in the town center had even been attached. Here the houses had just a strip of that brilliant grass between them. On the stoops of the houses people sat talking, making music, and waving to our group as we passed by—more to the Palunians than to me or Westalyn, of course.

As we continued toward the house I felt something cool on the top of my head. I turned to Westalyn, who flinched.

"What's happening?" She gasped, placing a hand to her scalp. There were drops of something falling onto her head and face. I looked around and saw they were starting to pour from the sky, hitting the ground all around us and soaking us in the process.

"Is this . . . rain?" I asked, in awe. Never in my memorable lifetime had I witnessed it. My mother often talked about the *last rain*, which happened when I was a child.

The group of us just stood there, drenched, as thousands of drops pelted our faces and bodies from the clouds above. Marlithan cheered, and we all laughed with bewilderment.

Rodiger closed his eyes and stuck his tongue out. At first I panicked, thinking of the acids and toxins that lived in our atmosphere back home. But here things were different. I stuck mine out, too, and found the water to be refreshingly clean.

To the locals we must have looked ridiculous, but we danced and played in the rain like children in an oil bath. The initial burst of water soon faded to a slower, steady rhythm. We passed about twenty more houses before Hel slowed down.

"Yes, I think this is it," he said, wiping the water from his eyes.

"How can you tell?" I asked. It looked like all the others to me.

"I was given the coordinates and the name. You see the sign on the post?" He pointed. There were steps leading up to the stoop and the door, and on either side of them were two posts. One had a sign affixed to it that said *Cedar*.

"What does it mean?" I asked.

"It's a type of wood," Rodiger chimed in. "On this world there are lots of types of trees."

"Enough to name hundreds of houses?" I looked around at nearby trees to try to spot the differences, but it was too dark.

"Each row is themed," Westalyn said. "I noticed on the way up. The one below us is named after fruit."

We walked up the stairs to the door and made our way inside. I couldn't get over just how *pleasant* this community was. I stuck a hand in my pocket and felt the key attached to the Omnilight. I had to go back, of course. But if Marlithan really wanted to stay, maybe the gem would be better left in her hands.

We came into the front room to find that it was bustling. It wasn't just our crew. Some of them were playing wooden instruments I'd never seen before, while others cheered them on and danced. In the far corner of the room, a group was huddled in what looked like a highly energetic conversation, with arms raising, fists banging on the table, and roaring laughter. Once the instrumentalists noticed us, they wrapped up their song on what I can only describe as a pleasant note, giving the attention of their audience to us.

"There you guys are!" Elhanizen, a crew member who'd hardly spoken a word to me, called, motioning for us to join her group with wine in hand. I noticed they didn't make eye contact with Westalyn as Elhanizen brought us over.

"Pen, Refat, Gus," she said, addressing the dancers. "This is Marlithan—one of the smartest Palunians I know. This is her student, Damaus. And here we have the great Rodiger and his good friend Helragizan."

"Hello!" the one I thought she referred to as Pen replied. He was enormously tall, though he was on the thin side for a Palunian. His eye caught mine. "A student, hey? What have you learned?"

"Well . . ." I started, but Marlithan spoke before I had a chance to get out anything intelligible.

"History mostly," she said. "As you can imagine, they teach the Lumes all kinds of nonsense."

"Oh, I'm sure of it," Pen muttered, cursing under his breath. "But this one's okay, hey?"

"Might be as good as they come," Hel butted in, winking at me. I smiled, though it may have looked more like a grimace. I was never one to want too much attention, and a room full of potentially hostile Palunians would not have been my first pick for center stage.

"Nothing compared with you guys," I said. "So are you all from Palunia?"

The one called Gus shook his head. "No, thank the sorcerers. We three are brothers. Grew up just a couple rows closer to town from here. We are the best at throwing parties, though. Rannigan asked us to make you all welcome."

"Who's Rannigan?" Rodiger asked. I could see the excitement in his eyes at the strangely dressed people surrounding him.

"Rannigan Thorip?" Hel confirmed, and Gus nodded enthusiastically. "Gonian's wife," he explained for the rest of us.

"Are they coming?" I asked. I hated the way he and I left things before the landing. I both really wanted to talk to him and really wanted to be gone before he arrived.

"Later, I'd guess," Pen said. "I'll bet the missus wanted some time to rekindle things, if you know what I mean."

"She certainly did," Refat chimed in. "Gave me the boot from her bed for the night as soon as he stepped off that ship."

I stared, dumbfounded at his blatant announcement of her betrayal. "You partnered with Gonian's rightful wife? And now he's back with her?"

He gaped back at me while the others laughed. Even Marlithan seemed to be in on a joke I wasn't getting.

"Damaus," she said, placing a hand on my shoulder. "Maybe we should have studied Palunian relations, too. We don't partner the way you Lumen do."

"Right, you're more strict about it," I said. "I know you have your so-called *marriages*, and that you don't separate for work and child-raising. And now I know that you live in communes and grow your families there. I get that she never planned on seeing her husband again, but now Refat here gets his heart broken and Gonian has to accept that she's been unfaithful? How is that fair?"

Marlithan smiled at me, which just frustrated me further.

"What?" I demanded.

"I didn't tell you about the family I left behind," Marlithan said, leading me away from the group to a nearby empty table. Westalyn followed us without a word. We sat and she took a wooden bottle from the center of the table and gave it a sniff. She then took a sip, nodded, and passed it to Westalyn to try. "I gave up three cherished partnerships back home by joining this crew. A husband, a wife, and a dear friend."

Westalyn and I exchanged a glance of concern. "You had multiple marriages?" I asked.

She nodded. "We stayed in a commune together, sharing our resources and responsibilities. We were all great friends who held the utmost respect for each other, until I put my name in the Cup."

"They didn't want you to go," Westalyn guessed.

Marlithan nodded. "Contrary to popular belief, we don't *all* put our names in. It was my first time entering. Because as awful as we had it, our family made the most of a dire situation. There's something about sharing in nothingness that makes it feel like something. Something special. The only one who stayed faithful to me until the end was the third—my friend, Thielan, who preferred leaving marriage out of our relationship, no matter how many times I asked them to share in ceremony with me."

"So why did you decide to leave?" I asked. "It sounds like you had it all right and this just messed things up for you."

She shook her head. "No, because as much as I love them dearly—and I do—I had to do what was right for me. Of course I wanted to stay with them, but my other friends were dying. One was forced to pull a carriage like a slug for days with nothing to drink. Another was taken and made to fight his brother, who won. I was either going to end up dead myself or wishing I'd been killed.

"The other thing is that while a life like that is comfortable, it isn't fulfilling. What do you do when you've read every book but live in a society where you can't talk about them? Here I can help establish a society. I can teach. I can learn to love new people. I can find new meaning within myself."

I nodded but found there was a lump in my throat. I guess I was feeling a bit of what her family had. The idea of a life without Marlithan was difficult to accept.

CHAPTER 18

GONIAN DIDN'T ARRIVE by the time I went to bed. I found a small room unoccupied upstairs with two cots. It was far from the comfort of our palaces back home, but many steps above my room on the ship. It didn't matter much, though, because Westalyn and I weren't going to sleep.

I took my notebook from my jacket and sat, scrawling letters slowly on the pages, trying to keep them legible. There were so many things I wanted to say, and yet none of the words I could come up with conveyed the right meaning or tone. So I kept it short and to the point.

The partially closed door swung open then. I folded the paper quickly and stuffed it back in my jacket as Westalyn appeared in the doorway.

"How much longer should we wait?" she asked, closing the door behind her. She didn't say anything about the note, and I'm not sure she noticed it. I let out the breath I was holding in and considered her question.

"We can either slip out when it's quiet or when it's loud," I said. "But nothing in between. We can go now through the window if you want." I nodded to the circular hole in the wall that was covered in large hung leaves.

Westalyn nodded but didn't move. She stared at the floor and sighed before speaking. "I see why you care for her," she said.

"Marlithan?"

She nodded. "She's . . . strong. She left everything she knew for a shot at a greater purpose. We Lumen have never *known* purpose. Except maybe Jiyorga, to make us all miserable."

I laughed. *The sorcerer of spirits does suit her*, I realized. "Marlithan is going to do wonders for this society. She's going to educate them. And I was thinking . . . if we make it back in one piece, maybe I could educate the Lumen."

I avoided looking up at Westalyn, nervously awaiting her judgment. Me taking work right away meant I wouldn't be raising children, defeating any societal purpose for our union. She didn't say anything. When I looked up she was shaking.

"Westalyn?" I sat next to her and instinctively put an arm around her. Realizing my error, I started to move away, but she nuzzled in close.

"It's a nice dream, Damaus," she said, once she caught her breath again. "But we both know we aren't going to make it back home."

I just sighed and held her.

I don't know exactly how much time passed when I fell asleep. We both had. I woke up and shook her. "Time to go," I whispered. The house was quiet.

She groaned but followed as I got up. When she turned to get the door, I placed the Omnilight on the bed with the note I'd prepared for Marlithan. I then followed Westalyn down the hall, down the stairs, and out into the rain.

Amazing as it was, the novelty of water falling from the charcoal sky wore off after walking about half an hour. And we had about double that to get to the ship.

"Do you know how to take off?" Westalyn asked.

I frowned. "Last time it happened automatically when we sealed the entry bay."

"And what happens if we just get stuck inside the ship and no one finds us?"

"It should sustain us for about a year. Besides, Marlithan's going to need her books eventually."

Rightfully, Westalyn continued to give me a hard time the whole way to the shipyard. It was hard to find in the dark, too. I don't know how many times we had to retrace our steps to make sure we'd gone over the hills in the right direction.

"I think that's it," she said as we came over the latest crest, pointing at something in the distance. I didn't see it immediately in the darkness, but in time I could make out the silhouette against the clouds.

We reached it in another quarter hour. I always forgot how big the thing was until I was standing in its shadow. "How do we get inside?" I asked. The entry bay was sitting flat in the landing device against the ground. Someone must have docked the ship properly after Welsia's landing.

"Don't these things usually have a hatch somewhere?" she asked.

"I haven't seen one on our ship," I said. It now sat tightly inside the structure of metal bars—four pillars with an empty square between them to fit the ship. Each pillar was a bit like a four-sided ladder made of several rungs. I sighed, knowing we were going to have to check anyway. We didn't have a lot of options.

I gripped a rung on the pillar closest to us and took a step. I looked up to see just how far I'd be climbing when something caught my eye. There was a figure sitting above, higher up the pillar.

"Westalyn!" I hissed. "Someone's there."

"Yes, indeed," a friendly voice called downward. "I thought you'd be faster. Not so considerate to those of us who have to sit in the rain."

"*Hel?*"

"One and the same," he noted.

"What are you doing here?" I asked, climbing up to meet him. There was room enough for two to a rung at least. Westalyn stuck to the ground. The metal was cold and slippery on my fingers.

"I could ask you the same question," he responded when I reached him. I sat and waited for more. Hel had a bigger stubborn streak than half the Lumen I knew. But eventually he spoke. "I sensed you might have more pressing engagements across the galaxy."

I nodded. "My people are dying, Hel. And yours are suffering. If there's any chance I can stop that, I need to."

"And how are you going to do that?" he asked. He wasn't smug about it, but the smile on his face suggested he knew something I didn't.

"We stick to the original plan," I explained. "It's not that I want to do anything for the contessa, but I'm not going to let my mother die out of spite."

He closed his eyes and nodded. I watched as the drops of rain slipped over his wrinkled forehead and fell to his sallow cheeks. "My dear Damaus," he said. "Did you ever consider that this whole journey might be yet another fabrication from the founding family?"

I frowned. "That would certainly complicate things. But we saw the tower. When I was a kid there was amber in it, and now there's not. Unless she's hoarding it somewhere else,

Palunia is out. And it wouldn't make sense to hoard that much for herself if she keeps her safety reserve in a vial anyway."

There was a banging noise next to us. I stood and watched as Westalyn walked along the plates of the ship.

"What are you *doing*?" I cried. "You're going to fall!"

"I borrowed those enchanted pads," she grunted. As she got closer, I saw that she was using the magnets to get herself across. She paused then, looking at something above. "Damaus, I think I found it."

"What?" I asked, trying to see what she was seeing.

"A hatch!" she exclaimed, moving carefully upward with the help of the pads. "Of course it's on the bottom. That's the liquid storage, right?"

I nodded, feeling nervous. "Westalyn, I don't know how well those work in the rain—"

But she was already down to one hand, loosening a safety valve with the other. "I think it's stuck!" she said.

I left a silent Hel then to go and stand below her. If she slipped I could at least help break her fall. From this far though, it would probably get both of us killed. That would be a heroic ending to our perilous journey.

"Be careful," Hel said when I reached the bottom. "If I'm right to doubt the contessa in this—"

"There!" Westalyn cried, spinning the safety away and giving the main latch a swift tug. The moment she did, a sheet of rain fell from the sky directly onto me. I backed away and toppled to the ground, wiping frantically at my eyes. I was sitting in a growing puddle of it, but the downpour had turn to splashing. I opened my eyes again and saw it was something thicker than water. I stood and leapt forward, back onto the rungs. Westalyn was still mounted to the ship, thank the wizards.

"What *is* that?" she cried. "This chamber is *filled* with it!"

I couldn't tell what color it was in the lighting. I smelled my uniform and didn't recognize the scent, but I was fairly certain it wasn't any kind of fuel.

"Amber," Hel said simply, as it continued to pour.

CHAPTER 19

WE ALL SAT on the rungs, Westalyn and I together above Hel's post, watching the puddle grow into a small lake below us. The latch had flung off and was now somewhere at the bottom of the amber sea. In the distance, an orange glow surfaced on the horizon.

"What does this mean?" I asked, feeling defeated. We'd just wasted what could have saved our people. *But why was it in the ship to begin with? Did the crew find a source here and load it for me?*

"You've studied the founding family quite extensively by now, haven't you, Damaus?" Hel said, not waiting for an answer. "What business do you think they might have in this?"

"Do you really think the contessa did this?" I frowned, unable to come up with a reason. "It makes no sense to kill off the Lumen."

"You're probably right in that," Hel agreed.

"But you knew about this," Westalyn said. "You just warned me, before the latch let go."

"I had my suspicions," he said. "You two don't really under-stand Palace-Palunian relations. Academically"—he put a hand up before I could protest—"I don't doubt you understand the facts, as a series of events mostly. But until you've witnessed being looked in the eye the way any families related to the founders look at us, you'd know that we are really, truly hated.

"I have a theory about the Drawing, and about the amber. How many names go into that Cup?"

"Tens of thousands," I said. "At least thirty. We put several of them in ourselves this time," I said, turning to Westalyn, who nodded.

"Well, that complicates the theory a little, I admit," Hel muttered. "But I still believe it. Do you truly think the Drawing is random?"

"Not precisely random," Westalyn said. "But with that number, it's close."

"Been studying math?" I asked. She smiled.

"Damaus, you're related to Jiyorga. Were you ever made aware of a second cup?"

"You mean the Cup itself?" I asked. "No, definitely not. It's unique. That's kind of the point of it."

Westalyn gasped. "There *is* a second cup!" I stared at her, willing her to keep talking. "I'm sorry, I just—too many thoughts."

She paused for a deep breath. "Okay," she continued. "Damaus, when we were watching—before your name was drawn, do you remember what I said to you?"

I flushed. "Honestly, no. Between having the attention of a pretty Lumen and being forced to head to the stage, I didn't exactly have the attention span."

This time she flushed, but she cleared her throat and explained. "I said the cup looked different. It was like . . . the gems were more brightly colored, and the paint more vibrant, compared to the one we put the names into. I said that!"

"Yeah, and I said it always looked that way in the afternoon sun," I reminded her. "Guess I do pay attention."

She shook her head. "But the only time you've seen it in the afternoon sun has been for the *Drawing*, hasn't it?"

I sighed. "Okay, maybe. But what you're proposing is ridiculous."

"It isn't," Hel said. "It seems Lady Westalyn and I have come to the same conclusion."

She nodded. "The cup used for the Drawing isn't random at all. They don't even use the same pieces of paper we put into the decoy cup. It's decided long before the event who's going on the journey."

"Okay, but how does that make sense if *I'm* here?" I demanded. "I put my name into that *decoy* cup and ended up drawn for a so-called Grey job."

"You must have done something," Westalyn said. "Something to upset the contessa? Or you were sent for the same reason the other drawn names were."

"It's the second," Hel said. Westalyn and I both looked at him, waiting for clarification. "Damaus, in the palace, Marlithan went to check on you. Do you remember?"

I nodded. "I thought I was dreaming."

"And did you tell Westalyn about your time in that room?"

I shook my head. She waited. I sighed.

"She keeps these . . . *secrets*, she calls them. Treasure chests that only she could open, containing information we can't handle. She takes them from Lumen and we just forget and go about our lives. She talked to me about one of mine, from when I was a child. It's . . . where that thing I said on stage came from," I admitted, embarrassed.

Westalyn looked stricken. "What you're describing . . . they aren't *secrets*, Damaus. They're *memories*. She sealed your thoughts away? And took them from your mind so you didn't even remember they existed? Do you think she's done that with many people?"

"It seems likely," Hel said. "You Lumen have been violated time and time again with this sort of rule. Damaus, though, has more than any other Lumen. Even more than the Lumen three times his age."

I gasped. "*What?* How would you know?"

"You wouldn't give it up," Hel said. "You kept finding your way back to us. You kept learning too much, empathizing too strongly. The last time you had a memory taken was the worst one yet in the contessa's eyes. I was there, of course."

"Why couldn't you have mentioned *any* of this before?" I demanded. "Seriously, I can't believe I thought we were all friends."

"Because telling a Lumen he isn't the smartest person in the room never goes well the first time," Hel noted, chuckling to himself. "I don't think the other crew members witnessed any of it, but I did a couple of times. And the last time you stepped out of line, it was in protection of Marlithan."

"*Marlithan?*" I exclaimed.

"She and I were two of about thirty who served the Lu Senhi palace."

"You worked for Roeni?"

"Indeed," Hel said, his expression dark. "Marlithan was being beaten for missing a round of wine-pouring by the woman of the house. Of course, when your fellow servant is being reprimanded for a failure they made, it would do another Palunian like myself no good to step in. I learned that well the first time." He raised his arm, revealing several deep scars.

"But that day you were sitting with the boy of the house—not quite men yet at that point—when the attack began. You came right over, and you went so far as to physically remove the woman from her. So, in the contessa's eyes, you assaulted a Lumen to protect a Grey, which made you terrifying to keep around."

"I don't remember that. I don't remember either of you at Roeni's at all," I said, frowning. "Memories stored as secrets?"

Hel nodded, turning to Westalyn. "The lady Westalyn thought of the decoy cup. I wonder—do you have a theory about the amber, too?"

"They go together," she murmured. "Assuming it's true."

"Okay, enough of this," I demanded. "What are you thinking?"

Westalyn was staring down at the enormous lake below us, its orange color now intensified in the light of the sunrise. "What if she isn't trying to kill us?"

I frowned. "It certainly looks like she is."

"What do you know about the founding family?" Hel asked me again.

I was growing impatient. "Well, let's see. When their planet became uninhabitable, they stole a new one. They tortured an entire society and beheaded its most outspoken leaders to control the narrative. They take our *memories*. We can't even think for ourselves. I guess I don't know much about anything, thanks to them."

"*Controlling the narrative*," Westalyn repeated. She and Hel exchanged a knowing look. I was about to lose it when she looked me in the eye. "Damaus, I don't think we actually need the amber. The tower has been emptying because she's been shipping it *out*, not *in*. It's just another made up Lumen story."

I blinked. I wasn't going to have to convince Westalyn about the Palunian side of things anymore. But this . . . had I really been that blind?

"Then what the hell is the point of any of this?"

"Silence," Hel said. I looked down at him, then glanced around us. The growing dawn was calm. It wasn't a command. "The point was to obtain silence."

"Are you saying she wanted each member of this crew removed *individually*, chosen from a cup with only our names, including mine, because we posed too much of a threat? Why not just take all our secrets?"

"She can't," Hel said. "However she does it, it doesn't seem to work on us. It's never worked on our kind, but it seems you were something of an enigma, too."

"And they chose the Killing Cup over execution because it was entertaining for the Lumen," I remembered. "Then the Traveler's Cup over the Killing Cup . . . So it really never mattered if we made it to Lor Annaius," I thought aloud, striking the rung above us with my fist. All this time I'd been worried sick about my family, and it was just another of the contessa's cruel tricks. "I guess the biggest slap in the face we can give her is to turn this thing around and go back to Palunia."

"You don't want to give her that satisfaction," Westalyn said.

I grinned widely at her until her face furrowed.

"What?"

"Seems to me that was what you wanted just a day ago."

She sighed. "Well, turns out you can learn a lot in a day."

"I think we should go back," I said seriously. No one replied. We all just sat and watched the valley turn into an orange basin below the ship.

The sun rose further toward the sky. If I were going to do this, I wanted to do it properly. "Hel," I said, "can you assemble everyone who migrated here from Palunia?"

There was a twinkle in his eye. "Assuming I ever get down from here, I think I could arrange that."

"What can I do?" Westalyn asked.

I hesitated. "Your relations with the people here still aren't great. But . . . if you could track down Welsia, you could get her to teach you and some others about mechanics."

She nodded. This was a good start.

The sun was now shining in a blue sky. With it came the people. We started to draw plenty of unwanted attention with our lake of amber. In small groups the townspeople made their way over the hillside to view the spill that was about as large as the town. Thankfully the hills around the valley kept it from spilling over.

"I don't think any of us are making a good impression now," Westalyn said.

"I'll probably be fine," Hel stated. We stared down at him, but he had nothing more to say.

"Thanks, Hel," I mumbled.

"What do you think they'll do with us?" Westalyn asked, the concern in her voice edging closer to fear.

"They could leave us up here until we die of natural causes," I offered.

"We have the hatch," she noted. "The flow is slowing. We could figure out a way through it to the rest of the ship."

"We could swim," I added, though the amber was wider and deeper than even Jiyorga's oil baths now.

"If we did get in the ship," Westalyn continued, "we could launch it and land somewhere else."

We all looked at each other, considering. And then we promptly burst out laughing.

A cry sounded from across the lake. I squinted as more voices joined in.

"That's the crew," I said. "Some of them anyway. I think I found a way to make Gonian even angrier."

"Not hard with that one," Hel said. "At least you've got some representation on the other side."

"Still not counting yourself in this, huh?" I grumbled. "Though with any luck they'll consider you worth saving and find us all a way."

I kept staring out at the crew, trying to see who exactly was among them. Though if I'm being completely honest, I was mostly confirming who wasn't. There was no sign of Marlithan.

"If we tip the ship over, it should reach to the other side," I offered. "Probably crush a few of our new friends in the process, though."

"Yeah, that'll get them to like us," Westalyn said. "Wait, what's that?"

"Hmm?" I followed her gaze to see two people coming over one of the hills separating the valley from the water. Between them was something that looked like a large slab, undoubtedly made of wood. As they descended, more people came into view—three on each side of the thing, and it was massive.

We watched as the crowd cleared for them and they marched the thing directly to the lake of amber, which was nearly at capacity. The two in front dropped it at the edge of the lake and moved to the back. They gave it a push, and the next two left their post and joined the others. They all shoved on it until it had slid into the amber and floated there. From somewhere in the back of his robe, one of them drew what looked like a large wooden paddle and hopped onto the floating object.

Next thing we knew, he was using the instrument to push against the amber, thrusting himself and the series of tree logs he was riding toward us.

"Think he'll knock one of us out with that thing?" Hel grinned up at us.

"Not if I can help it, old man," I said, rustling his hair and climbing down the few rungs that remained untouched by amber.

The man was across in no time. I saw as he got closer that he was small of frame but muscular. I guessed that he hadn't built this on a whim to save us. Crossing water must have been a regular activity for him.

"Get on!" he called when he completed the last stroke, lining up his vessel with our makeshift ladder. I had to hop a short distance, but I landed as gracefully as I felt I could have.

"Thank you," I said to him, taking a seat away from the structure where Westalyn and Hel were now climbing down. They both made it on, Hel the most gracefully out of all of us, of course, and our rescuer promptly got back to work paddling.

"Thank you very much," Westalyn said. "Is there any way we can repay you?"

He looked at her from the corner of his eye, not turning his head away from his destination. "A Lume? You gonna undo millennia of slavery?"

Westalyn gaped, then put a hand over her mouth. She didn't say another word. Instinctively I wanted to stand up for her, but the captain of our log ship wasn't really out of line. And the last thing I wanted to do was upset him and get sent back into the amber.

"So you did come for me," Hel said, filling the awkward pause.

The man gave him full eye contact as he spoke. "I was sent by the Council. If they think it's in our society's best interest, I suppose I trust their judgment."

It was as warm a welcome as I could hope for. It took us longer to get to the hillside with so much more weight on the logs, but I still had to admire his strength. When we did reach the shore, Gonian, Welsia, and more crew members helped us up and onto the grass.

"Thanks," we all muttered.

I looked Gonian in the eye, searching my mind for words. When none came, I gripped him in a fierce hug. He flinched back at first, then returned it. I let go to see that he was smiling.

"Council wants to see you three," he said, his thick eyebrows raised to a point in the center of his forehead.

"No chance we can get a bit of sleep or a bite to eat first?" I asked.

"It won't take long," someone said. We all turned. Coming through the crew was a familiar-looking face. His eyes met mine and he nodded. "Lord Ju Demma."

"You worked for us!" I blurted. "You cleaned my rooms."

He nodded. "Come with me?"

We waved to the crew and thanked them again before catching up to the man whose name I wished I'd bothered to learn. I hadn't seen him in a few years, and now I knew why. He must have been on the last ship. And, by the look of it, already a member of the Aneth Council.

When we got through the crowd full of ogling eyes, we continued over the hill and directly into the town center. We walked the length of the shops and long table before coming to a stop just on the other side of the stage.

"This is your planetary palace?" Westalyn asked, a hint of amazement in her voice. It was a simple wooden building, indistinguishable from the others.

"We don't have a palace," our escort said. "The Council is fair. Its members are impartial, and its impact minimal. This is a place of freedom, where no individual can rule over another. There are times, though, when we must rule on what's best for our society as a whole."

"Sorry about the lake," I mumbled as he opened the door and let us walk inside. He didn't follow.

CHAPTER 20

WE CLOSED THE door behind us to find a group of six people sitting around a table, including Fendaza, the one who'd given yesterday's welcome speech. I didn't recognize any other faces. They looked at each other with unease.

"Maybe it *is* best to keep the door closed," a woman who wore her hair in a tangled mess of flowers said.

"Transparency is everything," Fendaza replied. "If we start closing doors to official meetings, we're no better than them."

They didn't look at us when they said it, but I couldn't help but take that remark personally.

"We'll end up with a whole town of people in here if their fascination at the orange sea is any indication," another woman said with a deep voice. She was tall and stalky. She'd painted her lips a bright teal and wore several pieces of beautiful wooden jewelry.

"Fendaza, why don't you call your son in to take a transcript?" said an thin old man with a pointed beard that went to his hips. "Him and a common villager, if it'll put the people more at ease."

Fendaza considered the proposal as the three of us stood awkwardly just inside the doorway.

"All in favor of a closed door meeting with two scribes?" another member asked. This one had a robe on that was similar to what the Palunians wore back home, but it was neatly pressed and black.

Five hands went up—all but the one who posed the question. I guessed it was either because they disagreed with the motion themselves or because one couldn't participate in their own vote.

"You can have a seat," the larger woman with painted lips offered, motioning to the vacant end of the table opposite to where we stood.

"For a trial?" I asked, dumbfounded that we'd be given such a luxury as to sit next to our prosecutors.

They all shared a glance and laughter broke out. Fendaza howled as he stepped outside, presumably to find some scribes.

"This isn't a trial," the woman with flowers in her hair said as we took our seats, once they'd all managed to calm their laughter. "We just want to know what happened."

"And then what?" I asked. "The judgment comes once you've heard us out?"

"Unless you came to Aneth to cause harm to our people, we have no business judging you," the one in the black robe said. "But please save the story for the scribes. Everyone should be able to hear it."

We waited with nothing to do for a few minutes, which seemed to pass increasingly slowly. Our boredom was interrupted by the sound of Hel's stomach as it gave an audible *lurch*. Westalyn and I turned to him, horrified, but the Council all broke into another round of laughter. The broad woman stood, hardly able to contain herself.

"Let me see what we can do about that," she said, and sauntered through a doorway inside the building.

"I'll never understand," Hel began, speaking to the whole table, "how Lumen society ever decided that unpreventable bodily functions were impolite."

"You're right, Hel," Westalyn said. "I guess that doesn't make much sense."

"Oh, I like this one," the lady with the flowers said.

"Can any of you tell us what's really going on here?" I asked, changing the subject. As far as I was concerned, we could discuss bodily functions another time. "We tell you our story, and then what? Are we potentially deported? Imprisoned? Made to be servants?"

"Those are certainly interesting ideas!" the lady replied with enthusiasm. The person in the black cloak must have kicked her, because she looked at them incredulously and changed her tone. "But we'll discuss your ideas after we hear you out."

"Our . . . ideas?" Westalyn asked, as a tray of food was set in front of us. Leftovers from last night's feast. Back home we joked about eating leftovers, but we either fed them to the Palunians or tossed them. But these were the most delicious-looking leftovers I'd ever seen, and I immediately started grabbing from the tray.

"Thank you, uhh . . ." I trailed off.

"Dorelith," the broad woman said, taking her place back at the table.

As we stuffed our faces, I tried to picture the contessa personally serving anyone food. It was laughable. We had nearly cleared the tray when the outside door opened and in walked Fendaza, a boy of about thirteen turns, and Welsia.

We all must have been transfixed on her, because Fendaza turned to us to explain. "We believe the best way to be impartial is to have open and fair accounts. By having a transcript recorded by a member of your crew, we're attempting to remove an advantage from the narration."

"Thank you, Fendaza," the one in the black cloak said. "I'll be conducting today's meeting. Before I do, does anyone have reason to believe they may not be able to remain impartial in the matter of the orange sea?"

The man with the long beard stood from his seat and left the building without a word. One other member, a young woman who hadn't spoken to us yet, seemed to hesitate but remained in her seat. She couldn't have been more than fifteen turns old.

"Introductions, please," the one leading the meeting said. No one seemed to mind that they'd just lost a Council member.

I opened my mouth to speak, but the one with flowers in her hair went first. It seemed that *excited* was her default emotion.

"My name is Berilan, but you can call me Berry. I'm a lifer here on Aneth. My other contribution here, besides the Council, is carpentry, and my love is for flowers." I saw her wink at Westalyn then, as though they had something in common. Westalyn just looked confused.

"I'm Dorelith," our helpful host said through her painted lips. "Came from Palunia three waves ago. My contributions are to the Council, to art, and in particular the use of art for body expression."

"You know my name by now," Fendaza said. "A lifer like Berry, and much less interesting than the rest of this table. My great-grandfather came from Palunia. I contribute with the Council and village-planning."

"Stessa," the young woman said. "Born and raised on Aneth. I contribute here and with music. You may have seen me perform last night."

I did remember her singing. Then she'd been dressed in a costume, but I recognized her hair; it was lighter than the others. She was incredibly gifted in music, as far as my untrained ear could tell.

"I'm Zenthra," the cloaked one said. "I contribute with the Council and community event planning. I arrived here two waves ago. Prior to my Drawing, I was a direct servant of the Planetary Palace."

I started, wanting to know more, but the whole group was staring at us.

"I'm Damaus," I said. "I clearly come from Palunia. I'm here because I was Drawn, too."

They all stopped what they were doing or thinking and stared, mouths open.

"*Drawn?*" Dorelith gasped. "You mean the contessa sent you to investigate us?"

I shook my head. "No, *Drawn*. I put my name in the Cup and it came back out. The Lumen let me go, presumably as some kind of lesson. I'm starting to think I sealed that fate when I quoted one of your people in front of all of Centrisle." I left out the details of our working theory.

They kept staring at me and then looking back at one another. They clearly had the urge to gossip and theorize but couldn't without it being recorded by Welsia or their scribe.

"I'm Westalyn Chi Soha," Westalyn stated. "I went in search of Damaus and the crew after he stole a precious artifact from the contessa." I shot her a glare, but the Council seemed impressed. "He's since convinced me to think outside my Lumen ways. Thank you for welcoming us into your society, and I'm sorry for the mess we've caused."

"And I'm Helragizan," Hel said. "Was also Drawn. My skills are in writing, though I'm becoming old and useless these days. Looking forward to joining your community."

"Thank you," Zenthra said, lending Hel a slight smile. "Now, we will each ask you one question related to the event. If the answers are not sufficient, we'll ask another round. Let's begin."

And so they asked. It took two rounds to get our story out. They asked everything from why we did it to whether or not we liked the color orange. It took an hour and a half to answer everything, if I got the sundial reading correct this time. There was one outside the window at the back of the building, where they had a garden filled with beautiful plants. It felt shameful to be sitting inside.

At the end of the questions and answers, which included our plan to retrieve the amber and free the Palunians before saving the Lumen, the Council sat in silence.

"That's quite a story," Fendaza said. "But why would you care? Did your Palunian friend here put you up to scheming against the contessa?"

"No!" I said too loudly. "Erm . . . I learned from him, but I learned from the whole crew—particularly Marlithan. She gave me books. I studied about your history, about how the Lumen invaded Palunia and executed your people into silence and slavery. I get it now, and I'm very sorry for all of it. I want to make things as right as they can be."

"Who, besides Helragizan here, can validate your story?"

"I can!" came a voice from across the room. Welsia was waving eagerly. I smiled.

"Scribes are to be impartial," Zenthra reminded her.

"Oh, no one's truly impartial," Berry said. "Can anyone else in your crew vouch for you?"

I nodded. "Let me go back to the house for a moment?" I requested.

To my surprise they agreed. I got up and left the room, heading outside. I then ran as fast as I could up to our row and finally to the house marked *Cedar*. I must have done it in half the time it took us to walk.

"Marlithan?" I cried as I burst into the doorway.

But Gonian was sitting alone in the front room, lounging in one of the cushioned chairs.

"Damaus!" He stood up at once. "What's going on? Are you guys—"

"I need Marlithan!" I shouted, bolting up the stairs.

"She's not here!" he hollered up at me. "What's wrong?"

I checked every room and found no sign of her even being there, except that the note and the Omnilight were gone.

I came back down the stairs slowly, my adrenaline lost. "Where is she?" I asked, out of breath.

Gonian shook his head. "She was gone before I got up this morn. What happened with the Council? You look positively wretched."

I couldn't begin to phrase all the ways I needed Marlithan. "I need someone to testify that I've changed my Lumen ways," I settled on.

Gonian's eyes lit up. "Sure!" he said. "Let's go, then!"

He left the house before I could ask him anything. I smiled at our sudden ignition of friendship and followed him out.

When we got back, I told my story again, at Zenthra's insistence.

"Can you corroborate this telling of events?" they asked Gonian.

"Well, sure!" he agreed, bug-eyed. "S'that all? He's under-playin' it, to tell you true. Damaus here read more books in a month than I have in my whole life. He's a rising scholar and historian. Hell, you should give *him* a place on your Council, if it wouldn't send the wrong message. He says we all taught him, but he's learned me a thing or two, too. Part of that was patience, of course, but he's a good lad," he finished, laughing, then added, "for a Lume."

"How do I note sarcasm?" Welsia asked.

But Zenthra ignored her and kept on with the meeting. "Further questions for the Council?" No one spoke, but I noticed Berry smiling brightly at me. "On to the results," Zenthra continued. "Damaus, Westalyn, and Hel, please tell us any solutions you have to this problem."

We all sat in silence. We were going to be held responsible for this, and I had a feeling that even if they were fair, we wouldn't like any suggestions they had in mind.

"Will you give us a moment?" Westalyn asked. They nodded and we stepped outside with Gonian.

"Do you have something?" I asked her.

She shook her head. "Not quite, but a brainstorm could help. I want to know if there's any way to get it back in the ship."

"Not unless we can invert the flow of gravity," Gonian responded. "That stuff does harden though, donnit? We could suggest they make jewelry."

"With an entire military tankard full?" I pressed. "And export them for riches across the galaxy?"

"Suppose you're right," he grunted.

We went back in with nothing. We told them that, and they frowned.

"But there's more to our story," I said, calmly taking the closest available seat to Zenthra and looking them in the eye. "If our theory's right, each one of those ships in your yard is carrying the same amount of amber. I'd recommend you let us empty them *off world*."

They exchanged an uneasy glance.

"Can you prove it?" Stessa asked.

"Do you *want* us to?" Westalyn nearly snapped, shutting the young girl down.

"Where do you propose dumping hundreds of tankards when one causes such detriment?" Fendaza asked. "Surely no planet deserves this kind of environmental crisis."

You have plenty of planet left, I thought, suddenly bitter that someone who'd only ever known a beautiful world like this one would consider a small spill a crisis.

"I know a place," I said, and the Palunians in the room nodded with understanding. Zenthra's eyes grew wide and a slight smile came over their face.

"Is it empty now?" Zenthra asked, their tone warmer than before.

"Should be," I said. "Will you let me take a crew for every ship? We can send them back when all this is over."

"What are you two talking about? This sounds like it could be dangerous," Berry demanded.

But Dorelith shook her head. "If the people volunteer, we won't get in their way."

"Will someone explain what's going on?" Stessa demanded, and Fendaza nodded beside her.

"We're gonna bring the remaining amber back to Palunia and prove to the Lumen that the contessa is a liar," I said. "In short, I plan to dismantle a dictatorship."

CHAPTER 21

"ARE YOU READY for this?" Gonian asked at dinner that night. We were seated at the front of the table, nearest the stage.

I didn't feel ready. I'd managed to fit in just a few hours of sleep, and I still hadn't been able to track Marlithan down. "Yes," I lied.

"Good on ya, champ!" he said, giving me a swift punch in the shoulder. "You're up after this song."

I looked up, watching Stessa and the group performing something catchy. Several of the townspeople were dancing, and I had to say I understood the impulse.

"Do you know what you're going to say?" Westalyn asked.

"More or less, I suppose," I said, feeling my nerves rising inside me.

"I don't mean to discourage you, Damaus," she said, "but the last time you walked onto a stage and didn't know what to say, things took a pretty bad turn."

I let out a long, exaggerated sigh. "I'm a little more pre-pared than last time."

The song finished and the group moved to the back of the stage, where they sat with their instruments in hand, presumably to play again once I'd finished. I got up on shaking legs and looked out at the table and town center full of people, with several of them looking back at me with contempt. It was going to be a tough audience. I waited for their silence.

"People of Aneth," I said, my voice shaking. I wondered how Jiyorga did this on a regular basis. "I owe you several apologies. The first is for the new addition to your planet we dropped in the valley just beyond those hills. We Lumen seem to poison everything we touch. Would you believe we were just looking for a way into the ship?"

Not one smile, and not a hint of laughter.

"The second apology is for showing up here on your planet at all. I'm sure my face is not what you came here to see. I'm sorry that my friend and I disrupted your lives with our presence. I understand that you have every reason to despise us."

Some were starting to nod.

"I'll make a third apology that is only in part mine to make. But I have a request, if you're willing. Would those of you who come from Palunia please stand?"

I waited. At first no one moved. Then members of the crew were on their feet. Then some nearest them. Then some friends of those people. I was sure it wasn't all of them, but we had a couple hundred now.

"I'm sorry for the life you had in a place that should have been your rightful home," I said, looking into their faces. I felt my throat constricting. "I'm sorry for the way our people treated you. I had a part to play in that, and I neglected to stand up for you all, time and time again. But now I've learned, thanks to my crew, what it really means to be Palunian. I've learned how mistreated you've been for your entire lives, and I can't sit idly by anymore.

"You see, the contessa's lied to all of us. She sent us to get her precious amber, when she was really using us to take it *out* of Palunia. I've learned now that what the contessa craves is power, control, and silence. And I don't want any other Palunians to have to live in silence.

"So I ask you now, will you help me to form crews, to take these ships filled with amber, and to go take back your planet?"

No one moved. In fact, a few of the Palunians took their seats.

"Welsia?" I invited her forward as I took a step back.

"Right," she said, taking over. "So we've got another plan. Of course we know you're happy here. I am, too. By taking these ships and overthrowing the founding family, I plan to open up travel between Palunia and Aneth. First for Palunians and this community only. We have no intent of sending you back to be stuck there again or harmed in any way. You've earned your freedom, and we want to provide you with even more options while giving you the chance to see your loved ones again."

At the mention of loved ones, a few hooked their attention onto us. Welsia was getting somewhere with them that I couldn't.

"Furthermore," she said, "we need to be a united voice against the contessa. Damaus and Westalyn will stand up to their people, but they will not speak for us. We need to speak for ourselves, to have our own voices heard in a place that wanted to destroy us."

Several were nodding now. Not enough, but it was a start.

"Anyone who believes in this cause, we ask you to join us here, in front of the stage," I called out.

About twenty came forward, but most of the crowd averted their eyes. Some got up and left altogether. When the meal finished and everyone cleared their food, we gained six more—those who didn't want the public to know they'd volunteered, I suspected.

"Twenty-nine," Gonian counted. "That's thirty-five if you count us."

I frowned. "It's not enough. How many ships are there?"

"Intact, we estimate about eighty," Welsia said. *Not good.*

"We'll meet first thing in the morning, right here," I said to the group. "Before the morning meal."

I left them talking among themselves. Westalyn started after me, but I shook my head. What I needed was to be truly alone. I couldn't yet map the tightness in my chest to any words in my head.

I stopped first in my room to grab my notebook. Then I rushed back down the stairs, though I had nowhere to be, and took a scattered but mostly direct path uphill between the houses. I passed the last row and came to the crest of the large hill.

The view of the water from here was breathtaking. I was much higher up than the crest I'd come over last time. There were two chains of hills below, running parallel to this one, separating me from the sea.

I sat there and opened my notebook to the first page. It was tough reading those early notes again. Executions and torture, voice removal, enslavement, banishment . . . I couldn't blame them for not trusting my leadership. Yet nearly thirty had come forward and had agreed to leave behind a life of tranquility, presumably to save their loved ones.

I got why they wouldn't do it for me, but I didn't get their lack of desire for the Palunian community at large. Why didn't it matter that people were suffering? I refused to guilt anyone into helping, but at this point I wasn't sure I could if I wanted to. I sighed aloud and continued reading, glancing up every so often at the expanse of the deep green sea. The waves rolled in with enormous size and pressure, crashing into the sandy floor at its edge, frothing up onto land.

It was calming somehow, to sit safely away and observe the chaos and violence of nature. It had been a long day. The sun was already starting to go down, creating brilliant orange striping across the sky, reflecting on the swaying waves.

Then my eye caught sight of something bobbing in the distance. At a glance it looked like a person. I carefully started down the hill, studying it. I got over the next cliff and saw arms protruding up out of a wave. It *was* someone.

Without thinking I dropped my notebook on the hilltop. I stripped off the colorful, oversized dress Dorelith had given me to wear, and I bolted down the last hill, nearly losing my balance. I tumbled a little on my descent but managed to stay upright. The sea lurched again, and I saw the person go under.

Fear paralyzed me for about two seconds before I ran in spite of it, splashing through the curve of dying waves and foam at my feet. When I got waist-deep a large wave came for me, attempting to swallow me whole. I jumped—not high enough—and got a face full of thick salt water.

I coughed, spitting out as much as I could while preparing myself for the next wave. This time I had a new tactic in mind. I jumped over its tip, riding against it. I landed smoothly. When the sea calmed for a moment I looked around for the person. They had resurfaced but were farther out. I swam as hard and fast as I could, launching myself over each wave with improving grace, until they were nearly within reach.

As I approached, they turned to face me.

"*Damaus?*" she gasped, as a wave ran her under the water.

I dove in after her, but she'd already found her way back up, spitting water out with desperation.

"Marlithan!" I cried, grabbing onto her anyway. "Where have you—"

Another wave swallowed us and spit us out a little closer to the shore.

"Not a great time to talk!" she called, continuing back toward the sand. I followed her to the water's edge, a little embarrassed at how easy it was. The waves actually helped us along.

When we touched dry sand, Marlithan walked to the bottom of a hill not far from the one I'd scurried down. There I saw a pile of robes and a pair of shoes.

She sat on a rock next to her things and opened her hand. There the Omnilight shone majestically in the setting sun.

"You carried it into the sea?" I squealed. "What if you dropped it?"

She looked at it instead of me. "I wanted to know what activates it. Though maybe it would be better to drop it."

Instinctively I snatched it from her. Then, looking into her eyes, I cursed. "Sorry, Marl. It's just . . . I have so much to be responsible for. I guess it's getting to me."

She held me then. At first it startled me, but it felt right, too. I let myself relax in her arms, which first intensified my emotions and then seemed to release them.

"What's really troubling you?" she asked when we'd been quiet for too long.

I sat back on a rock next to her. There were too many things to count. But one thought remained at the front of it all.

"They don't care," I said. She looked at me with questioning eyes. "The people here don't care about what's happening on Palunia."

Marlithan was silent. When I looked up at her, her gaze was elsewhere and her expression wounded. I realized my mistake then.

"Oh, Marl," I said. "I know that you've already decided. I mean you at least gave it some consideration. I know you care. It's one thing to care and not have anything more to give, and another to just refuse to listen." I kept babbling until I'd told her everything that had happened in her absence.

But it was too late to take back the truth in my words. I understood their decision, but I couldn't respect it.

"Are you taking it back?" she asked, nodding at the Omnilight.

"I don't know if I should," I admitted. "If I do, it might help us somewhere along the way. But that could also put it back in the hands of the contessa. I think right now our only advantage is that she *doesn't* have it."

Marlithan hummed in agreement. "If you want, I can keep trying to figure it out until you leave," she offered.

"Yeah, okay," I agreed, handing it back to her. We sat together a while longer in silence, watching the ocean roar. I tried to capture the entirety of the memory for later. It was a good way to remember her.

I went to bed as soon as I managed to get myself back into town. Westalyn wasn't in the room yet when I crawled into my cot and fell asleep instantly. I dreamed I was home, sitting with Jona in one of our garden baths, talking about whatever we talked about when things were simpler. Food? Fashion? What our future palace extensions would look like? I should have hated it, but the comfort of home drew me in. I missed my brother, and I missed the simplicity of those times.

I was thinking of him when I woke up. It was still early. There was no sun in the sky outside my window. Westalyn was in the other bed, stirring in her sleep. I dressed myself quietly and tiptoed out of the room.

In the main room downstairs where we'd had our party the night we arrived, I found Gonian sitting in the corner in the same chair he had been that morning. I started, which caught him by surprise. We both grinned.

"Can't sleep?" I asked. I noticed he had a book in his lap.

He shook his head. "You?" I mirrored him, taking the lounge seat next to his.

"I just don't believe we can really do this," I admitted.

"Is that why you took off?" he asked. "We thought we lost our leader."

"It shouldn't be me," I said. "Welsia, maybe. It makes no sense for me to speak on any of your behalf. Reading a few books doesn't give me the whole story, and I'll never know how it felt firsthand."

"I s'pose," he agreed, holding up his own book. "Though you convinced me to read again. I'm not great at it. I'm sure I misunderstood half of what I read so far. But now that I've got my family again, and this mission to think about . . ." He trailed off.

I felt a pang of sadness for him. "Gonian, you don't have to come," I said. "You just found them again. They need you."

"Naw, they don't," he said. "I need *them*. They got by fine without me. This place is better for them than I could ever be. And my daughter's grown up a lot since then; she hardly remembers me. They'll be my reward for getting through this thing alive. But everything they've done, they've done without me."

"If you're sure," I said, sensing he wasn't telling me how he really felt.

"Some good news though," he added. "Your crew's grown to about triple."

"Triple?" I repeated.

"The volunteers kept spreading word. They knew who needed talking to and got it done. Much more effective than any of us. They've been holding meetings through the day and night."

I sat up straight. "So they don't need a leader after all."

Gonian winked. "I was just giving you a hard time."

"Thanks, Gonian!" I said, embracing him again and running out into the row. I cut between houses on the way down, trampling grass, but careful to avoid the flowers. I skidded into the town center where over a hundred people had gathered.

They were all looking up at the stage, where the most inspiring leader I'd ever set eyes on was speaking to a roaring, focused crowd. Marlithan.

CHAPTER 22

"WHILE WE WERE complacent, the Lumes learned to mistrust us. While we sat idly by, our loved ones had the vocal cords ripped from their throats. We've forgotten who we are. We've forgotten our great leaders—the councils past and the counsel they showed us—their teachings of what a functional society can look like.

"We've forgotten our education. We've stopped writing, and we choose wine over reading the warnings our forefathers wrote about.

"This life we have here—who are we to claim it if it isn't available to those we've left behind?" Marlithan's voice boomed over the growing crowd below.

"A traveler in my crew, with nothing to gain, is willing to risk his life for the cause. He'll stop at nothing to defy his own people for us, and yet you won't go back for your husbands? Wives? Sisters? The family you left behind in that commune?

"Is that what Naheizan Regalin risked her life for? Where is your fervor? *Where is your Palunian pride?*"

There was a thick roar from the crowd. Behind me were a hundred others, with more coming into town center from all directions. I saw Dorelith and Zenthra among them and a couple faces from our house party.

"Welsia, let's tell them the plan," Marlithan said, and Welsia took center stage.

"We've confirmed eighty-seven functional ships, each containing a tankard of amber, save the one that spilled. My team believes we can get twenty more ships operational by tomorrow. And if this mission goes successfully, we can grab what we need from Palunia's shipyard to repair the others.

"We need about fifty more of you to train on the consoles—you'll captain the ships. It's not hard, but your responsibility is vital. Volunteers?"

More than enough hands went up.

"Not your thing anymore?"

I turned. Gonian had managed to catch up and find me. I just smiled and kept watching my friends onstage. "I'd like to learn to fly one day, but I have other things to worry about at the moment." Thankfully, with this crew, my worry was lessening.

"Great!" Welsia exclaimed. Her face lit up in a way I hadn't seen before. "You guys come to the front, please, and wait behind the stage."

"We also need documentors," Hel called out. I hadn't even noticed him up there. "If you can write legibly and have a desire to record what's sure to be one of the most historical events of our time, please come forward!"

About ten more started moving, following the new captains. I was in awe of this crew. They had everything under control. They'd taken on this mission as their own and were making amazing strides. I should have expected it. It wasn't me who was crucial to this cause.

"Now," Marlithan said, "this quest is of two parts. We've got to show the Lumen they've been lied to—that I'll leave to our friends Damaus and Westalyn. Our part is *freeing our people!*" she cried. The cheer was enormous. It looked like the crowd had doubled in size, and still more were joining.

"Still, the question remains . . . how do we do it?" she asked. The cheering died down. Some watched her with unwavering confidence, but I heard doubtful whispers among the people, too. "While I'd like to think convincing the Lumen would be enough, I do have my doubts that this will put them all on our side. At least not right away, and it will definitely not educate them enough to change their ways. I fear we'll need to remove the contessa from her position if we hope to effect change, and for that we'll need something more powerful. And I've figured out what that is."

I watched as much in wonder as the rest while she held up the Omnilight. She uncorked the amber vial still attached to it and took a small sip. I instinctively tried to go to her, but I couldn't get through even the first wall of people. Gonian gripped my arm.

A moment passed in silence. Then I noticed her eyes. The black circles filled in to the edges. A whisper sounded as everyone tried to get a better look.

She held up the key for everyone to see. It was glowing under the Omnilight. It turned to white—to only a two-dimensional shape—and then that shape began to change. It became a musical instrument, like the ones they'd played at the Palace. Then it changed again into a sword. Then a long, thin needle. Then it turned back to white and expanded beyond the stage, the crowd, and the town. The town center grew dark at once. She'd made it a dome. The light came back in a flash. When I opened my pained eyes, I saw she was again holding a key.

"We believed this vial contained amber," Marlithan said. "But given our new assumption that the Lumes don't need it, that theory makes little sense. And so I went to my books on the Omnilight. They're filled with conflicting theories, but one of those mentions an *elixir given by the gods*. While there's clearly more research to be done on what this is," she said, holding up the vial, "I can confirm it gives me new sight and new senses. With it I can see and manipulate light itself. And I can see its true source. The Omnilight gives light to the suns and stars, which give light to us. It seems that any object bonded with the Omnilight can be bent to the controller's will. With this I believe we can overthrow the Planetary Palace."

A few cheers and cries came from the confused and impressed townspeople. It started slow, but the excitement grew like the waves of the sea as more joined in, crying out, stomping, and hammering on the central table. I caught Marlithan's bewildered eye as she surveyed the excitement below. And they refused to die down.

"So?" I asked Marlithan when I finally got her alone behind the stage. "What made you change your mind?"

"You gave me a puzzle to solve," she said. "That weighed on me. When I learned the truth of the Omnilight, I felt like it had to be for some kind of purpose. But, Damaus, I meant what I said about you. Against all odds, you're somehow the catalyst that's going to spur us on to victory."

"Not anymore," I said, nodding to the tens, if not hundreds, of people making their way behind the stage. A line was forming near us, filled with people looking to talk with Marlithan.

She frowned. "I should have talked more about the dangers and risks. What if I've just manipulated them into joining?"

"Marl," I began, but I found I didn't have any words of comfort. To be honest that was a fear of mine, too. "What you said was true, though, all right? You should never feel ashamed for speaking. You've had enough of that in your lifetime."

She jumped at me then, embracing me firmly, the weight of her body pressed against me. I squeezed her back and held her there for a moment. Looking past her I caught sight of Westalyn watching us, biting her lip, a hint of concern in her eyes. I grinned at her then and watched her expression slowly melt into a smile. She went to talk to Welsia, who was leading her group of mechanics and captains even farther from the stage.

This made room for Marlithan's line, which progressed quickly in our direction. "You got this?" I asked, and she gave me a stiff nod. I waved and went to look for Gonian.

I was lost again in the sea of people, but at least it was moving. I wandered back toward where we had stood during the speech, but there was no sign of him anymore. I needed some wisdom on another matter, and Marlithan and Hel had their hands full.

I searched for just a moment—that was about all I could take of the crowd, which was bustling about in all directions. I let myself get pushed to the edge, making a less than graceful escape between a couple of detached shops. Maybe if I got up higher I could spot him.

I leaned against the backside of one of the shops to catch my breath and cool down. A trip to the sea was sounding good right about now, if it weren't for the exhausting uphill journey.

"Damaus?"

I turned. Rodiger was leaning against the building next door.

"Hey," I greeted them, still waiting for my body to cool. They came to me.

"Why aren't you helping Hel and the others?" they asked.

"They don't need my help." I was wishing for one of my old Lumen cloaks right about now. The sun here wasn't as hot, but it sure wasn't helping.

Rodiger frowned. "They don't need mine either."

I had to admit I was glad the kid wasn't learning to fly a ship quite yet. "You learned writing from Hel, didn't you?"

"Yeah," they said, "but I'm not very good."

"You and me both, Rod," I murmured. "Are you gonna come back with us? See your mother again?"

Rodiger nodded. "Welsia says we can all be a crew again. Plus, I like riding in the ship."

"I do, too." I smiled. "Have you seen Gonian around?"

They shook their head. "Can I help you?"

I hesitated. "This is kind of . . . well, maybe. All I can really do is just spill out some thoughts, but you can chime in when they get too reckless if you want."

"Gonian *would* be good at that," they acknowledged, but they waited for me to speak.

"So I know we're trying to solve this whole thing diplomatically. And we should try. I know that some will respond when we show them the amber, or when they hear you guys speak. And Marlithan's figured out the Omnilight, which is huge. But some of those Lumen are a force to be reckoned with. Imagine telling Jiyorga he's wrong and asking him to step down? It's not just him, either—he's got plenty of friends who think the same way, and they've got hundreds of guards each. Honestly I'd guess that up to half of Lumen think like him.

"The Omnilight is great—Marl's done an amazing job, but unless she has some kind of master plan, I don't think just *having* it is enough. We're novices. The contessa used that thing for years, maybe centuries. She might have a way to take it right out of our hands.

"What if, despite this whole thing, she keeps the people under her control? What if a war breaks out? A *physical war*? Lumen versus Palunians, or Palunians versus themselves? Or any other combination. Things could end up worse than they began."

Rodiger was squinting up at me, nodding slowly.

"So," I continued, "I've been thinking. Maybe we need an army. I mean, I hate the idea, but what if we need to defend the Palunians? We could train everyone without jobs with whatever weapons we find on the ships. And now that I think about it, the contessa may have been trying to ship those off, too, to prevent resistance." I sighed.

Rodiger's eyes were now wide. I knew it wasn't fair to burden a kid with all this, but I'd lost track of my notebook, and the thoughts were coming too fast to contain.

"Hel told me the strongest weapons are words," they said, shrugging. It was a child's way of trying to find something relevant to say. But maybe they were onto something.

"Huh," I muttered. "Thanks, Rod."

They beamed, clearly glad to be of help, then their eyes wandered back toward the crowd below. "It's calming down," they said. "I see my friend. Do you mind if I go, Damaus?"

"Go ahead," I said, starting back toward the stage myself. *You gave me just the wisdom I needed.*

I pulled Marlithan from her ongoing conversation, ignoring the protests of the man she was speaking with.

"We have to teach them," I said. "Why we're doing this, how to do it."

"They get it," she said. "Did you hear the cheering? They know why it has to be done."

"Yes, okay," I agreed. "But you were right. You *did* manipulate them."

Her expression darkened. She didn't respond.

"Wait though!" I said, placing a hand on her shoulder. "It was a good start. It's just not enough. They believe you because you said some powerful things on a stage. But until they can think for themselves, manipulation is all they'll be capable of taking in. Like I was. I was willing to listen to anything that sounded good, but *I* didn't change until I read those books. Until I found the truth for myself. It'll be the same for them.

"They'll follow you as long as your voice is the loudest. If someone were to push hard at some other emotions—say fear—they'll act in their own best interest. You've got them thinking they'll be heroes and that this is all easy. But that's not the reality when we're dealing with the galaxy's most powerful woman, is it?

"Marl, I was ready to build an army—a ludicrous idea—but Rodiger had it right. The contessa won't care about bows and spears. That palace is probably impenetrable anyway. We need to teach our people to recognize her lies and to stand united behind factual history. We've got, what, a month on the ship back? Let's put books into their hands, generate discussions, answer questions. Let's admit what we don't know. We'll build knowledge and trust. Because the reality is, we may not win the first time. You said it—what about the risks? If the plan fails, and if our crew dies or is silenced in the process, at least the spirit of this thing can live on in the minds of an educated bunch of people."

Marlithan waited, making sure I was finally done spewing words, then let out a long sigh. "You're almost right, Damaus. But don't kid yourself; we need physical strength, too."

"We'd be slaughtered!"

"With spears and bows, yes," she said. "I have another plan."

CHAPTER 23

THERE'S NO SIGHT quite as marvelous as a hundred ships soaring together into space away from a planet like Aneth. Our usual crew was back together for the most part. The crews were set up to operate independently for day-to-day functions, but ours served as the core unit, sending members of our own over to the others, to teach, train, and solve any other problems we could.

Westalyn chose not to join us and instead flew her own crew as captain. I'd protested at first, but she reminded me she'd been able to track our ship when the contessa's mechanics failed for centuries. And that despite the outcome, she was the one to find and remove the storage hatch. And that she was her own independent person and I had no say in what she decided to do. She had a point and, according to Welsia, was doing a great job.

A couple of weeks passed quickly. Before we left Aneth I'd managed to form a team of my own who were already familiar with, and enraged by, the injustices on Palunia. We had our own discussions, checked our facts in books as best we could, and distributed ourselves by subfleet. With nearly a hundred ships in the air, there was no way I could spend time in each one, and on top of that, I was the least qualified. Though not all of the crews were interested in discussing history, they did seem to engage well in conversation once you warmed them up and asked the right questions.

Marlithan was nearly untraceable. I knew she was moving from ship to ship and it had something to do with her plan. I'd only caught sight of her a handful of times in passing, with her always running off somewhere. It took a week of far more effort than I wanted to dedicate to the task, but I finally managed to track her down.

I followed her when our unit locked bays with Captain Senrith's, leaving the group I was currently in discussions with to their own devices.

I crept through the tunnel after her on our ship, waiting for her to go up to the observation floor or down to the crates. She chose instead to go forward, locking the door to the communications chamber behind her. I waited several minutes. I paced up and down the tunnel at first. Then I considered going to grab a notebook from my room, but I'd put far too much effort into finding her to be reckless now. And so I sat. I sat and read a book a young traveler had recommended to me on dictated societies. It was a good choice. I'd ask him to lead the next discussion I had with his group.

I got another fifty pages in when the door finally clicked. I stood, ready to confront Marlithan, when Rodiger stepped out. Next came Hel, Welsia, and Gonian, followed by the rest of our original crew members. She came out last.

"What is this?" I demanded. They all stared at me, shocked and sheepish. "I know you guys don't need me, but you're leaving me out?"

They glanced at each other but not at me.

"Damaus," Marlithan said. "Why don't you come—"

"I want an explanation *now*," I stated. "If you're going off course again, Welsia, I swear—"

"Only slightly," Marlithan spoke for her. "And for a good reason. We met just now because there are certain things only we are capable of. If we believed you could help, of course we would have included you."

"Why not just tell me?" I asked. "I'm part of this crew, too."

"This isn't about crews," she responded. "I've spoken to all the Palunians."

"Oh, *that* makes it better!" I cried, my voice thick with sarcasm. "Just leave Damaus out because he's a Lumen!"

"Do I go into your group discussions?" Marlithan snapped. "Does Hel vet your books? Does Rodiger confirm if your material is graspable for children? No, because you have a job to do, and despite your lack of firsthand experience, we trust you to do it. Now let me do mine."

She stomped away, then started up the ladder. The others followed, lending me brief glances of sympathy as they passed. When they'd all gone I sat again and continued reading.

I just had a few pages remaining when the first rumble came. We felt them sometimes when our ships passed close together. I dismissed it and read another paragraph when the next one hit, stronger this time. I paused, glanced around the room, then turned back to the book. Then it began again, shaking more violently, and didn't stop. I stood immediately and scurried up the ladder, desperate for a chair to strap myself into and to see what was going on.

Most of the crew was standing in the dome, glowing as they had when we'd stopped the pulse dragon. Somewhere nearby they were affecting the flow of time. And I had a feeling it was whatever was responsible for the ongoing quake. I sat and locked in.

"Is it another dragon?" I asked. Marlithan, who stood at the window alone, nodded. I covered my mouth to contain the yelp that nearly escaped it. Marlithan wasn't glowing like the others. Instead she drank from the elixer.

I watched in stunned silence as she held up the Omnilight and pressed it to the dome. The key appeared on the other side, but the crystal remained in her hand. I watched the metal turn to pure white light, which grew longer and longer, like an oversized string flipping around in windless space.

She moved her arm, and the string moved according to its motion. Up, down, and in a wide circle her right arm went, like she was tying a knot. Whatever she was doing was happening just outside my range of view, and I wasn't about to unbuckle myself.

Marlithan suddenly pulled hard, as if tightening the knot of light. The quake intensified, thrashing me backward and forward in my seat. The others fell to the floor, and still Marlithan didn't break contact with the Omnilight or its path. It looked like she was struggling but holding firm. She fought for a while, then relaxed as the shaking stopped. She turned back to the crew, nodding. Their glow faded and they sat up, rubbing the areas of their bodies they'd fallen on.

I cautiously unbuckled myself and approached Marlithan and the crew. I opened my mouth to ask one of the dozen questions I had when something smashed against the dome window. I fell back into the front row of seats as a pulse dragon came into view, its face pressed up against the clear synthese. It bent the dome inward. I clawed my fingertips into the armrests of my chair, waiting for it to burst into the observation deck. Its head alone was the size of the window, and its large, hollow eye left me shaking.

"Marl?" I whispered. "Do you have a plan for this?"

"We wait," she said, not bothering to quiet her tone. She was tense but hadn't lost control.

"To get lasered?" I snapped.

"Two interesting facts about pulse dragons," Hel said, sitting with his legs spread in a V-shape on the floor. "When you constrict the throat the laser can't pass. Also, whoever wrangles one supposedly becomes its master. If our intergalactic biologists of the past are to be believed, anyway."

I blinked and ran the words over in my head. "So you just *wrangled* a *space dragon*. Good. Great. Nothing weird or terrifying about that."

"Wait . . ." Marlithan said. We sat in silence for a moment, and then the thing dropped away from the window. The dragon had fallen to somewhere below. Slowly, I rose again and accompanied the crew. I could see the blue glow of its laser as I approached, and then its body came into view. It was still moving, but with much less enthusiasm.

"Docile?" Gonian asked. As the others backed away and spoke, I leaned forward, unable to take my eyes from the terrifying creature below.

"Yeah," Marlithan said. "*Now* we've wrangled a dragon."

The conversation turned to jokes and all things irrelevant, but I just couldn't stop watching the dragon and worrying. There was laughter behind me, and it made my head pound.

"Why would you do that?" I demanded suddenly, turning to the group. They were unstrapped in the first two rows of chairs. "Did our trip off course have the express purpose of getting us a pet laser beast?"

Marlithan motioned to the empty seat beside her. I shook my head, but she started talking anyway. "We spoke at length about the importance of intellectual strength. It's key, more than anything. That's why we didn't take you away from the invaluable work you're doing.

"But the other reality, Damaus, is that the contessa likely has a great arsenal of enchanted weapons and maybe a crew of guards who know how to use them. She may arm herself against us, but worse still, she may use her power on the Palunians already submitted to her. The Omnilight could become a weapon, but it can also aid us in acquiring weapons. We will use diplomacy, but if necessary, we'll destroy her and the palace she sits in."

CHAPTER 24

"NOW APPROACHING PALUNIA!" came Welsia's voice over the fleet-wide radio she and Westalyn had configured. "Anyone changing ships must do so within the hour! Two hours to go before regulators must be off and helms on, prepared for landing."

"This is it," I told my current group. We were sitting in a meeting room identical to the one Marlithan and I used on the core ship. "Any questions? Ideas?"

"Plenty," a young boy nicknamed Chaz piped up, and the other agreed with nervous laughter.

"That's the spirit!" I stood and patted him on the shoulder. "I've got to go see your captain and then get back to mine. You can keep talking, of course, as long as you strap yourselves in and put some helms on." I waved to the group. This one was mostly older children, and they were way more eager to learn than I was at their age.

I followed the corridor to the ship's observation deck. It was identical to ours, just like each of the other rooms on each of the other ships, except this ship was piloted by a Lumen.

"Hello, Captain!" I greeted Westalyn.

"Little busy at the moment, Damaus," she called over her shoulder without bothering to turn from the console. "You'd better get back to Welsia before she starts bothering me, too."

"Soon," I said. "I just wanted to say I'm . . . uhh . . . proud of you?"

She turned this time to give me a sly smile. "Are you planning on never seeing me again? Off to risk your neck on a stupid idea of yours?"

"No, I value my neck quite a bit," I replied. "I like to think the stupid ideas are all behind me. Besides, the plan is all Marl. I've just had a particularly smooth ride on your ship today, and I thought I'd let you know. You're a good captain. And not that it's hard, but you're significantly better than I was."

"You'd do better now that you give a damn," she said. "Now, consider yourself banished from my vessel."

"Aye, aye." I smirked, waving before slipping down into the tunnel.

When I got back to the core ship, I sat in the kitchen and strapped myself in across from Marlithan.

"What, are you lonely?" she asked.

"Nope," I replied. "I've got friends in all directions again now that you've locked that dragon in our amber tankard. I just thought I'd read another book."

Her eyes narrowed. "In an hour's time?"

"This one's short," I said, revealing a packaged essay from inside my jacket.

"Where did you find *that*?" she exclaimed, motioning for it.

"Ah-ah!" I smirked. "You said anything in the crate."

"Fine," she grunted, waving a dismissive hand at me.

I cracked it open and began reading *A Future to Hope For* by Marlithan Izeyrin.

I didn't remember Palunia's atmosphere looking so bleak. Yellow and green dust rolled over us in fog-like clouds as we broke through them like a barrier.

"Think they see us yet?" Gonian asked no one in particular. He was watching from the front row of chairs facing the dome window.

"Some do," Hel said with certainty. "And we can guess the contessa will be waiting to witness our approach."

"We stick to the plan?" Marlithan eyed everyone in the room. It was her way of commanding. We all nodded as our fleet continued lowering toward the shipyard, then deferred east.

One by one we touched down in a series of circles, all surrounding the Planetary Palace. We sat in silence for a long moment until all one hundred ships had landed.

Marlithan unbuckled first, walking from the table to the console. Welsia selected something on the projection in front of her, nodding. They exchanged a smile before Marlithan bent over the console. "Let's move," she called out over the radio.

When our entrance bay opened and we walked down its ramp, we saw the other crews arriving on theirs. We all faced the Palace. A crowd as large as the Cup Festival's was gathering between us and the crater. But instead of the usual cheer I'd come to expect from Lumen, their expressions were concerned or set like stone. There was no red cloth in sight. If the plan had worked, most of the guards would all be at the shipyard.

The people below were looking in all directions. I followed one Lumen's pointing finger toward the Planetary Palace—toward a tower that stood high above the crowd. And there, somehow balancing upon its spiraled tip, she stood tall, as if she were a part of it.

I'd forgotten how tall she was, and how *menacing*. She was too far for me to see the details of her face, except that it was painted deep red. Her robes were black, blowing powerfully behind her as she stood motionless above us all, above even the ships. She wore the same spiked headpiece, which now bore no orbs.

"Contessa of Palunia!" Marlithan called out beside me, her voice echoing surprisingly well over the enormous but quiet crowd. There was a low gasp and murmur at the sound of her Palunian voice. "Surrender the planet to us, and we will let you live!"

The contessa lept into the air, her cloak flipping upward, then bolted straight for the ground below. She hovered just above the ground before landing softly, one foot at a time. She faced our crew but did not approach. She had black gems placed over her eyes—irregular stones this time.

"I should have known," she said. "Our traitor returns, looking to betray his people once again."

The crowd surged with mixed reactions. Most booed and snarled—the Lumen at us and the Palunians at her. I scanned those nearby for my friends and family, but they were nowhere to be found.

"This is bigger than me, and you know it!" I shouted, hoping my voice could reach those surrounding us as easily as hers.

She raised a hand then, holding her palm open. "Return what you stole, traitor."

"He can't," Marlithan said, holding up the Omnilight. It turned to white and then to a sort of javelin, wound with gold and many gems with the white light in its center. "Why don't you tell the people here all the secrets you've been hiding from them?"

Loathing and anger spread over the contessa's face, which turned into a smirk. "Foolish girl," she said slowly. "You may have taken my light, but do not think that makes me powerless."

Then, from the palm she had extended to receive the gem, fire emerged. She raised it, extruding a high wall of flame in front of Marlithan, blocking her view and nearly catching her arm. Marlithan jumped back, and the javelin soared toward the contessa.

The contessa ran and dodged, but barely. She growled with shock and hatred as she got back on her feet. The fire kept burning, but Marlithan had walked out of its path now and raised her hand at the object between them.

The contessa lurched forward, reaching for it. It lifted from the ground and shot toward her. She laughed aloud. "It still obeys me!" She cackled. But the javelin didn't slow on its approach. Her laugh turned to gape-mouthed horror as it pierced her abdomen.

Behind her, Gonian raised his hand and the Omnilight returned to it.

"There's something about Palunians you'll never understand!" Marlithan roared as the fire died at her feet. "Our power is not in the individual but in our community."

The contessa winced but smiled. She let out a quiet, breathy laugh, which grew louder and clearer as she stood back on her feet, her robes too thick to reveal her wound, and leaned against the closest palace tower. "You think you're the only ones with backup? Do you know what that little gem taught me? That there's always another way!"

She touched a hand to the smooth black surface of the tower. The ground began to rumble. Marlithan and I retreated to the bay with the others, but Gonian stood on the other side of the contessa, javelin in hand.

"We barely trained!" Marl whispered to me. "He doesn't know how to fight!"

I grimaced, watching Gonian try to balance himself as the dirt began to split beneath his feet.

"*Gonian, open the tankard!*" Marlithan shouted.

But it was too late. Below him a thin black object began to twist out of the ground. We stared at it, as transfixed as he was. It shot up so suddenly—another tower, with Gonian impaled on its tip. The Omnilight dropped to its base.

Marlithan let out a guttural scream and tried to run, but both Welsia and I held her back. It took the contessa only a few steps to pick up the javelin, which she turned into her signature staff.

"Now," she said. "It's about time we settled this, isn't it?"

"Your contessa is a liar!" a voice shouted from a few ships away. Everyone else turned to look at the speaker, but I didn't have to. It was Chaz. I'd have been proud if I weren't still in shock.

"These ships are full of amber! You never needed it to live! She sent it away on purpose!"

"We're not the simple creatures you think we are!"

"Her ancestors had Lor Annaius destroyed on purpose! They traded Lumen lives for power, just like she traded ours!"

Throughout our circle of ships, many helped in this simple act of shouting facts at the crowd. The contessa seethed but froze in place, as if at a loss for what to do.

"When one of us acts out, it's easy, right?" I asked her. "You just take away our thoughts or, in the case of the Palunians, their ability to speak. But what about when the whole planet rejects you?"

She turned to me, her staff raised. "This is over," she said.

Then a creaking sounded from above. I looked up to see the tankard latch had been opened. Westalyn was hanging there with magnet pads. A high-pitched scream pierced the palace grounds.

"Get her!" Marlithan called, as the dragon revealed itself to the sounds of panic and chaos below. Many ran, but others couldn't take their eyes off of the mass of blue light and bones—a sight that had never been seen on our desert planet.

A laser struck something in front of the contessa. She'd managed to turn the staff into a shield, but it cracked on impact and the gem flung toward our ship. The stones on her eyes shattered, too. The contessa ran behind the nearest tower and I dashed for the Omnilight. I grabbed it and took a swig of the elixir, ready to finish her off.

But when I tried to change the shape of the broken shield, nothing happened. I thought hard, picturing a variety of objects—swords, staffs, domes—but nothing worked.

"Marl, is it broken? *What do I do?*" I yelled to her.

Her eyes widened like she'd just realized something, and she ran over, snatching it from me. She took a quick drink from the vial and grabbed the gem from my hands, pulling the segments of the shield up into a chain. She commanded the chain to wrap around the contessa, and it did, binding her to the tower. She raised a hand to the dragon, and it stilled its laser. It was a magnificent sight to see, this ominous skeletal beast taking commands from one of us.

"Contessa!" Marlithan called. "Tell these people that what we've said is true. Tell them that they've been deceived—that you've lied to them, hurt them, and betrayed them, all for your own gain."

The contessa didn't even look at Marlithan. The dragon's blue light that had been reduced to the size of a stone in the void that was its belly began to vibrate, growing larger and brighter.

"Fine!" The contessa spat, staring down at her own feet. There was a gasp from the crowd. "That may be true, but doesn't our society work for us, for Lumenkind? Without me you wouldn't have your palaces, your great festivals, your meals, your wine. I've borne the burden of the darkness in this world so that you could live a simpler, happy life!"

"These people are not darkness!" Westalyn cried behind us. She jumped down off the side of the ship and marched between the contessa and the crowd, her arms spread wide. "These are some of the most joyful, loving, and knowledgeable people you will ever know. Those whom our houses have enslaved can actually be our teachers—our examples. This is the embodiment of darkness, right here!" She pointed at the contessa. The crews of our ships cheered, and some of the crowd joined in. "She taught us to hate one another so we wouldn't notice her. So she could maintain control of us, for herself. She deported anyone who said too much, like all the Palunians here and like our friend, Damaus!"

The next part happened too quickly for me to keep track of all the moving pieces. The contessa somehow broke free from her chains and started toward Westalyn. Westalyn sidestepped her, and a Lumen from the crowd took her place, pummeling their weight into the unexpecting tyrant and landing on her chest. The cloaked figure pressed their hands to her throat as we all watched in silence and stunned disbelief. No one moved to help.

The figure stood after a moment, with all eyes on them. "She's dead," she said, her voice low and solemn. Then her hood fell to her shoulders as she turned toward me.

"Mother," I said, not quite ready to smile.

Then a rumble came from the palace. I ran, shielding my mother from the debris that began to fly. I brought her safely back to where my brother Jona was standing. We exchanged a knowing nod before there was a large cracking noise. It was as though the contessa had told the palace what to do in her death, except—

Images washed over me. I could feel my body standing in place, but through my eyes I saw Marlithan. A younger Marlithan, serving in Roeni's garden. Hel was there, too, and I have to admit he didn't look so different. I watched as Roeni's mother hit Marl—watched her flinch—and then the view shifted. My own younger hand was outstretched in front of me, pushing against Roeni's mother before she could lay another finger on my friend.

More images came, a cycle of lost memories stolen from me by the contessa. When I snapped back to the moment, I saw them—glowing, colored orbs shooting up through the towers, splitting into beams of light, hitting many Lumen in the chest. The clouds above were a myriad of fading colors. It was somehow beautiful. Around me people were gasping as they came to confront their own truths.

I glanced toward Marlithan, who was holding up the Omnilight, back in the form of a key. The gem was split in two.

CHAPTER 25

AFTER PAYING OUR respects to Gonian, we sat around our palace's outdoor feast table. I never thought I'd see the day my family and my crew, including Westalyn, would break bread together.

Considering it had been so long since I'd seen my mother and Jona, and considering all that had happened in that time, we ate in a surprising silence. The sun was setting overhead, leaving a green glow in its path.

"Marlithan," I said, glancing to my right where she sat. She looked exhausted and worn. "You were incredible. And so is your book, for the record."

She gave me a weak nod. "I'm just glad it's over."

I took her hand, and noticed Jona raise a brow. "Do you know why the elixir didn't work for me?"

She smiled and sighed. "You won't believe it when I tell you." Now all eyes at the table were on her. She was a natural leader, though, and never seemed to notice things like that. "It wasn't any fault of yours. It's in an early Palunian book of theories on how to control the Omnilight—one of the many takes. I found a few that mention elixirs as a possibility, but in this one the author theorizes that there's an elixir that could work for our people. For Palunians."

I waited for her to say more, but she didn't elaborate. "You mean *only* for Palunians? Not for Lumen?"

She nodded.

"Marlithan, don't you think there's a flaw in that theory?" I smirked. "That would mean the contessa was . . . well, *Grey*."

"I know," she said quietly, returning to the meal we had all made together. Everyone continued to eat in silence as we thought it over.

"Why would she do that to her own people?" Jona asked after a moment. The awkward, contemplative silence carried on.

Then Marlithan opened her mouth, visibly searching for words. "It doesn't matter. The Lumen were well on the path of hatred before the contessa came to power. Even if she had been one of us, she internalized that hatred herself. It may be worth our pity, but never our forgiveness. She became what she wanted to be, at the expense of all the rest of us. We can't keep asking why. We need to ask, what now?"

There were thoughtful, distant nods around the table.

"Sorry, but I think I'd like to go for a walk," I blurted out.

My mother looked at me, then nodded. "You've been through enough to do whatever you want, Damaus."

"Thanks." I smiled. "Wes? Marl?"

The two on either side of me stood, following my lead. We left the Ju Demma palace hand in hand, heading toward the city center.

"This place is going to look a lot different soon, I think," I mumbled.

"It won't be easy, though," Westalyn said. "I saw their faces. The ones without memories aren't exactly on our side—they just don't know what to believe. Even some who had those visions will likely deny them."

"I guess we need to start thinking about how we can even begin to turn this planet into something respectable." It was hard to imagine what this island would look like without all the Lumen riches on display.

"I consider it my duty," Marlithan said. "Though after things settle down, I might head back to Aneth."

For a second I felt a pang in my chest, but it faded. "Yeah, you should." I squeezed her hand, and she squeezed back.

We had reached the center, which was normally dark at night when there were no festivities to attend to. But in the distance shone the orange glow of a flame.

"What is that?" Westalyn asked, though none of us could answer.

We approached, making our way closer, along with others who had wandered into the square from all directions. They were mostly Lumen. And standing under a torch of fire were three young Palunians, telling stories of early Palunian conquests—of heroes with grey faces who wore bold colors and stood up to anyone who got in their way. The fire was bright, its embers gleaming and refracting off the bowl that contained it. It wasn't a torch at all, I realized. They were using the Cup. An apt choice.

There, with Marlithan's hand in my right and Westalyn's in my left, we learned something new together, in the company of about a hundred Lumen people. People who wanted to hear what a few of *them* had to say. The Palunians hadn't won over the masses that day, but they had done something valuable. Marlithan and her crew had opened the doors of a few Lumen minds to finally listen to the people they'd once enslaved.

I grinned to myself, observing what I would have called the unbelievable around me. It turns out that, for some of us at least, when the message you've been force-fed all your life crumbles at your feet, you can't help but start thinking for yourself. And these Palunians, paired with a hundred Lumen who were willing to listen for once, had the power to change the world. At least that was my hope.

GRAND PATRONS

INKSHARES

Printed in the USA
CPSIA information can be obtained
at www.ICGtesting.com
JSHW022217140824
68134JS00018B/1110